9/13

Yesterday's Secrets, Tomorrow's Promises

Yesterday's Secrets, Tomorrow's Promises

Colleen Sutherland

Yesterday's Secrets, Tomorrow's Promises
Copyright © 2013 Colleen Sutherland
All rights reserved.

*For Gary, who is by my side whenever needed but out of sight
when I am at the keyboard.
The perfect writer's companion.*
— CS

Chapter One

"Jodi!" The tall man in the gray business suit bellowed as he caught sight of his thirteen-year-old daughter sauntering down the street two blocks away.

"Jodi!" he shouted again, charging from the courthouse steps, abandoning his associates, who stared after him. He shoved his black leather briefcase under one arm and quickened his pace in his dash to catch up with the teenager. Darn that girl! He had put her on a bus to the girls' camp not an hour ago, but made the mistake of hurrying off to a Bar Association meeting without waiting for the bus to leave. And there she was, strolling down Stephenson Avenue in Iron Mountain, Michigan, as casually as if she belonged there. There was no mistaking that long, almost white-blond braid that hung down her back or the distinctive sway of the slender, jeans-clad hips.

He could hear the chorus of whistles of a construction crew as his daughter passed their project, a new office complex. He swore again under his breath. Couldn't that girl walk without a wiggle? He had tried to discuss it with her just a week ago, but she only giggled at him and squealed, "Oh, Daddy! I can't help the way I walk!"

No thirteen-year-old should attract that much attention. As she strutted down the street, he noticed how men's heads turned in her wake, almost as if they had been choreographed. He began to jog, swerving to avoid pedestrians, and was soon within a block of her. "Jodi!" he shouted once more. She paid no attention to his voice and turned into the parking lot of a large shopping mall. He put on a new surge of speed, perspiring in the unusual heat and humidity of the June day, cursing his leather-soled oxfords.

The electronic eye of the discount store's automatic door already had her in its sight when he grasped her arm.

"Listen, young lady . . . " His lecture ground to a premature halt as he gaped at the most extraordinary green eyes. Green, not brown. It was not his daughter.

The woman standing before him was the same height and build as his daughter. Little tendrils of hair the exact shade of Jodi's framed the same oval face, but there the resemblance ended. His daughter could be described as cute, perhaps even pretty. This woman was beautiful, though even that adjective was inadequate.

He scanned her face as he mentally tallied the details that were the sum of her stunning beauty. A perfectly clear complexion, free of all cosmetics. A straight little nose with only a slight tilt that added character. A slight indentation on one cheek that might become a dimple with the right provocation. Wide emerald eyes, shining with jewel-like brilliance under impossibly long lashes set under pale, slanted brows. A mouth that . . .

A mouth that was twisted downward in a frown as she glared at the hand that still restrained her arm. Her angry eyes flashed up to meet his. He quickly released her, dropping his hand to his side, flushing with embarrassment.

"I'm so sorry," he apologized lamely. "I thought you were my daughter."

She stared into his bemused gray eyes, momentarily astonished. She examined his lean face, weighing the possible truthfulness of his claim. But as his lips began to curve up into a smile, she laughed.

"That's a new one," she said and twirled around, once more activating the sliding door.

"Wait!"

"Yes?" Her voice was frosty as she glanced at him over her shoulder.

"I . . . I . . . " he stammered, realizing that he had no reason whatsoever to detain her. He shook his head, trying to clear away the unusual buzzing that had taken over his brain. He reddened as she waited, her hands shoved into the pockets of her sleeveless pink sweatshirt. His mouth was dry and he swallowed painfully, retreating under her caustic scrutiny. He brushed the back of his hand against his forehead, pushing away the thick dark hair to wipe away the perspiration.

"Nothing . . . It's nothing," he muttered, turning away from her. Dazed, he began to walk back to the courthouse, then wheeled once more to watch as she entered the mall.

What had happened to him? The cool, competent attorney, so collected before judge and jury, had fallen apart under the cool gaze of a slender blonde. In one moment, his life had been torn apart and thrown back together, now incomplete, missing an essential element. His fist tightened around the handle of his briefcase.

Through the plate glass of the store, he saw the woman moving through the aisles, her almost white braid swinging in rhythm with her swaying hips. His eyes strained to follow her until she was out of sight, not appreciating the irony: he was now thoroughly enjoying the same undulating movements he found so aggravating in his daughter.

Lisa Fratelli stared at the stacks of silky lingerie piled in the aisle of the store. She fingered the soft material in pastel shades of pinks, yellows and greens, but her mind's eye was seeing the gray eyes of her tall accoster. Who was he? Michigan's Upper Peninsula was a rural area where everyone kept track of the other residents. Her young friends surely would have told her about such an attractive man if he had been in Iron Mountain for long. Had she seen him before, she would have noticed those broad shoulders, that strong jaw, the nearly black hair.

Lisa put a trembling finger to her mouth as she absentmindedly examined panties that were several sizes too large for her. She rubbed her arm at the spot where he had grasped her so roughly, but there was no pain there, only a tingling sensation, a pleasurable reminder of strong male hands touching her. A warmth spread through her body and her legs weakened. Stop it, she whispered, unmindful of the curious stares of fellow shoppers.

Lisa was not an innocent. She recognized desire and understood feminine needs, long repressed. She closed her eyes tightly and shook her head to relieve the tension. A minor sexual attraction, she told herself, that was all. It was simply nature's way of telling her she was a normal woman with normal physical reactions. It meant nothing more than that.

She let out a long breath, blinked, and continued her aimless stroll through the mall, trying to remember why she had come there.

******

3

Jake Gannett had been warned that there were more car-deer accidents on the short stretch of Highway Two between Iron Mountain and the little town of Norway than there were anywhere else in the state of Michigan. He turned off his cell phone, kept his white Corvette well within the speed limit, and carefully watched the brush on either side of the road.

As he followed the curves through the towering hills, he thought about the changes in his life, but the green-eyed beauty he encountered three days before intruded into his reveries. Before she destroyed his self-image, he had viewed himself as a mature man, beyond the hormonal urges of the young. He had a teenage daughter, for heaven's sake. He should be beyond sexual adventures, he groaned, yet his desire flashed again, as he envisioned her lush breasts, slender waist and curving derriere.

Jake could not exorcise the woman from his mind. She crept into his mind at inconvenient moments during the day and disturbed his dreams at night. In his law office, in the courtroom, at times when he needed all his powers of concentration, he found himself woolgathering.

He wished he had had his wits about him that day. He didn't know her name. Hell, he did even know if she was married. He sighed. As soon as he had his life organized, he would have to make a point of tracking the lady down. Someone in the county would be sure to know about a woman that beautiful.

But what if she were a tourist? Jake frowned as he considered the possibility – and decided it was a probability. The beautifully forested area surrounding Iron Mountain encompassed Northeastern Wisconsin and the Upper Peninsula of Michigan and it drew visitors in all seasons. In the summer, it backpackers and vacationers tramped through the woods. In the fall, bus companies brought hoards of nature lovers to see the glorious autumn colors, ranging from the deep greens of the conifers to the vivid reds of the sumac and the vibrant oranges of the sugar maples. In the winter, snowmobilers, hunters and skiers arrived, to enjoy the fine slopes on several small mountains. Championship skiers tried their skills on the jump Iron Mountain claimed was the biggest in the world.

Jake first discovered the blue lakes and rivers as a boy,

when his parents brought him here on vacations. His family were city people who came to the cool north woods in the summer to escape the heat of paved sidewalks. He loved the freedom he had to explore the woods and enjoyed the long, lazy days of boating and fishing with his father. Though he was now planning on becoming a full-fledged "U-per", as Upper Peninsula natives termed themselves, he still viewed his surroundings with the appreciative enthusiasm of a visitor.

He wondered again about the green-eyed vision. It was Monday now. With another weekend over, it was unlikely that he would see her again, if indeed she were a tourist. But he could make a few discreet inquiries to be certain.

Meanwhile, he must find a home for his daughter Jodi. As Jake carefully maneuvered his car over the smooth black-topped highway that twisted through the hills, he pondered the problem his daughter posed. A year ago, Christine, his wife of eighteen years, died suddenly of a heart disease that she had long known about, yet kept a secret from him. He had been left to raise their daughter alone.

In the emotional turmoil of the funeral, one of his elderly uncles revealed to Jodi that she was adopted, something Christine had always insisted she never be told. Jodi, already upset at suddenly losing her adored mother, recoiled sharply and went into a deep depression. Jake found counselors to help her deal with her grief and constantly reminded her how much he loved her. He thought she was making progress, but when Jodi finally came out of her withdrawal, it was to become rebellious. He could not approve of the new friends she made. Her grades, once excellent, began to drop. She began to wear flamboyant clothes, usually filthy. The blond hair her father was so proud of was sometimes pink, sometimes blue, sometimes a combination of both, but usually dirty. Thank God she had never cut it, he thought ruefully.

When Jake came home on a school day to find Jodi in a bedroom reeking of marijuana, he made a decision. He resigned from his busy law firm and looked for a location to start his own practice as a country lawyer. After some consideration, he remembered the Iron Mountain area from past family vacations. Surely, this would be an ideal setting to raise his daughter.

For the past few weeks, he and Jodi had lived in a furnished motel apartment while he prepared to hang out his

5

shingle. He passed the Michigan bar examination easily, hired a secretary and found a pleasant office in a trendy new building near the courthouse. Now he was looking for a permanent home for his daughter and himself, preferably in a nearby small town. Some time during the next two weeks, he would make his decision about a house while Jodi was at the well supervised Lake Hope Girls Camp. He had heard wonderful things about Norway from his legal associates. Today, he had an appointment with a real estate agent there. With any luck, he would have a livable home for Jodi when she returned.

"Rainy days and Mondays," Lisa hummed to herself as she unlocked the door to her little office on Norway's Main Street, but she changed her tune to "Oh, What a Beautiful Morning" as she realized that this sunny Monday was not "getting her down" at all! After a weekend of dissatisfied pacing in her tiny cabin in the hills near town, unable to walk out her restlessness on the forested trails because of torrential June downpours, she saw work as her salvation.

At thirty-one, Lisa had long resigned herself to her life as a small town spinster, and even managed an enviable serenity, measuring her hours between Fratelli Realty, her church and civic activities, her brother, and her wooded hideaway. If anyone were to have the temerity to question her about her life, she could truthfully answer that it was satisfactory. If she had no children of her own, she unconsciously mothered the teenagers in her church's youth group, which she served as advisor. She had no husband, but she poured out her love to Richard, her brother. Her many good friends had become her extended family. If she occasionally missed a close physical relationship, well, she could cope with that, too.

There was always hard work, she thought, there was the satisfaction of building her real estate business. Lisa had been only eighteen when she began to study for her real estate boards, nineteen when she made her first sale, quickly moving from a secretary's desk to sales in an Iron Mountain firm, then on to her own realty firm in Norway. There were times she thought wistfully of her first dream of becoming a teacher, but that had been impossible for a young woman with no money for college and only a high school equivalency diploma to show scholarship boards. She accepted her life and made the best of it, but she took winter courses at a nearby community college, juggling her schedule between house showings and classes.

She checked her voice mail for the few messages from the weekend and looked at her calendar. Only one showing today, a Mr. Jake Gannett, who was looking for a single family dwelling. During their brief phone conversation, he had not been specific about his requirements, but it seemed that price would be no problem. She sank into her chair, switched on her computer, and ran through the real estates listings, selecting all the house descriptions that might appeal to him. As the sheets came out of the printer, she sorted them into stacks, one of rural and the other of village homes, according to size. She put them into a folder and slipped it into her desk. She glanced at her watch, calculating how many phone calls she could make before her appointment.

Jake gaped in surprise as he turned a bend on Highway Two and looked down a steep slope into a fairytale setting. The little village of Norway nestled in the midst of high, forest-covered hills. Church steeples gleamed in the sunlight. Neat white houses seemed to be painted against the lush green of the trees and shrubs. He smiled at a setting that seemed created out of the bright memories of a Grandma Moses.

The Corvette coasted down the hill, passing a small park that boasted a sparkling waterfall. With quarter of an hour before his late afternoon appointment, Jake cruised through the town, taking the time to explore. He turned south on Highway Eight, finding the golf course. He thought about his golf clubs, still in storage. He smiled when he spotted the county fairgrounds, imagining Jodi eating cotton candy and enjoying lighthearted carnival fun with small town friends. He scrutinized the well-tended bicycle paths with approval. Jodi, who had always lived in a high-rise apartment, had never had a bicycle before. She would love it here.

He turned his car around, returning to the center of Norway, noting the churches, the schools and the library as he drove. This was what he wanted for his daughter, he thought, as he parked in front of the little real estate office on Main Street.

Eager now, he opened the door of the car and slid out, then hesitated as the warm air of the June day spread into the air-conditioned interior. He undid his tie, tossing it to the passenger seat, removed the jacket of his business suit, folding it carefully and placing it on top of the tie. He opened three buttons of his white shirt and rolled up the sleeves. He breathed in deeply and turned to look at the business section.

Norway's downtown looked much like others in this part of the Midwest. Storefronts of assorted businesses abutted onto narrow sidewalks with high curbs or low curbs depending on the condition of the streets adjacent. The neatly marked parallel parking spaces were almost vacant this late in the day. As he strolled past the gift shop next to the realtor's, Jake paused to view the display of arts and crafts that spoke volumes of the Scandinavian heritage of the town. He glanced down the street where, to his surprise, a large band shell dominated the square.

Jake had seen small gazebo-bandstand structures in towns across Wisconsin and Michigan, usually constructed of wood and painted white. But this bandstand was shaped like an upended bowl, the exterior a dull red brick, the interior, white wainscoting in a tongue and groove design. It was set back from the street, fronted by a grassy area that invited concert goers. Jake inspected it hopefully, considering the possibility of classical concerts. Was there an orchestra here? He turned and walked briskly into Fratelli Realty, filled with enthusiasm for this new venture.

There was no one seated at the computer console at the rear of the room but Jake heard the clinking of dishes in the adjacent room and smelled freshly brewed coffee. He examined the office. It was simple. Besides the desk and chair, there were a couple of filing cabinets, with several comfortable chairs for customers. The pale yellow walls held little in the way of decoration save for the mandatory licenses and an aerial photograph of Norway. The few magazines on the small table dealt with real estate business. Functional, Jake decided, in no way competing with the houses sold here.

The only bright spot in the room was a corner with tiny cabinets, chairs and a table, devoted to children's toys, books and games. Hands in his pockets, Jake rocked a little doll's cradle with a toe, glancing at the exquisite soft-sculptured baby doll within. An old hand carved train circled the area on its wooden track. Everything was attractive and durable. In this corner, at least, some time had been spent in selection.

Jake stepped up to the desk and rapped on it. "Hello?" he called out to the rattling in the rear room.

"Be out in a minute. Have a seat."

Jake recognized the husky female voice from his telephone conversation of the week before, a sexy voice, he had thought then. It probably in no way matched the woman he was about to meet. He had been disappointed too many times to put much credence in telephone impressions.

He sprawled onto a faded chair that was not really adequate for his six-foot-plus frame and took up one of the magazines, scanning it for anything of interest, finding at last something on condominiums and the real estate laws that pertained to them. Somehow, he mused, he never expected the condo craze to reach this far north. He became engrossed in the article, settling into the chair and stretching his long legs out under the desk.

Crockery smacked down sharply. Startled, Jake glanced up to meet the fiery glare of a pair of furious green eyes.

"Don 't you think it's going a bit too far, following me all the way here?"

Jake stared at the woman, stunned, and rose swiftly to his feet, cracking his shin painfully on the desk. He ignored the ache in his surprise. It was the fair-haired beauty of his mall encounter, now wearing a cotton shirt with a matching skirt, both in a bright color Jodi had once described to him as raspberry. The color could have given a blond a washed-out look, but instead it emphasized the vivid emerald of her eyes. Her hair, now smoothly bound in a French twist, gleamed in the sunlight streaming in through the picture window at the office's front. She was even lovelier than he remembered.

Jake grinned at her, extending his right hand. "Jake Gannett, Ms . . . . ?"

The woman hesitated, for a brief moment searching his intense gray eyes. Her lashes lowered as she quickly scanned his tall figure, taking in the wide shoulders and the long arm outstretched to her, before checking her desk calendar, where she noted his name. Recovering quickly, she raised her own hand to meet his, shaking it briskly in a businesslike way.

"Lisa Fratelli," she responded, then smiled. Jake was delighted to see that he had been right about that dimple, which flashed on one cheek, lending a charming gaiety to her face. He was absolutely enchanted with it. He held her hand, admiring the cool smoothness of her skin.

"Then you aren't chasing me today?"

"It's a total surprise to see you here, but a delightful surprise all the same," he beamed.

She pulled her hand away. Jake released his grasp reluctantly.

"And you really have a daughter that looks like me?" she dubiously contemplated his dark brown, almost black hair. He watched her as her eyes followed the short sideburns to his tanned cheeks. Did she like prominent cheekbones, he wondered. He saw her glance lower to the thick column of his throat, exposed by the open shirt, catching a glimpse of dark, curly hair at the vee. He chuckled and she quickly raised her eyes to meet his amused twinkle.

"You don't seem old enough to have a daughter," she blurted out, then blushed.

"She's only thirteen. And she looks like you only from behind, believe me." He pointedly inspected her curves, caressing her breasts with his eyes.

Lisa stiffened angrily. "What can I do for you today, Mr. Gannett?" She reddened further as his grin widened. She dropped her eyes to her desk and rearranged some papers that lay there.

Jake realized she was struggling to find some sane way to control this conversation, and took pity on her. "What I need, Ms. Fratelli, is a family home, as I told you on the phone. Your firm was highly recommended to me. Is your boss available?"

She straightened to her full height which, given even the added inches of the heels of her leather sandals, brought her only to the level of his eyes. She told him firmly, "I am the boss here. As a matter of fact, I am the entire business."

"Sorry," he apologized quickly. "I'm not a chauvinist, you know, it's just that when I made this appointment . . ."

"It was with me," she finished for him. "I suppose I didn't tell you that at the time. But I'm sure I can provide exactly what you need. Actually," she continued quickly before he could misconstrue that remark, "we have several houses on the market here in Norway." She reached into the desk drawer and handed him a folder containing home listings. He took them from her, noting with delight that she wore no wedding ring. She motioned him to a seat and placed herself safely behind her desk.

"I suggest we look at the first three in that stack today," she said, pouring him some coffee. "They're all vacant so immediate possession would be possible provided your financing went through quickly. You did tell me that was important to you."

Jake looked over the photocopied papers while he sipped from his cup. Most of them described very large homes, much too big for two people. He was about to reject several, then reconsidered as he glanced at the attractive woman across the desk from him. The more houses they viewed, the longer he would be in her company.

He cleared his throat. "They all look as if they could have potential. Shall we start?"

Chapter Two

They elected to use Lisa's Bronco, a sturdy copper-colored four-wheel drive vehicle that was practical in northern winters. Lisa observed that he made no argument over her taking the wheel and buckled his seat belt without her urging, two points in his favor. Perhaps he really was a liberated male. Then she noticed his eyes on her legs. Her skirt had slipped up when she climbed into the SUV. She inched her clothing down, he grinned in amusement, and she revised her opinion.

"Shall I give you the grand tour of Norway first?" she suggested, then wondered where that had come from. Just part of a new kind of sales pitch, she tried to tell herself; if this man fell in love with the village and decided to live here, selling him a piece of property would be easy.

She chided herself then. The man was married, he wore a gold ring on his left hand. He had a child. He would be a nuisance, a temptation if he were to move here. She told herself these things, but still continued the tour, aware of every movement beside her and thankful for the shifting mechanism that separated them.

Lisa took the Bronco south on Highway Eight, proudly showing Jake the city-owned golf course and fairgrounds.

"Wonderful!" Jake exclaimed, never mentioning that he had already seen them, and was not really looking at them now. His gaze more often wandered to the pure profile beside him, wondering how long it would be before he could place a kiss on the tilted nose and considering various strategies to accomplish the same. But his attention returned to the road as she drove even farther, almost to the bridge that crossed the Menominee River and marked the Wisconsin border.

As she turned down a road marked by a sign that read "Piers Gorge," he threw her a glance. Her dimple flashed as she smiled at him. It was all he could do to keep from reaching out to touch it. She turned off the air conditioning and rolled down a window.

"Can you hear it?"

Jake tore his gaze away and opened his window, too, to listen to the roaring that could be heard over the sound of the engine and the rushing wind. "A waterfall?"

Lisa nodded as she parked the vehicle at a spot where they could look at the twelve-foot Mishicot Falls that spanned the wide river. The water flew over the rocks, crashing onto a huge boulder that looked like a Volkswagon bug, swirling madly over and around ledges and crevices and flowing into a narrow channel towered over by 75-foot granite bluffs.

"Stunning," Jake murmured, his voice almost lost in the thunder of the rushing water.

Lisa gave him another gamine smile as she drove them back to the highway. She explained that there were whitewater enthusiasts going down the river every weekend and most weekdays in rubber rafts, canoes, and kayaks, supplied by several local outfitters.

Jake grimaced. "You wouldn't get me on one of those things. That crazy I'm not."

"But it's fun!"

He shuddered. "No way! I can think of better ways to end my life. I'll stick to swimming pools."

She laughed, a bell-like tinkling over the grumble of the falls. Damn, he thought, the first woman in years I've wanted to impress and she's zeroing in on my one phobia. He hoped he could avoid any further discussion about whitewater.

Jake struggled to bring back his usual self-containment as they continued on their way, back through the town and eastward, passing the little hamlet of Vulcan.

"Vulcan?" Jake questioned. "Home of Spock?"

Lisa groaned.

"O.K., O.K," he laughed. "So Star Trek jokes are out. But why call it Vulcan and not something Scandinavian?"

"This entire area was heavily mined for iron through the Depression and on into World War Two. Who better to name an iron town after than the Roman god of fire who gave the secret of working with iron to mankind?" Lisa gestured at the hills that towered above the road, indicating the remnants of old mine shafts, ghostly reminders of the past. She explained that besides the old mines, there were many pits and holes that unwary hikers could fall into. New openings could be found every spring as the earth shifted and old mines collapsed. They should be avoided.

"Aren't you exaggerating just a little?" he asked. "You make it sound as if the earth is hollow beneath us."

"When we get back to town, I'll show you our lake. It was created when the buildings at the center of town began to sink into an old iron mine."

"You're kidding!"

"No, I'm not!" she said. "It's the truth. The people just moved a block or two and now there are houses all around the edge of the lake."

"And you're trying to sell me a house there?" Jake teased, thinking that even if he were faced with the possibility of the ground opening up and swallowing him whole, the prospect of living in Norway near this intriguing woman looked more and more inviting. The breeze blowing through the still-open car windows had loosened her chignon, freeing wisps of hair that fluttered around her face. He longed to smooth them back, to slide his fingers through the silvery luster of her loosened hair.

"It's perfectly safe, you know," Lisa hastened to reassure him. There are plenty of geologists around here who keep track of the old mines. But you should stay away from the hills until you know them better or have a guide. It would be a good idea to warn your daughter about them, too."

Jake nodded, liking her immediate concern for their well-being and her assumption that he would be living here. As a matter of fact, he liked everything about her. He was so entranced with her nearness, it took some moments for him to notice that they were now bumping along yet another dirt road. Over the engine's roar, he could hear another rumbling sound.

"Are you still trying to get me excited about whitewater?" he asked sternly. "It won't work, you know."

She chuckled, not even trying to talk over the combined roar of the four-wheel drive Bronco and the rush of water through turbines. Jake was astonished to see the enormous hydro-electric dam hidden away in this remote spot. It stretched across the river, grumbling as it did its work, spouting foamy water through its outlets. Jake turned to Lisa as she switched off the car engine. "What's this?"

"This dam belongs to the city of Norway," she shouted over the noise. "The city has its own power source so our electric rates are about a third of what they would be anywhere else."

"The city built this?" Jake was interested despite the familiar tightening in his throat.

"Oh no, it was left behind when the iron companies closed down the mines and the city kept it running," Lisa explained with pride. "It's hard to keep it going sometimes because of the shortage of parts for such an old dam, but I think it's a wonderful asset for the city, don't you?"

He did not answer and she turned to see his lips pressed together and perspiration beaded on his forehead as he gazed out at the monster spanning the river. Without another word, Lisa started the Bronco and threw it into reverse, managing the narrow Y-turn easily enough, though he grasped the arm rest tightly and braced himself against the dashboard as she came near to the edge of the riverbank.

"Does that help?" she asked dryly, glancing over at him.

The corners of his lips lifted slightly as they drove out of sight of the dam. "Just a reaction."

"Phobia?"

"You might say that." Jake changed his position to gaze out the passenger window. So, he thought, now she knows my one weakness. I wonder if I can convince her it's endearing and sweet.

Lisa chattered away, extolling the virtues of her hometown, showing him the entrance to one large mine that had been turned into a tourist attraction that she recommended highly.

"Unless, of course, you're claustrophobic, too?" she teased.

"Hey," he objected, "I'm not a total basket case."

She grinned at him and he relaxed as he realized she was trying to put him at ease. He returned her smile, put his tensions away and prepared to enjoy the day and his charming companion.

The last stop on their tour was a huge cemetery. Lisa drove a long avenue of flagpoles, their banners of red, white and blue snapping smartly in the warm breeze. She explained that a flagpole was erected for each soldier from Norway who had died in battle. At the circle that marked the center of the cemetery, Jake motioned to Lisa to stop.

Hands on the steering wheel, Lisa watched him in surprise as he uncoiled his tail frame from the car, circled the front of the vehicle and opened her door to assist her out.

"Time to stretch our legs," he smiled, as he pulled her to his side and tucked her hand under his arm. She made a tiny attempt to pull away, but he held her firmly with his other hand. She turned to him to object, but found herself trapped, enthralled by his gray eyes. She caught her breath, startled at the desire she saw there. He wanted her and was making no attempt to hide it. Did he think it was flattering? Well, other men had wanted her, too, and she had dealt with them. She could handle this one. She thought about jerking her hand from his, forcing the issue immediately. But somehow, her hand felt comfortable where it was. She shrugged and allowed him to lead her down a path.

They strolled through the cemetery, meandering aimlessly from tombstone to tombstone, silently reading the inscriptions. They looked at each other sadly when they happened on a group of small markers whose dates indicated the deaths of infants and children, all from the same family. They ran their fingertips over the now worn carvings on old headstones, trying to decipher their secrets. Lisa wandered along, dreamily content to go where he led. His head towered over her, his strong jaw thrust forward as he examined a newer stone.

"Why are there so many Italian names here? I thought they would be Norwegians."

It took Lisa a moment to focus on his questions. All her concentration had been on the spot where the back of her hand met the firm warmth of his ribs.

"And how is it that a blonde has an Italian name? Or are you married?" His careless question did not mask the intensity of his concern and she could not help smiling.

She explained that the mines had drawn many nationalities to the region and that most of the townspeople were Cornish, Swedish or Italian. "You know," she mused, "I noticed the other day that of the dozens of dentists in Iron Mountain, there are only two who *aren't* Italian." She turned away, shielding her eyes from him, a slight catch in her voice. "Northern Italians are often blond, but I'm actually one of the few true Norwegians left in Norway, Michigan. My foster parents were Italians. I was with them so long, I finally changed my name to theirs, once I was of age."

"So you aren't married," Jake grinned, honing in on what he obviously considered the most important piece of information.

"No." She slid her hand away from him. How had she allowed this? Her eyes became iceberg cool and she marched back to the parking area, glancing at her watch. "I think we had better be going. Do you realize that we've spent an hour and a half looking at the town and you haven't seen any of the houses on our list yet."

They looked at two large, modern four-bedroom ranch homes that Jake rejected quickly before they came to the last of Lisa's prospects, a large gray and white Victorian three-story that stood on a long tree-lined street.

"This will probably be much too large for us." Jake sighed as they approached the wide turn-of-the-century porch that stretched around three sides of the home.

"Oh, I don't know," Lisa protested. "It's only four bedrooms. How many children do you and your wife have?"

"There's just the two of us, my daughter and me."

She looked pointedly at his left hand.

"Oh. I'd forgotten about that." He turned the ring slowly around on his finger, considering. Taking his ring off now would only add to her suspicion, he knew. He had to explain. He drew a breath. "My wife died this past year, I just haven't taken it off." He hastened on, trying to make her understand his dilemma. "I took the ring off at the time, but Jodi, my daughter, was having some problems dealing with her grief and . . . other things. She was so upset when she noticed it was gone, I agreed to wear it until such time as she could feel comfortable about it. I had no inclination to date. Christine had just died . . ." His voice trailed off, his eyes shuttered, his thoughts far away, reliving those painful months.

Lisa stood quietly, waiting for him to return to the present. As he became aware of her silence, he shook his head. Lisa was cool springtime after a long winter. "And you?" he asked. "Have you always been single?"

She opened the front door hastily, answering sharply, "Yes! And likely to stay that way!"

Satisfied with his progress, Jake hummed to himself as he followed her into the house, enjoying the swish of her skirt as she strode before him, and admiring the shapely legs.

The place had been empty for some time. There was dust in the corners of the hallway and cobwebs covered the halls, but

Jake immediately saw what a treasure lay beneath the dirt. He admired the curving grand staircase in the entry and knew that the grandfather clock that had been in his family since the eighteenth century would fit perfectly in the alcove beside it. Christine had always thought of the clock as an anachronism, out of place in her carefully structured digital world. It had been shunted aside into his dressing room where he tended to its needs. But in this Victorian setting, the morning ritual of setting the hands on the brass face and pulling the chain to raise the old lead weights would seem appropriate.

Large sunny rooms opened onto the hallway. Jake whistled as he explored the kitchen where he found an original stone oven set in the wall near a built-in breakfast nook. He was singing by the time he found the big shelf-lined library with its brick fireplace. He mentally furnished the room with his collection of books, his century-old rolltop desk and an Irish setter on an oriental rug in front of the fireplace. Jodi would love that, he thought wistfully. Christine's perfect housekeeping had never allowed a pet.

He followed Lisa up the winding staircase to a wide hallway where four doors led to each of the bedrooms. He wandered through the small bedrooms first, finding one with faded blue-and-white flowered wallpaper. He provided an imaginary bed with a frilly canopy for his daughter. Then he rejected the idea, chuckling at himself. Jodi would want something more modern than that!

He strolled into the master bedroom and stopped short. Light streamed through several large windows on the west wall, the late afternoon sun lighting up a massive oak bed. The entire frame, head and foot and sides, was beautifully carved with animals, birds, trees, shrubs, grasses, what seemed to be all of the flora and fauna of the Michigan forests. The room was immense, covering at least a third of the second story, yet it was dominated by the king-sized bed.

Jake had never seen anything like it. He looked to his realtor for an explanation.

"It comes with the house," Lisa said. "The whole thing was built and carved from several solid pieces of oak that were fitted together right here in this room, so no one has ever been able to get it out. You would have to take an ax to it to remove it." She was visibly embarrassed and Jake did not say a word, waiting.

"Actually," she said after a pause, "I've always discouraged anyone from buying the house who would do that to the bed. I'd buy the place myself before I'd let that happen and I have no idea what I would do with such a large home."

Jake surveyed the room thoughtfully. He looked once more at the fantastic bed and pictured it with a brocade bedspread, maybe in green. Yes, green would appropriate, in fact, emerald, about the color of . . . her eyes. Suddenly, he pictured her lying on it, her blond hair loose, spread gossamer fine over that imaginary bedspread. His eyes lowered to take in the vision of her face, eyes slumberous, mouth parted in passion, a pulse beating in her throat, the fine bones of her delicate shoulders, her . . . breasts. Sensations he hadn't felt in a year rippled through his body.

He turned abruptly, before he could embarrass himself in front of her and hastened from the room. Lisa trailed behind, thankfully not speaking to him, letting him explore the house unhindered. He groaned under his breath. He could see the bewilderment in her face as she tried to gauge what he found offensive in the old pantry. His physical warmth lessened as he paced, inspecting the rooms on the lower floor once more.

It really was too large a house for two people, he thought, surveying the spacious living room. He thought about furniture and found himself wondering if Lisa might like the Chippendale he had in storage. He watched the play of the sun across the floor and all at once, he pictured a playpen with toys scattered about. Damn! What was he thinking of? He was forty years old!

Jake and Lisa left the big white house without speaking and stood together on the old porch. He gave the ancient swing a push. Lisa listened to its gentle creak. The setting sun gave the white gingerbread trim a rosy hue. Lisa admired his classic profile in the glow of the fading light. He is a handsome specimen, she thought woefully, there's no denying that.

"Look," he suggested quietly, catching her eye on him, "it's getting late. Why don't I take you out for dinner and we'll talk about this house?"

Startled, she spun away. "No!" she cried, panic-stricken, then chided herself for her frightened reaction.

"Why not? Do you have other plans?"

"Well . . . no," she floundered. "Actually . . . my brother has guests . . . but I don't like to leave . . . " She ground to a halt as he pinned her with his gray gaze.

"Oh, come," he teased her. "Whatever happened to woman's liberation? All I'm doing is asking you out for a simple meal to discuss business. Let's be sophisticated about this."

She gave him a skeptical glance, finding the twinkle in his eyes. In that corner of her brain that retained sanity, she knew that this was no simple invitation to a business dinner. Oh, she had plenty of those in the past. She also had become an expert over the years at discouraging unwanted attention from men, knew just the right things to say, the perfect attitudes to take. Her cool, calm efficiency dampened any ardent attentions from her associates.

Ordinarily, she would have accepted the invitation in a business-like way and kept the conversation during dinner strictly on real estate. But Jake Gannett was different. For one thing, she really didn't have the time. For another, he was so blatantly male! And finally, she wasn't altogether certain that she was going to be immune to his personality. She opened her mouth to refuse him.

"The Highway Supper Club has good steaks," she said.

Chapter Three

As she parked the car in the gravel-covered parking lot of the Highway Supper club, Lisa Fratelli was still trying to analyze why she had agreed to have dinner with the man seated beside her. She had avoided male-female relationships over the past fifteen years devoting herself to her family, her home, her business, her church and a handful of civic organizations. She had always busied herself enough to sleep well at night, which was her idea of a satisfactory life. Though she considered herself to be a small town spinster, archaic as the term was, she told herself she was happy with her lot.

In her early twenties, she had had her share of local admirers pestering her with their attentions, but one by one they had given up. While not totally ignorant of her beauty, she did not really understand why they had persisted so long. Perhaps they had sensed the warmth and sensuality that lay just beneath the cool surface. Yet none of them had had the strength of character to overcome her steady, calm rejection.

As the years passed, Lisa celebrated her friends' joys in engagement, wedding, anniversary and christening gifts, and never regretted the choices she had made. She easily squelched any matchmaking attempts her closest friends had attempted. By now, she assumed that the rest of the population of Norway had grown used to both her appearance and idiosyncrasies and accepted her for what she was.

But Jake Gannett, an outsider, was looking at her from a different perspective than the men and women she had grown up with. He knew nothing of her past history or reputation. He considered her available, that was certain, and she knew that she would have to tread carefully to keep him at arm's length. So why had she so foolishly agreed to have this dinner with him? It was simply not in character for her.

She observed him as she met him at the rear of the Bronco and walked silently to the door of the little country inn. What was it about this man that broke through her natural reserve? She usually shied away from big men with their casual air of physical superiority. She never judged anyone on surface perfections or imperfections, so why should a simple glance at his profile send a ripple of pleasure through her body? And why, oh why, was she here at the Highway Supper Club?

Because Lisa Fratelli was an honest woman, she admitted to herself that she was here simply because he was the most attractive man she had ever met.

The little country tavern held only six tables and five booths, each lit with what Jake had always thought of as bug lights, green vases holding votive candles. The larger part of the club was a typical north country bar, a gleaming horseshoe curve surrounded by padded, high-backed bar stools. Behind the bar was a mirrored wall which reflected racks of liquor bottles and glasses. Efforts had obviously been made to maintain a degree of elegance, but Jake scanned with amusement the usual little cards with homespun humor and wisdom, provided, no doubt by the patrons, which had found their way into the corners of the mirrors.

The few people seated at the bar on this weekday evening turned in unison to greet the new arrivals. They all seemed to know Lisa, smiling genuinely when they saw her. Even the women like her, Jake noted with mild surprise, calling out greetings and asking her to stop by for coffee sometime. Her stunning beauty seemed to be no threat to them. Lisa, in turn, asked about health, children, farming problems, or whatever else might apply, leaving each of them with a smile as she and Jake proceeded through the tavern.

For a moment, Jake considered staying at the bar to get to know some of the folk in the community he was planning to join, but he thought better of it and steered Lisa to the farthest corner, ushering her into a secluded booth. When she glanced at him and then looked toward the better lit parts of the supper club, he grinned. "I like to keep my business dealings private," he told her.

She laughed and reached for the water glass the plump bartender who doubled as the waitress brought them, along with menus. "If you want privacy, you'd better reconsider moving to Norway. Everyone knows everybody's business here. If you have any secrets, somebody is sure to ferret them out."

"Oh, come now," he scoffed. "How would you know? You don't strike me as the kind of woman who would have any dark, deep-hidden secrets in her life."

To his consternation, her eyes flew up to meet his in alarm. The hand holding the green glass shook and her water splashed onto the table.

"What's wrong?" he demanded, seizing the napkin dispenser to help her mop up the small, damp spot.

"Nothing." Her low voice was even huskier and her eyes were shuttered against his compassionate gaze. Her lips trembled. God, he groaned inwardly, she looks so miserable. What on earth did I say? He wanted to gather her into his arms, hold her head to his chest and comfort her but he knew the time for that had not yet come.

They were interrupted again by the waitress. By the time they agreed, under Lisa's advisement and the waitress's concurrence, on a simple meal of beef tenderloin, baked potatoes and salads, Lisa had regained her composure.

"What was that all about?" he quizzed.

"None of your business."

"Ah, but as a future resident of Norway, I want practice in ferreting," he explained with a straight face, "so your business is my business."

"If it's business you want to talk about, let's consider the Johnson house."

He raised an eyebrow.

"The old Victorian three-story," she clarified.

Jake waved his hand. "We can talk about that later. No serious matters until we've eaten. That's the way to avoid indigestion." He straightened the silverware in front of him as he considered his strategy. "Tell me about Norway instead."

"I can't think of anything I haven't told you."

He pondered for a moment then brightened. "How about some of its past history? You know, background is important if I decide to buy here. For example, have you lived here all your life?"

"No. I came here when I was six," she sighed, playing with a bread stick.

"You said something about a brother."

25

"Yes, I have a brother." She was not volunteering any information, but Jake had always relied on persistence to get to the heart of a matter.

"Parents, any other family?"

"No, none, just the two of us," she said irritably, snapping her bread stick in half. "I thought you wanted to hear about Norway."

"Oh, I do, I do!"

"Then ask me about Norway."

"Isn't that way I was doing?" he asked innocently. "So . . . you were born . . . in Norway . . . what, about twenty-five years ago?"

"Thirty-one, and I'm an old maid," she retorted, "and I don't want to talk about me anymore, please. Stick to Norway."

"Right, right. Let's see, how about Norway's social life?" She nodded.

"Good. If you and the current man in your life want to go out for fun, where does he take you?"

"I don't have . . ." Lisa tried to catch herself but Jake had found out what he wanted to know. He chuckled as she glared at him, those green eyes snapping. She was beautiful! And unattached! He was batting a thousand.

"I'm sorry," he said in mock contrition, struggling to keep a straight face.

"You should be." A small smile was forming on her lips despite her best efforts. "Now, ask me about Norway. Only Norway."

"Fine, fine, we'll stick to the town." He stretched his long legs under the booth table, nudging hers, exploring her slender ankles. To his delight, she didn't move away. "So . . . ," he continued, "where . . . in Norway . . . do you live?"

She started to laugh and he joined in as the patrons sitting at the bar eyed them curiously.

"And I suppose," she gasped, "that next you'll want to hear about the Norway telephone company and my private number will come into that?"

"It crossed my mind."

Several emotions he could not comprehend flitted across her face. For a moment, a frown creased her forehead. Before he could follow his impulse to reach out and smooth it away, it disappeared and her lips formed a pleasant but distinctly polite

26

smile. "Look," she said coolly, "I'm willing to tell you all about Norway. You know my business address and business telephone number and those are all you are going to need, because all we have here is a business relationship. Is that understood?"

"Understood," he said, suitably penitent. Understood, he thought, but not accepted.

The salads arrived at that moment and Lisa slipped her legs away from his. She had been aware that he had physical strategies he was using besides the clever little games he played so well but somehow, his body next to hers did not feel threatening at all. In fact, it was almost . . . welcoming, as if he were a cozy fire to warm the coldness that surrounded her.

She tried not to think about it and concentrated instead on the crisp lettuce garnished with cherry tomatoes, strips of colorful red cabbage and carrots, toasted croutons and grated cheese, all topped with a hot bacon dressing she had never tried before. Her mouth watered as she realized how hungry she was. She had missed lunch and it really was very late!

"If the steaks are as good as this salad, I'll be in heaven," Jake vowed after his first bite. "Now, tell me about Norway."

Lisa's head shot up.

"No, really!" he laughed. "I'm serious this time. Tell me about that bandstand for starters. Who plays there?"

Lisa, relieved that the man was going to desist in his ridiculous gambits, launched into the history of the Norway City Band, the oldest continually performing marching band in the United States, formed around 1880. The members rehearsed year-round, marched in all the local parades and gave concerts in the band shell on Main Street every other week all summer.

"Who plays in it?"

"Just about anybody who plays an instrument," she answered enthusiastically. "Men and women of all ages. Quite a few high school students. There's a lot of civic involvement so you might be interested. Do you or your daughter play anything?"

"Jodi, but just a piano, unfortunately. Unless we can push it down the street."

She laughed. "Oh, well, we'll have to find something else for her."

"I'd like that. Any suggestions?"

They were discussing other organizations and activities

that Jodi might enjoy when the steaks arrived, sizzling on their heavy steel platters. The corner booth became quiet as they began to work their way through the meal, but occasionally Jake's fork would pause in midair as he studied Lisa. She caught him staring at her for the third time. "What are you looking at?" she asked, pausing in her mad dash through her meal.

"Nothing, nothing . . . " He turned his head away for a moment, then confessed sheepishly, "Well, actually, I was admiring your appetite. You have what Joseph Heller would have called a good mouth.

"Oh," she cried, delighted. "You're a Heller fan?"

Realtor and lawyer immediately forgot business as they set themselves to discussing literature. After debating the merits of **Catch-22** and **Good as Gold**, they learned that they found equal delight in Kurt Vonnegut, Richard Brautigan and John Irving. Jake urged Lisa to try some short stories by Joyce Carol Oates. She suggested John Barth's novels. He mentioned Agatha Christie. She championed Dorothy Sayers.

They had long since finished their meal and polished off some delectable cheesecake. They were on their third cup of coffee. They wandered into movies and then into music, finding they had many similar interests there as well. They were arguing about the differences between country and folk music, trying to define the dividing line between the two, when she glanced at her watch.

"Oh no, I'm late!" She rose abruptly, pulled a cell phone from her purse and scurried away to a quiet corner of the supper club to make her call. Jake made a move to rise but she gave him her fiercest glare to drive him back to the booth. She dialed frantically and listened impatiently as the phone rang in her brother's cabin, clenching and unclenching her fist in her frustration. She had never been late before, never! What would Richard think!

A lilting soprano answered.

"Oh, Marlene! Thank God you're still there . . . No, no, I'm all right . . . Nothing happened, I just lost track of time, that's all . . . The Highway Supper Club . . . Well, a client . . . I know it's eleven, but . . . Marlene, I'll get there as soon as I can!"

Lisa could see Jake at the booth, staring at the bill. How had he managed this? How had she forgotten her responsibilities? Damn him, he had that devious smile again. He wasn't calculating the tip, he was planning something else, she could swear to it.

"Marlene, I'll be home in half an hour. Just hang on a little while longer, please? I'll make it up to you . . . No, I will **not** tell you all about it when I get home!"

Lisa anxiously hurried back to the booth. Jake was still drinking coffee, those long legs taking up two-thirds of the area beneath the table. She wanted to kick him.

"Look," she said irritably, "I have to get back now. Are you ready?"

"Nope!" he replied calmly. "We still haven't talked about the Johnson house."

She frowned. What was he going to try next? "You know that house is too big for you. You said so!"

"Maybe, maybe not," he said, as if he were considering the matter. "I want to see it again, I think. How about tomorrow? And perhaps you have some other houses I could look at?"

"Couldn't you just call me tomorrow?" she asked, flustered as she searched in her purse for her share of the meal. He had already placed his portion of the tab on the table and she smiled slightly, pleased to see that he had made no move to fight her for the check. Then she saw the amused glint in his eye and realized he had second-guessed her on that, too! Her temperature rose another notch. This man knew too much about women! She didn't know if she could deal with that.

"Listen," he was saying, "I hope to find a place by the end of this week and get a start toward moving in before my daughter gets back from camp."

"Don't you want her opinion on the house?" Lisa asked, rapidly counting out her money and figuring the tip. She felt awkward standing there. Why didn't he stand up?

"She doesn't want to be up here at all right now. She still hopes we'll move back to Milwaukee. She wouldn't like anything you showed her anyhow."

"But about tomorrow . . . "

"I'll pick you up at ten tomorrow morning."

"No . . . oh, can't you just call me in the morning?"

Jake took another leisurely sip from his cup, making no move to stand. He crossed his legs and motioned her to her seat. "I don't think I can leave here until I have all this settled. I would upset my indiges . . . "

"I know, your indigestion," she interrupted with exasperation, her normally husky voice becoming shrill as she struggled for control. "Don't you think you should carry around

29

some Maalox or Kaopectate or something? Or should I get you some Tums? She motioned to the bar, only to notice that the good citizens sitting there had become interested in their discussion. Oh great, that's all I need, she groaned inwardly. She swung back to him, gritting her teeth.

Jake stretched his legs out comfortably, now taking up three-fourths of the floor space beneath the booth. "I'm fine as long as I don't get upset and my life follows nice, smooth lines," he explained with equanimity.

" I could just leave you here."

"Nope, I don't think you could do that," he smiled confidently. "There are some kind of realtor ethics involved, I'm sure. You can't abandon a client."

Lisa stared at the irritating man so comfortably ensconced in the corner. You couldn't force a man that big to move. She could feel the eyes of the patrons on them. She glanced at her watch again. Defeated, she finally surrendered.

"O.K. Ten o'clock. I'll have several houses to look at, but some are occupied and the owners will need more notice. There really aren't that many vacant houses in Norway, just now."

"I could consider even larger houses. Or maybe something smaller. Maybe a duplex? Or an apartment?"

"How about an old sawmill? A farmhouse? An outhouse?" she added sarcastically, understanding at once his plan of action.

"Sounds fine. He slid toward her and extricated his long frame from the booth. "Tell you what. Why don't we spend the whole day on the project? I'll bring the picnic lunch this time. You can bring the next one."

"Picnic lunch? Who said anything about a picnic lunch? No way!" She was waving her arms in agitation.

To her disgust, Jake sighed and sat down again, pointedly looking at his watch. "Do we have to discuss that, too? Why don't you sit down and we'll talk it over. I'll order more coffee. Would you like more dessert?"

"I don't have time for this!" she wailed. There was a sudden hush at the bar and she knew without looking that their audience was hanging on every word. She counted to ten. "All right," she said between clenched teeth. "I'll have a picnic with you. But this is a business relationship, nothing more, got that?"

"Absolutely. We'll get right down to business tomorrow," he assured her. She groaned and several patrons snickered. Jake rose and placed several bills on the booth table as a tip, winking at her. She glared at him and twirled around, her flying skirt revealing her shapely thighs. He whistled. Damn the man, he actually whistled at her! She marched out the door past the wide grins of the bar clientele, whose chairs had swung around 180 degrees. Jake followed at her heels. Out of the corner of her eye, she could see him waving to one and all as they left, executing a neat bow when they applauded.

Jake was still laughing as Lisa stamped through the parking lot, kicking gravel in every direction in her fury. He followed at a safe distance behind her, admiring her spirited show of temper. Lord, she was even more beautiful when she was angry, her cheeks flushed, her eyes the color of jade, but he had the good sense not to mention it. He had really pushed the joke farther than he had intended. It was a good thing he would furnish the picnic lunch tomorrow. In this mood, she would be sure to poison it.

He smiled as he watched her which angered her even more. She pushed the door of the Bronco open as he tried to help her in, hitting him across the chest with a resounding "thunk". He winced as she clambered into the vehicle and thrust her key into the ignition. She was starting the motor as he dashed around and climbed in the passenger side, shutting his door just as she threw the car into gear. They roared out of the parking lot, tires spinning on the loose gravel before they caught on the paved surface of the highway.

Almost immediately, Lisa put her foot on the brake and pulled the squealing vehicle to the side of the highway. Jake threw his hands in front of himself to brace himself on the dashboard just in time.

After the fireworks of the last few minutes, the silence was a sudden shock and it took Jake a moment to adjust to it. Lisa had switched off the engine, he realized. The mountain road was pitch black before them. A small amount of light from the tavern parking lot behind them lit the interior of the car. Lisa's hands were tightly gripped on the steering wheel. She stared ahead into the dark night, breathing hard, trembling as if in shock.

"What is it, Lisa?" Jake asked anxiously. "What's wrong, honey?" He touched her arm and she flinched.

Her voice was low and Jake strained to catch her words. "I was angry. I drove out of that lot as mad as hell. I didn't even look to see if anyone was coming. Oh, God," she cried, pounding her fist on the steering wheel, "I even forgot to put on the headlights!" She twisted her body to face him and even by the faint lights of the Highway Supper Club behind them, he could see how white she was, her tear-damp eyes luminous.

"You aren't wearing a seat belt," she whispered. "Please . . . please buckle up."

"What's the matter, Lisa?" Jake repeated, reaching out to grasp her arm as she began to shake. "Lisa, what's wrong?"

"Buckle up, damn it!" she screamed at him.

He dropped her arm and hurried to comply, shocked at the emotion in her voice. He faced her again and opened his mouth to question her, but she put trembling fingers to his lips, quieting him. He quickly grasped her cold hand and held it with both of his, rubbing her fingers to warm them. What had he done?

"Lisa?"

"Please don't talk to me for a minute," she begged, misery in her voice. Jake nodded, watching in silence as she fought to control her emotions, forcing the tears back. He caressed her soft hand, trying with this one small gesture to show her his willingness to help her through this turmoil. He was touched by the fragility of her slender wrist and circled it with the massive span of his fingers. Such a woman should not be facing this pain alone. Yet she was not ready to accept him, she had known him such a short time. Had they only met this afternoon? It seemed like he had been waiting for her forever. Wasn't it the same for her?

He knew the moment she became aware of his hands on her. Gently, reluctantly, he released her hand from his grip.

"Are you all right?"

"Yes, " she whispered. "This isn't like me. I don't know why . . . "

"Because I teased you until you lost your temper."

"No . . . well, yes. But that was no excuse for the way I drove out of there."

"Everyone does something like that once in a while."

"No! At least they shouldn't." She shook her head vehemently. "Look, I had a bad experience once . . . I don't want to go into it, but I never drive unless I'm fully aware of what's going on around me. I never drink and drive and I never drive when I'm emotional. And I don't ever, ever get into a car without buckling my seat belt." She drew a long breath as she now reached for it.

"It's all right, Lisa," Jake reassured her. "I always watch those things, too. I don't know why I forgot the seat belt this time. And I am sorry for stirring you up that way." He hesitated, wondering what he could do to comfort her. "Want to tell me what happened? About your bad experience?"

"No!" she said sharply, and repeated it more calmly. "No." She turned on the headlights and put the engine in gear, driving off more slowly this time. She said nothing more to him during the ride back to her office and remained silent when they reached his car. But before he got out of the Bronco, he held his hand out to squeeze hers and leaned over to kiss her gently on her cheek. It was a kiss of comfort, from one human soul to another, and he expected no response. He received none. She sat like a statue, staring out at the lights of the little town.

"Good-bye, Lisa," he murmured. "I'll see you in the morning."

Chapter Four

Jake entered Fratelli Realty exactly at ten, carrying a wicker picnic basket. He could have left it in the car, but he expected a battle after the night before, and the basket was part of his artillery. He had traded his business suit for blue jeans and a sleeveless blue sweatshirt bearing the University of Chicago logo, which he had selected for comfort on this sunny June day. On another level, he admitted that he wanted to impress her with his muscular arms. If that didn't work, maybe his prestigious *alma mater* would do the trick. Ridiculous, he told himself. Idiotic. You're acting like a fourteen-year-old. But he couldn't help feeling good, just thinking about her, and he broke out in a grin when he saw her.

Lisa met him head on. "I can't go on a picnic with you. I remembered a previous commitment."

"Dressed like that?" he scoffed.

She blushed as his eyes raked over her. He recognized the same pair of faded Levis she had been wearing the first time he saw her. Her old pink T-shirt read, "I Love John Philip Sousa" and her dingy gray tennis shoes sported prominent holes revealing her pink-tinted toes. She was charming, but certainly no business woman today. Her classic chignon had disappeared, replaced once again with the long braid that reminded him so much of Jodi's.

"And what about our appointment? I could have worked in my office today, but I really do need to buy a house soon."

"I can show you some houses later," she quickly interjected, "but I have to meet my church's youth group at ten-thirty for their monthly outing. That doesn't leave any time for a picnic. I tried to reach you this morning, but I didn't have your cell phone number and you didn't answer at your apartment, and . . . ."

". . . I was out shopping for this stuff." Jake mournfully

showed her his basket. "I slaved all morning to put together a great lunch and you back out."

"I'm sorry."

"Sorry, she says. What on earth can I do with all of this?" He knew he sounded like a shrewish housewife, but his plans to spend time with her were slipping away. He considered the problem silently for a moment. "You're sure you can't get out of this thing?"

She shook her head, her long braid flying behind her. "No way. There simply aren't enough people who are willing to chaperon a trip like this. We're short one adult as it is."

"Great!" he spotted his opportunity at once. "You need a chaperon. I'll be the chaperon."

"You don't understand," she objected. It's a bunch of teenagers and . . . "

"I have one of those, remember?" he remarked, taking her keys from her hand and hustling her out the door, locking it behind them.

"But you have to be able to . . . "

"What's the matter, you think I'm too old or something?"

"No, not at all! But . . . . ."

"Then I'm going along and that's final." They reached the low-slung Corvette and he leaned into the car to place the basket behind the seats. She said nothing and he looked over his shoulder at her. The minx! She was examining his thighs! He grinned at her and she grinned back as he pushed the passenger seat back.

"You're sure I can't talk you out of this?"

"I want to go," he insisted and turned to help her into the car. He noticed that her grin had taken a decidedly feline slant, as if she knew something he didn't. "So . . . where are we going?" he asked her suspiciously.

"Piers Gorge." Her grin widened.

"But that's where . . . "

"Right. That's where we're going whitewater rafting."

"Damn." He looked at her, at his picnic basket and once more at her.

"You really don't have to go," she remarked casually.

He stared at her complacent face. Why did he feel that this was a test? If he failed now, would he ever have a second chance with her? His gray eyes blinked twice as they met hers. The corners of her mouth quirked up and the dimple mocked him. Damn it, the woman was laughing at him!

He approached the problem from another angle. "Are you sure it's safe?"

"Well, I should hope so. We're taking eighteen kids along." She leaned against the Corvette with her arms crossed, amused at his predicament.

"You've got some professional supervision?"

"Of course!" She straightened, scanning his muscular arms and chest. "What's the matter with you anyhow?"

He knew that she was perplexed. How could he explain that although he was a mature adult, he had this one little area of cowardice. It all sounded so childish and he had never told anyone about it. Should he tell her?

He weakly tried another tack. "I was scared in my formative years by a movie."

"What movie?" she asked.

"*Deliverance*?" he pressed on.

"How old did you say you are?"

"Forty."

"*Deliverance*? In your formative years?"

"Damn! The woman knows her movies. Well . . . "

"O.K. Spill it!" She poked a slender finger into his chest, pinning him down with her eyes. He sought ways of wriggling out of confessing, but she was merciless. Who would have thought such a petite woman could be so . . . tough? For a moment, he toyed with the idea of a good lie. Something about the Gulf War? No, that was desert, not water. Besides, he hadn't been stationed overseas, as she was sure to figure out.

Then he discovered that he really wanted to tell her! He wanted to be intimate with this woman, certainly physically, but also intellectually and emotionally. He gave in.

"There really was a movie. *Huckleberry Finn*."

"In your formative years?"

"I was nine. I was so impressed I built a raft and sneaked it into the river near our home without my parents knowing anything about it, and . . . "

"Yes, go on," she prodded. "Where was this?"

"It was the Fox River, in Wisconsin, near Appleton. I ended up going over a couple of dams before I got out of the water." At her gasp of consternation, he hastily added, "Oh, they were little ones, lucky for me, or I would have been killed. But I still get a bit nervous when I think about going down a river in anything, even a boat. And rapids, well . . . "

"You went over two dams and a home-made raft stuck together?" she asked incredulously.

"Well, it stuck together for the first one."

"You're lucky you didn't drown!" she exclaimed. "Just how far did you go?"

"Must have been eight miles. It took me all night to get home."

"You walked home? At night?"

"Yeah." Now why had he told her about that? He cursed himself silently.

"Your parents must have been frantic!"

"Yeah, I guess they were."

"Why didn't you ask for help?"

He reddened with embarrassment. He felt like he was nine again, explaining it all to his mother, who had been alternately laughing and crying. "I don't think I want to tell you."

She waited, tapping her foot on the pavement, crossing her arms once more.

"Uh . . . my clothes were sort of ripped to shreds by the time I managed to get to the river bank."

"Ripped to shreds?"

"Yeah. On the rocks."

"Oh, Lord. If I'd been your mother I would have killed you about then. But what has that to do with your walking home at night?"

Uh . . . I could only move around at night. I kind of . . . hid out . . . in the shrubs during the day."

He knew that she had caught on: her lips began to twitch. "Oh, really?"

"In the shrubs?"

"In the shrubs," he growled in irritation as she began to chuckle. He tried to be an offended male, but her throaty laugh was infectious. His lips began to curl upwards and suddenly he was rumbling with deep bass laughter as he saw the humor in his predicament for the first time. Each time he thought he could stop laughing, he caught sight of her, tears flowing from her eyes, and he would be off again. She slid to the curb and leaned weakly against the Corvette, holding an arm to her side.

"Well," she finally gasped, "if that's the problem maybe you'd be safer going on home. I don't have any extra pants for you."

"Next time I'll bring some to leave with you," he chucked.

38

Her back stiffened.

"You know," he went on, trying to ignore the frown that creased her forehead. "I never told anyone else about that, even Christine. I don't know how you wormed it out of me."

"I don't know what you mean," she said, rising gracefully, ignoring the hand he held out to her. "I'm going to be late. Why don't you call me tomorrow so I can organize some showings."

"Hey, I'm coming with you."

"What?"

"I'm coming with you. It's about time I put this fear to rest. I'm with you all the way. No doubt about it."

In the five short minutes it took them to drive to Lisa's church, her mind spun off in several directions at once, or so it seemed. Drat the man! She had been so sure she had a certain escape from spending the day with him, yet here he was again. There was no way she could convince him to forgo this trip. He was single-minded and she was afraid she had been targeted.

Yet he had shown that he could be vulnerable, too. It took a strong man to show that side of himself. She felt herself warming to him more and more and she knew it was her long-submerged maternal instincts that led her to picture him as a little boy, a brave little Tom Sawyer setting off on an adventure. She smiled slightly, trying to find that boy in the profile of the man beside her, searching the strong, blunt fingers on the steering wheel for signs of the chubby fingers that built a raft one summer day. An elusive picture of a small, naked boy, running and dodging through night-time shadows flitted through her mind, but she suppressed it, not wanting to imagine a nude Jake at any age. That prospect both attracted and frightened her.

What did he want of her? Was it simply to share her bed? There was nothing "simple" about that, no one knew that better than Lisa. Besides, a man like Jake would have no trouble finding eager female companions. No, he wanted more from Lisa than sex, she felt that instinctively. He had confessed his childish prank to her and made himself vulnerable. He had taken that step despite his embarrassment, knowing that she might ridicule him, yet wanting that openness between them.

It was that intimacy that bothered her. If he persisted in this relationship, would he demand the same of her? Would she be forced to tell him of her past? She was still fretting about it as they drew up to the front of the old gray church.

The crowd of teenagers lounging around the steps were suitably impressed at Lisa and Jake's arrival. The boys immediately circled around the sporty Corvette. The girls formed another circle around Jake and Lisa, preening and prancing, practicing their Lolita flirtations on him.

"Where did you find him, Lisa?" a tiny brunette giggled, fluttering her eyelashes as she gazed up his tall length and admired his rugged features. To Lisa's intense irritation, his gray eyes sparkled as he winked at them.

Lisa coolly described Jake as a client of hers, explaining that he was thinking about moving to Norway, had a teenage daughter and had agreed to chaperon, wanting to learn more about the church. If any of the girls believed that initially, they changed their minds as Jake slipped his arm around her waist possessively and gave her a quick hug. He left it there, ignoring her glaring eyes as he busily complimented and teased the awe-struck girls. Lisa shifted from one leg to another, wondering if she should remove that hand from her side. Perhaps in a few moments, when she could do it surreptitiously, casually. Meanwhile . . . oh, no, he was drawing her against his thigh! She lifted her hand to push against his shoulder, only to come into contact with his rock-hard biceps. Her trembling fingers slipped down his arm as the shove became a caress. Her legs weakened as she melted against him. The sun, it must be the sun, she thought, as Jake glanced down at her, supporting her weight with ease.

She averted her face and straightened. She asked an inane question of one of the group's officers and tried desperately to force her thoughts away from the warm male body.

It took a strident horn to pull the boys away from the sports car and the girls from the most interesting man to set foot in Norway in the past year. The teenagers clambered aboard the yellow school bus, pushing past the driver who struggled against the flood. The girls screeched and laughed as they vied for seats that would give them the best view of Jake and Lisa.

"Whew!" The driver, Lisa's pastor, pulled off his baseball cap and wiped his balding head. "I don't know how you and the kids talk me into these things every month, Fratelli."

"You love it and you know it, Neil," said the tall, slender redhead who had appeared at the church door and was maneuvering to keep it open with her hip as she shoved box after box of soft drinks and picnic lunches out the opening. Lisa rushed to hold the door open as Neil and Jake began to cart the supplies to the bus, the young people stowing everything away.

"What I want to know is how I always get involved in these things," the redhead groused cheerfully. "I knew I would have to go to church every Sunday for the rest of my life. I figured on playing the organ, singing in the choir, and pouring a lot of tea at endless church social events. But you never warned me about this."

Her husband confided to Jake, "She's been grumbling about being a minister's wife for twelve years now, but she'd be even more upset if we left her behind." He extended his hand. "Hi, I'm Neil Franke, and the redhead is my wife, Beth."

Lisa hastily introduced Jake, once again maintaining that he was simply a client of hers. Beth's eyes gleamed immediately as she looked at the two of them, drawing her own conclusions, and Lisa knew she was in trouble.

"And are you planning on furnishing us with future chaperons from your real estate files, Lisa?" Neil asked innocently. "Wish I'd though of that years ago."

Lisa's sputtered retort was interrupted as the church door was suddenly thrust open, knocking her neatly off the steps and into Jake's arms waiting arms. He paused only a second before sweeping her into an exaggerated Fred Astaire dip and kissing her with a resounding smack. Cheers erupted from the bus. Beth was in raptures.

"Ooooooh!" Lisa shrieked angrily as she struggled to extricate herself from Jake's arms. How dare he?

"Rats!" a tenor voice exploded at the same time. They all turned to see a sandy-haired boy of about fifteen at the church door, loaded with three more twelve-packs of soft drinks, staring balefully down at them from the top of the steps like an avenging angel. "Did I hurt you, Lisa?" he asked in concern, then glared at Jake who was still holding her in his arms. "Who's he?" He took a menacing step forward.

Jake met the blue eyes squarely and cheerfully and introduced himself, as he set the wriggling Lisa back on her feet. Making a great show of straightening her clothing, he asked, *sotto voce*, "Who's your Sir Galahad?"

Lisa slapped his hands away. She would think about implications of that kiss later when her head cleared and her heart stopped thumping.

41

"That's Gordie Ruggeri, our right-hand man around here," she said quietly.

"He's crazy about you."

"You're crazy!"

"I recognize puppy love when I see it," he whispered. "I know it when I feel it, too."

"Are you all right?" Gordie repeated loudly. "What's going on here?"

"Nothing!" Lisa shrilly insisted. "Gordie, Jake's going to be a chaperon."

"Some chaperon!" Gordon muttered audibly as he headed past the four adults, carrying his load of soda to the bus. Shrugging her way out of Jake's grasp, Lisa followed, clambering aboard the bus to find a seat next to one of the quieter girls, only to find Jake taking the seat across the aisle.

During the short bus trip, the adults never spoke a word over the roar of teenage voices, giggling, and boombox rock music, but Lisa watched Jake surreptitiously, wondering if he would lose his temper at the raucous teasing he received about his necking tactics. He was taking it all good-naturedly, to her chagrin. If only there was something she could hate about him! She licked her lips, tasting him there. A baseball came rolling down the aisle and reaching for it, she lurched against his thigh. He caught her and their eyes met, and she read in his glance what the kiss had meant to him. No, she screamed silently, please no.

At Piers Gorge, the kids poured out of the bus and climbed all over it, pulling down the rafts and grabbing for paddles and preservers. A professional guide was waiting for them, ready to supervise the sendoff of each raft and to drive the bus to their destination. Jake could see that Norway kids were obviously old hands at this sort of thing. Jodi would enjoy this, more than he would.

He thought ruefully of the bottle of wine getting warm in his trunk. The day wasn't going at all as he planned, though he had managed to get Lisa into his arms at least once. As he helped unload the picnic supplies, he watched the rafts move down into the gorge and noticed all the life preservers they held. The falling water roared ahead and the bus began to look inviting. He could so easily volunteer to drive the bus to the rendezvous. He hesitated, looked at Lisa, who was in serious conversation with

42

Beth, and remembered the electric contact of her body against his. He couldn't quit now. He squared his chin like a gladiator entering the coliseum and climbed down the hill.

"I suppose you've done this before," he glumly asked Lisa, who followed just behind him.

"At least once every summer since I was twelve."

"Then you're in charge of our raft," he said. "I expect you to save me if I go overboard."

"No way," she grinned at him. "A good captain goes down with the ship."

"Down with the ship? What does that mean?" He anxiously queried her about all aspects of the trip as they clambered down the slope leading to their vessel, which was already in place.

There were three eight-man rafts waiting at the landing, each loaded with an equal share of teenagers. Neil commandeered one, Beth another, and Lisa gracefully settled into the last. Jake followed clumsily, tripping over legs and lines. He looked down to meet the malevolent stare of a silent Gordie, who was holding the raft steady against the shore. Oh no, he though in alarm, all I need is to worry about somebody pushing me overboard. As the raft bounced up and down, tossed by the current and the jostling of six rowdy young people, it was only his concern over Lisa's opinion of him that kept him from leaping back to the bank.

Lisa silently handed Jake a life jacket and helped him fasten it with quick, efficient movements. Her hands stilled as she inadvertently touched his chest. He was instantly lost in the verdant depths of her eyes, his panic forgotten. He grasped her hand, holding it over his pounding heart. The river, the teenagers, the pastor and his wife, all disappeared from his sight and he saw Lisa, only Lisa. She flushed and licked her lips, a provocation he could not resist. He lowered his head to hers, gently cupping her chin. Now, yes now, she would know what it was to be truly kissed.

Their lips had not yet met when a cheer rang out. The two adults were thrown apart as, with a splash, Gordie pushed the raft from the shore with an angry thrust. They were pulled into the raging maelstrom of the Menominee River.

Jake grabbed for his line, hunkering deep into their rubber vessel as the current found the first of the ledges that formed the bottom of the narrows. With a whoosh, they slid over the first of the rocks. A massive wave swept over the entire raft, drenching all the adventurers, and effectively cooling Jake's ardor.

He had just caught his breath when he noticed a long chute dead ahead of them, leading into a churning cauldron of boiling water. He moaned, his hands grasping for anything, hanging on tightly as they started down a long roller-coaster ride through the convulsing water. He closed his eyes, feeling only the spray on his face and the hollow feeling in his belly. He was thankful that he had skipped breakfast that morning and was not likely to embarrass himself in front of Lisa.

Then they were sliding down, down, down. Lisa cried out and someone else screamed. Oh, my God, Jake thought, I'm screaming. They hit the bottom, turning and twisting through the narrow channel. Everyone on the raft was shouting as they burst through to be tossed into another whirlpool. They surged into a second run past rock after rock, whirling past the green blur that was the shore.

And then it was over and they were floating serenely past sylvan banks, lush with foliage. The beautiful green of Wisconsin and Michigan scenery on opposite shores surrounded the deep blue of the gently flowing river. Jake slowly opened his eyes to a forest paradise. A great blue heron fed near the shore. Turtles sunned themselves on a log.

"Did I die?" he wondered aloud. Someone chuckled beside him and he turned to see Lisa, her hair soaked and sticking to her head. She leaned back against the raft, watching him in amusement. Her face was rosy and her eyes glowed. Her clothes were wet enough so that he could discern her lacy bra through her pink T-shirt. Front clasp, he thought, filing the fact away for future reference.

"Well?"

He thought about it for a moment, letting his adrenaline subside and analyzing his present mental and physical condition. "It wasn't bad," he admitted in surprise. "In fact, it was a lot like making . . . . " He stopped just in time, realizing the others were listening, and hastened to correct himself. " . . . *taking* one of those rides at Disney World. It really was fun!"

"So you're all right now?"

"I feel great!" he grinned.

"Then you can let go of my thigh." Everyone on board the

raft laughed as Jake realized, to his chagrin, that he had been holding onto her for dear life.

"Well," he sighed, "at least I've put that fear to rest. I'll be able to enjoy rivers from now on. But I'm glad it's over, just the same."

"Over?" she asked softly, just as Jake became aware of the roar of falling water straight ahead of them.

Chapter Five

The hot mid-afternoon sun was beating down on the landing as Lisa scampered lightly out of the raft, then turned to assist a sodden Jake. She giggled as he made a big production of straightening his stiff, aching legs. Clutching her to his side, he managed to pull himself to the shore, take a few steps and collapse on the bank, taking her with him. Around them, the teenagers formed teams to pull the rafts and equipment from the river, hauling it all up to the waiting bus.

"Where do they get the energy?" he groaned.

"They know that there's no picnic until everything is packed up," Lisa was tempted to stay right where she was, held gently against his solid chest. He had been holding on to her for dear life for the past two hours anyway, though she had sensed that the last hour-and-a-half had nothing to do with his fears. But she glimpsed Beth regarding them thoughtfully and she was immediately on her feet, tugging at Jake.

"Come on. You won't get to eat unless you help."

"Ah, but I brought my own lunch," he said craftily.

Lisa put her hands on her hips and glowered at him.

"You remind me of Miss Selmer," he said wearily, propping himself up on an elbow.

"Who's Miss Selmer?"

"My Sunday school teacher when I was nine. Boy, was she strict."

"She must not have done her job very well, or you wouldn't have gone down the river on your raft and lost your . . ."

"Don't bring that up!" Jake exclaimed, looking around at two curious girls who were hanging on every word. "I'm going! I'm going!"

Laughing, Lisa used all her slender strength to pull him up. The idiot! He was enjoying this! He threw an arm over her shoulder and slouched up the bank, whispering in her ear.

"It was a lie, you know."

"What's a lie?"

"About Miss Selmer."

"Miss Selmer? She wasn't your Sunday school teacher?"

"Oh, she was, all right. But you don't look anything like her."

"Oh?"

"She never looked like a winner in a wet T-shirt contest."

She punched him in the arm and chuckling, squished up the incline to charge into the fray.

A mere twenty minutes later, four exhausted grownups were sprawled on a blanket at Marlon Park in Norway, watching eighteen crazed kids playing frisbee, squirting each other with soft drinks, romping on the playground equipment and generally charging around the park. They had gobbled down their lunches before the four tired adults barely started on theirs. Lisa waved a chicken leg she had found in Jake's wicker basket.

"Slaving over lunch, ha! Kentucky Fried!"

"Somehow, I don't think I've done a very good job of impressing you today," Jake said ruefully as he sipped his Coke. He was admiring her well-shaped feet, with their tiny pink toes, now loosed from the still-damp tennis shoes. She had shaken her hair loose from her braid to let it dry, raking it with her fingers. It fell over her shoulders like a platinum cape as she sat cross-legged on the blanket. It was all Jake could do to keep his hands at his sides. He wanted to throw her back and nuzzle that tempting throat, to slide his hands inside her pink shirt and find that front clasp.

He cursed under his breath. Even on a sunny day, surrounded by people, and exhausted by his recent trauma, he could not escape lascivious thoughts. With a minister sitting beside him, too! He moved slightly to ease his discomfort.

"So, you're moving to Norway," the Reverend Neil said thoughtfully, his eyes gleaming at the prospect of a new member for his church.

"Well, I'm thinking about it. So far, I haven't been sold a house. The real estate agent I've been dealing with doesn't seem anxious to make a sale."

Lisa choked on her soft drink. "Just a minute here . . . ."

"What about the old Johnson place?" Beth suggested. "Didn't I hear you say something about a daughter? I always thought it would be a good place to raise a family."

"There are just the two of us, Jodi and me. I don't know, it seems to be rather big. On the other hand, if all these kids show

48

up at one time . . . " He waved a hand at the motley assortment racing around the park. "Maybe an extra bathroom or two would come in handy."

"And you never know," Beth remarked sagely, "you may not be single forever."

Jake pounded Lisa on the back as she choked again, and Beth wisely changed the subject. As the Frankes discussed all the possible houses for sale in the area, Jake soon realized that Lisa was right, there were no secrets among the residents. Neil and Beth seemed to know everything about the homes, including the floor plans, lot lines, the history of all the past residents and why they were selling the houses. And the Frankes were relative newcomers to the area!

"I could show you several other places this afternoon," Lisa offered, packing up the picnic leftovers as Beth and Neil strolled off to round up their gang.

Jake reached out to retrieve some empty aluminum cans. "It's well into the afternoon already. Besides, I'm too soggy. I have a better idea. Why don't you join me for supper in Iron Mountain?"

"No thanks."

Jake sat back on his heels, surprised. He had thought he was making progress with her. He couldn't have imagined her responses on the raft. She hadn't pulled away from him, not once.

"Why not?" he asked.

"Look, I don't have to answer to you," she replied coolly. "I have other plans."

"A date?"

"Other plans, that's all you need to know. I can't get away. Besides, I think it's time to get our relationship back on a business footing."

"Oh, do we have a relationship?" he teased.

She gave him her disdainful, Queen Victoria "I am amused" look. "We do not. I'm going to show you several houses, if not this afternoon, some other day. Right now, you are going home. Either you buy a house in Norway or you don't buy a house in Norway. Either I handle the transaction or I don't. That much is up to you. But I am not going out with you again. Understood?"

"Understood," he said meekly, but thought once again: Understood. Not accepted.

*****

49

The warm water cascading over Lisa's head as she showered forced her to close her eyes. She wished there was a way she could close off her mind as well. Her moods had been shifting capriciously all day. It had nothing to do with her biological clock. It had everything to do with that exasperating man.

He had been toying with her for the past two days, setting off unprecedented fireworks. She, who was always even-tempered, had blown up in a display of pyrotechnics she was ashamed to remember. She, whose daily smile quota could be counted on one hand, had spent today giggling and laughing like a junior high schooler. She, whose life had been an open book since she was a teenager, was now linked romantically with that man and was now the prime source of gossip in Norway, she was certain of it. And Beth . . . oh, what Beth must be thinking!

She cringed against the side of the bath tiles as she thought of her physical reaction to Jake. She had made a fool of herself, melting against him on the raft, allowing him to put his arm around her at the church, letting him kiss her! If he thought she was available for further amorous adventures, she had only herself to blame.

When her legs had touched his thighs, she had grown warm. Had he sensed that? Had he discovered that her body grew weak when his hand touched her? When he looked at her, her breasts swelled. Had he noticed? Of course he had, he noticed everything about her.

She touched her breasts delicately with her fingertips. She knew he liked looking at her body, the body she had taken for granted since she left puberty. Now, because of him, she was aware of it. She slipped out of the tub and stood before the full-length mirror, examining herself. Long legs, slender waist, tight little tummy, ample breasts. Yes, she supposed he would find her satisfactory.

But then, she had always known she could arouse a man's desires. She angrily thrust her arms into the sleeves of a terry cloth robe and covered her body. She had had enough of men's passions. She just wanted to be left alone. All Jake could bring to her was more pain, more heartache. She wandered into her bedroom, brushing her long wet hair as she walked, and reached for the bedside phone to call her brother.

The trees and hills took on an eerie glow from the setting sun as Jake found himself driving once more down the seven-mile stretch of road that led from Iron Mountain to Norway. It was ridiculous for him to be doing this. He knew that she would not be at her office this evening and he had no idea where she lived. He looked in the telephone directory to find her residential number but it was unlisted. He found a Richard Fratelli in the listings who lived somewhere on Route Two, but that was no help at all. He could hardly ask Lisa's brother to give him the number she had refused him.

Jake was well aware that the logical thing would be to hole up in his motel suite tonight and go over legal briefs. True, he still had little business, but he ought to get the few cases he had in perfect shape if he wanted a future in Dickinson County. He had accumulated a healthy savings account and stock portfolio during his Milwaukee years, but his earnings could slip away quickly if his new law practice failed.

But here he was, like an old Crosby-Hope movie, on the road to Norway. A picture of Lisa in a sarong flashed through his head and he grinned. He couldn't keep away from her. He was making a fool of himself, mooning over her. Here he was, a rational adult male, acting like an eighteen-year-old. Perhaps it was male menopause.

He decided to wander up and down the streets for a while this evening, get the feel of the town, talk to some of the townspeople. Maybe he could find out where Lisa had gone tonight. But what if she had a date? He would feel like a jackass if he ran across her on the arm of another man. Jake almost turned the Corvette around at the thought. He vacillated, considered his options, and finally compromised, deciding he would limit himself to a leisurely half-hour stroll around the square, then go home.

To his surprise, Jake had difficulty finding a spot for his car on Main Street. All the parallel parking slots were filled. He finally gave up and slipped his car into the space next to Lisa's Bronco in the small lot beside her unlit office. Wondering what she was doing in town, he switched off his engine, then frowned as his car radio continued to play. He turned the ignition on and off once more before he realized that the music was coming from outside the car, and looked down the street to see the bandshell brightly lit, filled with musicians playing a lively Sousa march.

He leaned against the car, staring. Up and down the street, people were standing, some listening, others trying to chat, shouting to be heard above the blare of trumpets, trombones, clarinets and drums.

A figure peeled away from a nearby group of teenage boys. "Hey, Mr. Gannett!"

"Oh, hi there, Gordie," Jake answered, straightening up. He suspiciously wondered why the boy was now being friendly, after treating him like some slimy lab specimen, ripe for dissection, all day. "Hey, what's going on here?" He nodded toward the band.

"Oh, the band plays every other Tuesday night all summer. It's the regular concert. Noisy, huh?"

"Yeah, it's loud all . . . " Jake's attention was caught by the sight of one very blond clarinetist. "Well, well," he murmured.

Gordie followed his line of vision and grinned sheepishly. "Uh, Mr. Gannett . . . "

"Jake."

"Uh, yeah, well, Jake, I'm sorry about this afternoon, for being such a crud and all. Mrs. Franke explained everything to me."

"Everything?" Jake said absently, as he rocked on his heels, his concentration on the clarinet section. If Gordie said anything further to him on the subject, he missed it, though it could have been because of the loud march the band was playing. With a dismissive wave of his hand, he left the boy and set off briskly, not slowing his pace until he was directly in front of the open air stage. He leaned against the platform, gazing up at the first clarinetist with star struck eyes.

Lisa was paying serious attention to her music, glancing at her director from time to time, tapping out the beat with her right foot. She did not see Jake at first. She wore the regulation band uniform, a light blue blazer over a white shirt and black tie, with a dark pair of slacks. A navy blue band cap that looked like a policeman's hat perched jauntily on her head. Her blond braid escaped to wind around her neck and over her shoulder. Jake had never seen anyone that sexy in a uniform. He rested his chin on his hands and gloried in her beauty.

All at once she noticed him. There was a very sour note in the reed section and she threw an apologetic glance at the surprised director. She kept her eyes fixed on her music, concentrating on each note until she came to a long rest, and could turn to Jake.

"What are you doing here?" she mouthed over the music.

52

"I'm a marching band groupie," he yelled at the top of his lungs. Several nearby listeners smiled. They might even have laughed, but no one could hear them.

Lisa tried to wave him away and he cheerfully waved back. "Go somewhere else," she motioned with frantic hand gestures, then noticed the director glaring at her. She had missed her entrance at the end of the rest. She hastily began to play, making several obvious and squeaky mistakes as she tried to find her place.

Jake stood his ground, watching and listening with rapt attention. He hadn't enjoyed anything so much since the last season of the Chicago Symphony. When the music ended, he applauded wildly, drawing the attention of everyone in the square who had not noticed him before.

As their audience grew, Lisa pleaded with him. "Will you please go listen from somewhere else?"

"But this is the best seat in the house!"

"You could hear just as well from the street!" You could hear us from the edge of town, as far as that goes."

"But I wouldn't have the great view."

"Please."

Jake saw that she was becoming agitated. Well, he wouldn't tease her much longer, but he certainly was going to take advantage of the situation. "Hmm. I might consider moving under certain conditions."

"Such as?"

"What are you doing after this set, baby?" he asked in his best tavern voice. This time the audience roared with laughter.

"Please!" she wailed, her face bright pink.

Jake relented. "I'm leaving, Lisa. I can take a hint. But I'll be at the stage door when you're through. When is that anyhow?"

"Half an hour!" a trumpet player called out.

Lisa groaned as Jake turned away, then called out, "Wait! We don't have a stage door!" The Norway City Band joined the audience in laughter as she covered her face with her hands.

Jake blew her a kiss and received the biggest applause given for any performance that night. Lisa blushed hotly and fixed her eyes on her music for the rest of the concert.

Lisa was putting her clarinet in its case, trying to be a good sport about the merciless teasing from the other band members, when Jake reappeared, carrying a bouquet of pink carnations. He solemnly presented them to her.

"How on earth . . . ?"

"It was Gordie Ruggeri's idea. His dad is the florist and Gordie got him to open up his stop for the occasion. It seems we stage-door Johnnies have certain traditions to uphold." He helped her gather her music. "What do you suppose Beth Franke said to that boy to make him mend his ways?"

"Beth talked to him? About us? You and me?"

Jake nodded.

"Oh, no," she moaned. "She's the worst matchmaker in Norway. We're doomed."

Jake chuckled as she lowered her head to smell the sweet scent of the blossoms. She touched a bud gently with trembling fingers, holding her face away from his gaze. Jake instinctively knew when her mood changed. Because of the din of the musicians around them, he sensed rather than heard her tiny sniff. He placed on finger on her delicate ear and traced a line from her jaw to her chin, lifting her face when he found it. He gently wiped away the single tear that had slipped from her eye.

"What is it?"

"I've never . . . "

"Never what?"

She shook her head, too close to tears.

"Surely you've received flowers before?"

Her emerald eyes, wet and shining with the tears she was holding back, met his. She whispered, "No. Never."

Shocked, Jake turned her to face him, his eyes burning into hers. A beautiful woman who had never been given flowers? What was wrong with the men in this town? Couldn't they see that Lisa was a treasure to be cherished, a goddess to be worshiped? He caressed her cheek. Her lips parted at his touch and he caught his breath. God, she was lovely! The masculine cut of the band uniform only emphasized her total femininity.

He gently removed the jaunty hat, smoothed her hair back and drew her closer, unaware of the bustle of band members getting ready to go home, until a musician swung his trombone into the two of them. It was Neil.

"Sorry, Fratelli," he apologized cheerfully. "Well, Jake, good to see you here. Thinking of joining the band?"

Neither answered, lost in each other. As the minister realized that neither was interested in anything he had to say, he saw his wife gesturing at him frantically from the square. "Oh. Uh . . . see you next Tuesday at practice," he remarked to no one in particular.

Lisa might have stood there forever if Jake had not finally picked up her clarinet case and led her down the steps of the band shell. Something had happened to her there, some subtle shift in her psyche that she would have to analyze when she was alone. Jake wasn't going to stop this pursuit, and suddenly, a tiny part of her was happy he wasn't.

"Does this mean you're tied up every Tuesday night?" Jake asked.

She nodded, her thoughts elsewhere.

"Hmm. What about Saturdays and Sundays? Anything going on those nights?"

"Well, no, but . . . ."

"Great. Put me on your calendar. We're making progress. And how about Wednesdays, Thursdays and Fridays?"

"Just a minute here," she sputtered. "You can't . . . " A thought occurred to her. "What about Mondays?"

"You can wash your hair on Mondays," he explained generously.

"What? I wash my hair more than once a week! Besides, you can't just take over my whole week like that!" she argued as they walked down the darkening street.

"Think not?"

"I know not! It's not all right with me, you know. Maybe I don't want to get involved with a . . . a . . .a . . . "

"Stage-door Johnny?" he suggested.

"With anybody! And besides, you're rushing me!"

He stopped her in the protective shadow of the real estate building. "Look, Lisa. I don't want to rush you." He negated that immediately. "Well, maybe I do. But you know we're good together. We like the same things, Vonnegut and folk music and teenagers and . . . ."

"Whitewater and marching bands?"

"Right! O.K., so we'll take it one night at a time. How about I pick you up tomorrow night and we'll go to a movie. Tom Hanks' new one?"

"But . . . "

He rushed ahead, searching madly for his best arguments.

"Look, maybe we'll get sick of each other soon. I don't know. But don't we owe ourselves the chance? Lisa," he begged earnestly, "please say yes. Don't let this thing between us get away. I get so lonely sometimes. Don't you."

"Oh, yes," she whispered almost against her will. She could see the moonlight reflected in those expressive gray eyes. What should she do? She wanted him to go away, to leave her alone. No, if he left, she would lose something vital and she would be miserable. But he would leave her sooner or later anyway, so wouldn't it be the same thing? Torn, she looked at him helplessly and her tears began to fall. Jake groaned and dropped her instrument case carelessly, reaching for her, crushing her against his chest.

"No, honey, don't please don't," he crooned, rocking her gently, stroking her hair, pushing her cap from her head. She nestled into him, melting into the comfort of his arms. Her hands were imprisoned between them. His heart seemed to be beating as one with the pulse in her wrists. She sighed as he placed tender little kisses on her forehead, on her eyes, tasting the salt of her tears. He comforted her, caressed, and petted her, gliding his hands along her back.

His tongue found the trail of an errant teardrop and followed it down her cheek, suddenly finding her lips. He licked away the salty remnants from the curve of her lower lip and then he was kissing her, softly at first, testing her response. She drew away slightly, but her resistance collapsed as he gathered her even closer, molding her hips to his thighs..

His tongue traveled to the small indentation on her cheek, finding it unerringly. She moaned, opening her lips slightly, and he slipped his tongue into her mouth, darting in and out so quickly she was scarcely aware of it.

She wanted more, to her surprise. Her hands glided up his chest, hesitating for a moment at the whorl of hair exposed by the vee of the knit sports shirt, then climbing to his neck. She slipped her fingers into his hair, sensitively examining the shorter hairs, then thrusting her hands into the thick waves. She instinctively swayed, rubbing her breasts against his hard body, loving the differences between them.

Jake gasped, astonished by her responses. He wrapped his arm around her waist and deepened their kiss. She opened her mouth to his and he quickly tasted her soft recesses, finding her tongue with his. Shocked, she closed her lips, capturing his tongue for an instant. She pushed at his chest and stepped back, confused and appalled at her own reactions to his lovemaking.

Jake grasped her shoulders to keep her from escaping. He sighed and rested his forehead on hers, fighting to control himself. After a moment, he straightened and searched her wide, frightened eyes.

"I think," he murmured, "that it's time we went home."

Chapter Six

It was the wrong thing to say. With a soft cry, Lisa scurried to the Bronco, searching in her pants pocket for her keys. It was obvious what he was thinking – that she was ready to share his bed! How could she have allowed things to go this far? She belonged at home, her own home, alone, without him! She stashed her clarinet case in the back as Jake watched silently, hands clenched at his sides. She straightened, still holding her carnations in her left arm.

"Did you want to look at any more houses tomorrow?" she asked huskily, picking at the blossoms nervously, avoiding his eyes.

"This evening isn't over yet," he growled.

"I think it is."

"We can't just let it go at that, Lisa." There was desperation in his voice as he stilled her hand. "Why don't I meet you at your house? Or you could come back to the motel with me."

She gasped.

"Damn it, I don't mean it like that!" Jake dropped her hand and ran his fingers through his hair. "You know I won't press the physical side of this relationship if you don't want me to. Good God, Lisa, I'm not a rapist!"

"Oh!" she cried, shocked. "Jake, I never thought that!"

They stared at each other for a long minute, not knowing what to say.

"O.K." Jake finally said, "so tonight is over. What about that movie tomorrow night?"

"I don't know . . . ."

"Have you seen it?"

"No . . ."

"Do you want to see it?"

"I guess so, but . . ."

"But, what?" he demanded, exasperated. "Look, we both want to see the movie and we both plan on seeing it, so why not see it together? I won't even hold your hand, if that's what's bothering you. If it would make you feel any better, you buy the popcorn."

Still she hesitated and he threw his hands up in the air. Lisa felt his frustration and hurt and she ached for him. Why was she denying him anyway? She wanted to be with him, on one level anyway, and he wouldn't pressure her on the other, the physical side. She had his word on that and she trusted him.

She searched inside herself and found her unvoiced concern. What she wanted was some reassurance that he wasn't entering into this affair lightly, that he was going to invest as much of himself as she was. But how could she know that? And how could he prove it to her?

Then she noticed his hand. He was not wearing the wedding ring! She realized that he had made a commitment of sorts. Could she do any less? She smiled.

"The barrel?" she asked.

"What?"

"A barrel of popcorn? How much can you eat?"

Jake's grin covered his face.

"And does this mean I have to buy the soft drinks?" she bargained. "And what about the Raisinettes?"

His laughter rang down the empty street "What's the matter? Don't you think you can afford me?"

"Maybe not. I haven't sold a house for a while."

"You haven't, have you?"

She grinned impishly back at him. "Nope."

He considered her cash flow problem. "I have meetings tomorrow morning and I have to be in court in the afternoon, but how about looking at houses Thursday? Maybe you can even talk me into buying one. And about tomorrow night, if you need a loan for the Raisinettes . . . ."

"I think I can just about swing that," she said wryly.

On Saturday evening, Jake again wound his way through the forest on Highway Two, turning onto a dirt road just before the Norway city limits. He whistled soundlessly as he thought about the happiest week he had had in over a year.

His life was shaping up nicely, Jake reflected, as he maneuvered the sports car through the twisting roads, ever watchful for north woods animals. Since he started making these daily pilgrimages, he had spotted porcupines, foxes, rabbits, skunks, and coyotes. He had even seen a bear rummaging through the garbage behind Fisher's Restaurant. Some of the local residents claimed to have seen moose, wolves and cougars in the area.

Lisa was another elusive wild creature and Jake knew he had to keep her off guard or she would flit away from him. True to his carefully thought-out plan, he had kept her too busy the whole week to think about slipping out of their blossoming relationship. He teased her, complimented her (how easy that was!) , courted her, and enjoyed every minute of it.

On Thursday and Friday, Lisa showed him every house for sale in and around Norway. By late Friday afternoon, he finally admitted that the only house he liked was the old Victorian she had shown him the first day. It somehow seemed to have been waiting all along for him and Jodi, though it was, he realized, far too big and he would have to hire a housekeeper. It wasn't a rational choice of homes, because all along, lodged in his imagination was the vision of Lisa, sharing that old carved bed with him. The thought of another couple in the bed was abhorrent to him.

He took one more look at the house and made an offer. By today, the Johnsons would have replied. Jake figured it would be a quick sale, the house being vacant and the family eager to close the estate. He had been assured by the loan officer at his bank that his credit was excellent. The banker was well aware that Jake could have paid cash if he so desired and was taking out a loan only as a tax advantage. As a lawyer, Jake planned on drawing up the documents and researching the title himself.

Jake knew he was making progress in other areas, too. On Wednesday evening, Lisa met him in Iron Mountain, where they saw the movie, afterward spending several hours at Grandma's Old Fashioned Ice Cream Emporium. Over coffee and enormous hot fudge sundaes, they argued about movies. Jake liked big, historical extravaganzas with swashbuckling adventurers, while Lisa preferred light comedies and tearjerkers. After a lengthy but friendly debate, they agreed to disagree.

"Why don't we meet here once a week," she suggested. "We could see movies separately, just to keep it impartial, mind you, and rate them here."

"Like a weekly series?" he scoffed. "No way! We're going to be a soap opera instead."

"A soap opera!"

61

"Right! Five times a week, lots of romance, but we'll skip the tragedies."

She laughed, somewhat nervously, he thought. He wondered what there could possibly be in her past that kept intruding into her thoughts. She was still skittish with him. Taking no chances, he only called out a pleasant goodnight as they climbed into their respective vehicles to find their separate ways home.

To his delight, while showing him yet another prospective real estate bargain the next afternoon, Lisa asked him to join her in a house concert, which was to be held at the Franke's that evening. The informality of a concert held in a home intrigued Jake. Neil and Beth provided food and drink and the guests passed the hat to cover the entertainer's fees.

"A musical Tupperware party," Beth explained with a laugh when they arrived.

The performer was an area folksinger, a truly gifted artist with a lovely alto voice, who sang an assortment of folk songs, accompanying herself on instruments ranging from a hammer dulcimer to an Irish harp. While the guests listened to the soft music wafting across the living room, they nibbled on a variety of Scandinavian delicacies and sipped fruity homemade wine served in long-stemmed crystal goblets.

By the end of the evening, Jake was relaxing on the rug in front of the Franke's fireplace, his head on Lisa's lap. She shyly examined his thick black hair with her fingertips.

"Counting my gray hairs?" he asked lazily.

"Looking for bald spots."

He quirked an eye to catch the laughter in her eyes and the quick flash of her dimple. He seize her hand and kissed it, over and over, working up over the smooth skin to reach her fingers, nibbling and kissing until he reach the tips, where he gave her a strong nip.

"Ouch! What was that for!"

"For damaging my male ego."

"I couldn't dent your ego with a Sherman tank."

"You'd be surprised," he murmured and laid his head back on its warm nest. After a moment, she resumed her soft forays through his hair. Behind her, Jake saw Beth grinning.   An ally, he thought.

That night, Jake gave Lisa a circumspect peck on her cheek

as they parted at her office, she to return home in her own car. With a sense of satisfaction, he noted her small sigh of disappointment as she turned away.

On Friday, the two attended a fish boil prepared by a local men's club. They sat beneath the stars at the park to watch the fantastic fireworks as the wood fire brought the fish and vegetables to a boil, the oil water overflowing to burst into flames on the fire below. Beth and Neil brought their plates to join them at their picnic table. To Jake's delight and Lisa's chagrin, Beth suggested they join the church's couples club.

"You encourage her!" Lisa accused Jake later, as he drove her to her office. "Next thing you know, she'll be planning our wedding."

"You mean she hasn't started yet? I'll have to talk to her. But first things first," he continued, as he helped her out of the low-slung car, "how about another movie tomorrow night? I haven't checked the listings, but . . . ."

"No thanks, Jake." He looked at her with concern as she took a deep breath, staring shyly at his shoes. Jake felt she was about to say something momentous.

"Now just a minute . . . " he began.

"How would you like to come for dinner? I'll cook spaghetti." She glanced up at his stunned silence. "I *can* cook, you know."

Jake recovered rapidly. He seized her, swung her around and kissed her.

"At last," he leered. "I have you in my clutches. I will chain you to the stove and I will never eat in a fast-food joint again." He released her with one last hug.

Lisa tilted her head, warily considering him as she might a wild cougar in the woods, but when he made no further advances, she gave him the directions to her home.

Now Jake was traveling to meet the woman he was falling in love with for an intimate dinner for two. Yes, he thought, as he turned down yet another dirt road, life is sweet, and getting sweeter all the time.

Lisa Fratelli paced her small living room nervously. Everything was ready for their dinner: her finest Italian sauce, a family secret, was simmering on the stove, a crisp green salad was waiting in the refrigerator, and the antipasto plate was laying on the counter. She had even picked fresh strawberries that afternoon at a local farm to grace her homemade shortcake. The table was waiting, set with her finest china and silverware, ceramic chalices were cooling for the wine Jake said he would bring.

She smoothed her shirt, checking for the dark stains that were almost inevitable with spaghetti sauce. Miraculously, her knit emerald green pullover seemed to have been spared. Lisa, who never thought much about clothes after they were purchased, had long debated over what to wear, trying on clothes for over an hour before she finally decided on this top and its matching full-length flowing skirt. A few minutes ago, she changed to white slacks in a sudden panic, concluding that a casual look would be less suggestive. She considered yet another blouse, maybe something more tailored, then groaned. *What is wrong with me?* she thought, and then irrationally, knowing he was not late, spoke out loud, "Where is he?"

She threw open the back door and slipped out to the wide deck that overlooked the little lake. The moonlight was reflected on the peaceful waters, yet she felt far from tranquil. A fresh breeze sprang up, keeping the insects at bay. Her hair escaped the combs that held it and she cursed her impulse to let it fall free. She knew instinctively that Jake would like it that way. He was forever touching her silver hair when he thought she was unaware of it. But she always knew when he was near, aware of his every movement.

She turned abruptly and re-entered the cabin, scrutinizing it for flaws she could correct before his arrival. It was immaculate. She glanced out the window again, caught herself and laughed.

"Why bother looking?" she said aloud. "You know he'll come."

He certainly made no secret of his interest in her. And she was interested in him, too, when she allowed herself to be honest. No, it was worse than that, she was rapidly becoming emotionally dependent on him. He was so much fun, so likeable. He teased her, complimented her, made her laugh, but more than that, tantalized her. If he brought her happiness, he also made her ache for fulfillment. It was all she could do to keep her hands off him! Sometimes she wanted to cry, sometimes she had to laugh out loud for the sheer joy of him. Either way, she felt totally alive.

But would he still want her if he learned her secret? But why should he learn anything? No one knew . . . no, that was wrong. One person in Norway knew all about it, but he certainly would never tell anyone, let alone someone Lisa was interested in. Her secret was safe. Why not take the chance, why not let herself try for some happiness?

Because it could lead to unhappiness, she mused, it had before. And because this time, she would not be able to suffer the loss if she let herself fall in love.

"Don't be a fool," she lectured herself. "Your life was fine without him. Now's the time to stop this foolishness."

She peered out another window and saw Richard's lights below. Her cabin perched on a rocky ledge, reached by a winding outside staircase that led visitors up from the garage at the roadside. Far below, near the lake, stood her brother's home. Richard was still awake. He would quiz her in the morning about her visitor. What should she tell him? He'd been pressing her for years to find a husband. "Lisa," he had said only a month ago, "isn't it time you made me an uncle?" She had laughed at him, and mourned in her heart over what she could never have.

She snapped out of her reverie as she heard the rumble of tires going over the bridge two miles away. The sound always reverberated over the river that fed the lake, giving her several minutes warning of impending guests.

She scurried to the table and checked the place settings. Something was missing. She dashed panic-stricken to the mantelpiece, seized the two candles resting there and rushed them to her centerpiece. She lit them and stood back, studying the effect.

What would Jake think if he saw a candlelight setting? That she was ripe for romance? No! She blew out the candles and quickly placed them back on the mantel, just as she heard his knock. Breathless, she flew to the door.

Jake, as short of breath as Lisa, was mesmerized by the vision before him. She was flushed, her cheeks pink, her breasts gently rising and falling as she struggled to control her breathing. Jake could not resist the beauty of her windswept hair. He reached out his hand to caress it, adding a simple kiss on her soft, parted lips.

Lisa lips trembled, staring at him without a word, her eyes shining as she inspected him. Jake had purposely donned a black silk shirt that emphasized the width of his shoulders and rolled up the sleeves to reveal the dark hair on his arms. Tonight, he wanted no doubt about who was male and who was female so he had selected white jeans that fitted snugly over his hips.

He winked at her. "Are you going to let me in?" he asked plaintively. "Though the view is superb up here, all those steps wore me out."

"Oh!" She quickly ushered him into the living room. He waved the bottle of Chianti at her.

"Will this do? Italian wine for an Italian meal."

"Perfect," she replied in a husky little voice, her hands shaking as she took the bottle from Jake. She scurried back behind the kitchen counter like a frightened rabbit, to check the sauce and start the water boiling for the spaghetti. Jake chuckled as he watched her retreat. Did she think he would leap at her? But he appreciated what courage it had taken for her to invite him here. He knew he would have to be gentle with her tonight. This was no time to tease her.

While Lisa puttered in her kitchen, Jake wandered through the small cabin, examining its delightful little nooks and crannies. The living room and kitchen were one, separated only by a counter. A table set for two took up a corner of the kitchen area. The living room, delineated by a long, stuffed couch, faced a fireplace containing a pleasant fire that was taking off the early summer chill. Cozy and charming, Jake decided, that was how he would describe Lisa's home.

He stuck his head in a few doors and discovered the tiny bathroom, an office-library filled with well-worn books and an oversized desk, and finally, her bedroom. He gazed thoughtfully at the double brass bed with its hand-stitched patchwork quilt for a few moments, then drew back into the living room. Lisa was waiting for him there, her face solemn and pinched. Such a simple thing, Jake mused, for him to look at her bed, yet not simple when it was inevitable that some time, some day, they would share it. He knew she was thinking the same thing.

"Did you have any problems finding this place?" she said in a tiny voice, trying to make conversation.

How idiotic, Jake groaned inwardly. We've never had trouble finding topics for discussion before. He constantly thought about things all day that he wanted to tell her, things that he wanted to ask her. But everything had flown out of his head at the sight of that bed. It wasn't going to help if all she could make was polite chitchat. But this was her home ground and he was willing to play by her rules.

"None," he replied to her question, "though I thought that by the time I got here, I would be traveling down deer trails. The roads get worse and worse, don't they?"

"Yes, I guess they do."

"I can see why you need that four-wheel drive Bronco what with all these dirt roads and Michigan winters. I was surprised to see you have a paved driveway. Isn't it odd to have a black-topped drive off a dirt road?"

"Well, yes. Richard, my brother, wanted it that way, you see."

"That's his cabin down by the lake? The place with the big van?"

"That's right," she nodded, slipping back to the kitchen to stir the sauce yet again. Jake sensed her withdrawal, her avoidance of that topic.

With a lawyer's cross-examining instinct, he pressed on, following her and leaning against the counter as she worked.

"Any reason you don't live in the same house?"

"Richard wanted it that way. He thinks I should live my own life."

"I can see that. I suppose a sister would interfere with his social life, too. Yet you live next door?"

"He needs me to take care of him and I like to be near him."

"Is that why you never married, Lisa?" Jake asked seriously.

"No!" she exploded, dropping the spoon into the sauce with an angry splash. "Yes . . . oh, I don't want to talk about that. I don't think I could explain it all anyway." She grabbed for a cloth and with vigor scrubbed at some bright red spots on the stove.

Jake straightened, perplexed. He certainly had not expected her reaction to what was, after all, an innocent question.

Lisa sighed. "Maybe you should wait until you meet him. You'll understand then."

"Good idea," he smiled, slipping an arm around her waist and hugging her as he slipped a spoon into the sauce for a taste. "I don't want to talk about him anyhow. All I really wanted to know is whether or not he's going to rush in here and threaten me with bodily injury for making eyes at his sister." He neatly nabbed a fresh strawberry and eyed the antipasto with interest.

"He won't. He never comes up here at all, so I can promise you that you're safe." Noticing what Jake was up to, Lisa laughed and gave him a little shove, effectively removing him from her kitchen. He enjoyed the picture she made as she bustled around, tossing the salad with a vinaigrette dressing, adding a spice here, a dash of freshly ground pepper there.

As she piled the steaming spaghetti on plates, Jake was contemplating the centerpiece. Something was missing here. He snapped his fingers and crossed to the fireplace, seized the two candles there and brought them back to the table. He lit them with the matches resting there and grinned when he realized the two scented candles had only recently been blown out.

As Lisa brought their dinner to the table, he walked around the room, turning off some lights, turning others on, until the intimate mood he wanted was created. His eyes questioned hers over the candlelight, silently seeking her approval. Blushing again, she gave an almost imperceptible nod.

While Lisa returned to the kitchen for the salad and antipasto, Jake examined the compact disk resting on her stereo.

"Julian Breem? What's this?"

"Sixteenth century lute music. I found it at the library last week."

"Sounds perfect."

"Well . . . maybe something else would be better."

"In other words," he interpreted, "it's exactly the right thing for candlelight and romance. You don't want to admit you're a romantic at heart, Lisa. Lute music it is."

In a moment, the room filled with the splendid little melodies of the Elizabethan period. Jake listened with pleasure and turned to her in the manner of a courtier, using the grand gestures of a Sir Walter Raleigh. He bowed to her curtsy, and lifting her hand high, led her to the table, seating her and kissing her hand before finding his own place, to the sound of her delighted laugher.

The antipasto and salad were long gone and very little spaghetti remained. As Jake sipped the last of his Chianti, Lisa expressed her amazement at what she and Jake had consumed.

"Good mouths," he said lazily, leaning back in his chair. "I don't know where you put it though." His eyes raked her slender frame, as if looking for some clue.

Lisa smiled mysteriously, deciding to keep her secret, long sessions of aerobic exercises, to herself.

"Do you realize how long it's been since I've had a decent

home-cooked meal?" he went on. "Jodi and I eat out at restaurants most of the time to avoid my cooking."

"Oh, really?"

"Yes, really! I don't think Jodi even knows about grocery stores and butcher shops. She thinks you get hamburger at McDonalds's and roast beef at Arby's."

"And steak at Ponderosa?"

"Right!"

"And chicken at Kentucky Fried!"

"Exactly!"

"I think you're just playing on my sympathy, hoping for another free meal."

"Will it work?" he asked hopefully.

"What do you think?"

"All I know, woman, is that if you continue to ply me with spaghetti, you may have your way with me," he offered with an expansive wave of his hand.

Lisa laughed at him. She was unaccustomed to drinking and the wine was going to her head, but she didn't care. Her eyes sparkled in the candlelight. She knew that Jake's eyes were riveted on her and she basked in his admiration. No longer was she Lisa Fratelli, small-town spinster. She was an enchanted princess, beautiful and desirable. How marvelous that such a handsome, virile man should want her!

It was a magical evening with a magical man, who could make her forget everything but the possibilities of what could be between them. Perhaps Jake was right, she was a romantic who believed in happily-ever-after. Anything could happen now that Jake was in her life.

She started as he took her hand and rubbed her palm with his thumb. The corners of her brows shot up, as her eyes questioned him.

"That was delicious, Lisa. What now?"

"Oh!" she exclaimed, pushing her chair back. "I almost forgot our dessert."

"Dessert? How can you think about it?" he groaned, still holding her hand as he rose. "Maybe later. Let's go sit by the fire."

"N...no, not yet," she stammered, panic-stricken. "Let's have our coffee first."

Lisa occupied herself in the kitchen for some minutes, brewing the coffee, clearing plates, loading the dishwasher, scrubbing the counter. She avoided looking at the corner of the table where he sat patiently waiting for her. What would happen now? She didn't really know what he expected of her. Well, she knew what he wanted all right, she wasn't that naive! But she hadn't been alone with a man other than Richard in years. She wasn't ready for this. Romance was one thing, reality was another. Reality was that man sitting at the table, a man she had to face. Who was he, anyway? Some stranger she had known only a week! But no, he was Jake, wonderful Jake, she argued with herself, Jake who could be someone to fall in love with.

The coffee was ready, the kitchen immaculate. Lisa swallowed hard and lifted the coffee tray, turning to face the table. He wasn't there! Where had he gone to now? She hesitated, searching the room for him, and saw a movement beyond the big, over-stuffed couch. She took her courage in hand, skirted it and found him there, stretched out on several cushions he had placed on the floor before the fire. He had removed his shoes and set them aside. His stocking feet were up on the fender, his head propped against the couch with several quilted pillows behind his dark head.

Lisa surveyed the length of him and was speechless. The cups rattled on her tray. He was so big!

"Put the coffee down and get comfortable," Jake invited.

She couldn't, she was frozen to the spot.

He growled irritably, "Oh, come on, Lisa, we've been on the floor in front of a fireplace before, remember?"

"At the house concert? That was different."

"How, for Pete's sake?"

Her voiced quavered, "Well, there were other people around there."

"Use your imagination. Pretend you have company. That lamp over there, for example, that can be Neil."

The lamp in question was a modern contraption, with a shiny, dome-shaped top. Lisa smiled wanly. It did bear a resemblance to Neil's bald head. Her lips trembled but she settled on the floor and began to pour the coffee into the mugs. She automatically added a spoon of sugar to Jake's and handed it to him. Knowing how he took his coffee made the scene more domestic, and that calmed her a little, yet she tried not to look at him.

"Do I make you nervous, Lisa?" He rolled over to face her.

She peeped at him through lowered lashes, not knowing what to say. He cupped her chin, studying her pink cheeks.

"You are such an enigma, Lisa," Jake murmured. "You are a woman in so many ways, yet there's something of a little girl about you, too."

Lisa watched the play of emotions on his expressive face and knew the moment the suspicion flickered into his mind. "Lisa, you aren't a virgin, are you?" His hand tightened on her chin.

Her eyes flew up to meet his. She put her hand on his, trying to loosen his grip.

"Jake . . . ."

"Are you?" he demanded hoarsely, sitting up and sliding his hands up her arms to grasp her shoulders firmly. She turned her head away, but he forced her to look at him.

"Lisa?"

"N . . .no," she admitted and lowered her head in shame, agony in her slumped frame. Jake groaned and tugged her into his arms. He drew her onto his lap, held her and rocked her as she struggled with her tears.

"Oh, honey, honey, it's all right. I'm not accusing of anything. I never expected you to be an innocent. We're both mature adults, Lisa, and I think you're perfect just the way you are. We aren't kids, after all." Jake faltered, fumbling for words. He ran his fingers lightly up her spine, finding the base of her neck and massaging it as he crooned soft words to her. He drew the combs from her hair, allowing it to flow wildly over her shoulders, covering his arms. She burrowed into his chest, nestling against his throat, seeking his warmth and loving the clean, male scent of him.

"It's O.K. It's O.K.," he muttered. "I shouldn't have asked you that. You're a grown woman. It was just . . . you don't seem very experienced either." He wiped a tear from her cheek. "Lisa, honey . . . listen to me. Whatever happened before we met, can't we put it all behind us? Can't we begin now? I find that I don't want to hear about your past lovers," he admitted ruefully, "and I don't suppose you want to hear about my lurid past either."

Lisa smiled a little through her misted eyes. "You have a lurid past?" she croaked.

"Scandalous," he chuckled. He lowered his head to hers and kissed the tears, licking each one away. One of his hands glided down her back to find a soft thigh while he firmly held her head with the other. She quivered in response and gazed open-mouthed at him. His clear gray eyes darkened as he caressed her.

He lowered his head once more, examining her face with his tongue, learning its delicate contours, finding the hidden dimple that she knew he coveted.

Lisa lifted a hand helplessly, as if to stop him, then timidly rested it on his chest. What had frightened her so was now all she desired. He hastily unbuttoned his shirt to the waist. Her eyes flew open in confusion. Jake smiled at her encouragingly and leaned down to kiss her gently. Her lashes lowered once more and she made no objection when he took her hand and placed it inside his shirt. She touched him delicately, as if she were first discovering the differences between a man and a woman. His chest was so warm and she could feel the beating of his heart.

Jake kissed her again, with more passion, and she moaned. He opened his mouth slightly, daring her to match him. He drew back almost imperceptibly and she moved with him, asking for more with her response. Her hand slipped deeper into his shirt. She paused to explore the nipple. He groaned, tearing his lips from hers. She opened her eyes, her glance a question mark.

"Oh, baby, you are making this tough," he whispered hoarsely. He pushed the coffee tray to the end of the fender, rearranged the pillows and slipped her from his lap, laying her against the cushions and nestling her in his arms. He stretched his long legs against hers and lifted her hands against his chest once again. He lowered his lips to hers. Now he demanded more and she met his demands with her own. When he opened his mouth, her tongue darted to meet his and each made forays into the dark recesses that promised so much.

Her mind grew hazy and she was only dimly aware that his hand had crept under her knit blouse. She felt his fingers on her breast, gently caressing it, lifting it, cupping it. She started, as if an electric current had whipped through her body. Her eyes flew open in panic. A tiny corner of her mind urged her to stop this insanity.

"Love?" Jake asked, begging her with a single word, and her heart melted.

Her lashes drooped languorously. She sighed and wrapped an arm around his neck, pulling him closer. He kissed her exuberantly, grinding his mouth to hers. He rubbed a thumb against her nipple and she arched toward him. Her leg slipped against his involuntarily, finally resting on top of his thigh.

He ran his fingers around her ribs, warmly caressing her, unerringly found the front clasp of her bra, and unhooked it. He pushed her cotton shirt aside, releasing her generous breasts from their strictures. He lifted his head to gaze down at the pale peaks, tinted a soft rose in the firelight.

"Oh, God, Lisa," he groaned. "You are so lovely." He placed a reverent kiss on each breast. She placed a trembling hand on his dark head. His eyes met hers. The gray irises took on new color as they reflected the flames from the hearth. Her lips widened into a tiny smile, encouraging him. Enchanted, he crushed her to him, burying her tender breasts against the mat of hair on his chest. Already sensitized, her nipples hardened as they burrowed in the wiry curls. Her heartbeat quickened to match his.

He rose above her and lifted her slightly, pulling the emerald shirt over her head and sliding her bra away. Her face flushed in embarrassment and she crossed her arms, covering her breasts, but Jake took her hands and tugged them to her sides, surveying her body in wonderment, murmuring little words of love to her. He quickly removed his own shirt and slipped back to lie beside her. The flames in the fireplace danced, throwing a play of light and shadow across their trembling figures.

Jake wrapped his arms around Lisa and nuzzled the tender and sensitive cord at her throat. He cupped her soft bottom and held her tightly to him, showing her the full extent of his arousal.

Lisa was frantic with need. She stroked his bare back, loving the smoothness of his firm skin, yet coveting the roughness of his furry chest against her breasts. She shook with emotion and desire. She had never known such sensations. She wanted him! She wanted him to complete her, to fill the emptiness of her. She was beyond rational thought.

"Jake," she cried. "Oh, Jake!"

But Jake slipped down to tantalize her even more. He nibbled the underside of her breasts and ran his tongue along the valley between them. His journey was leisurely and she wriggled in frustration. The ache reached deep into her belly, then lower. She arched against him frantically, finally grasping his head and urging him to her breast. She sighed with pleasure as his lips found her nipple. But he continued to tease her, tapping the tip lightly with his tongue. She whimpered little entreaties to him and held him tightly to her, begging for more.

He surrendered to her pleas and sucked her breast deeply into his mouth. Her nipples hardened into erect buttons. When she thought she could bear no more, he moved to her other breast while still caressing the now wet nipple with his thumb. She cried

73

aloud and twisted her hips, rubbing against him in unconscious invitation. She thought she would go mad with longing.

Jake lifted his head to gaze into her passion-glazed eyes, looking with satisfaction at her swollen lips, now slightly open in invitation. He took her trembling hand in his and drew it to him.

"Feel what you are doing to me, darling," he whispered huskily, sliding her hand along his hardness. She recoiled at the unexpected intimacy, but he reached for her once more, bringing her back to him.

"It's all right, Lisa," he reassured her in a tender whisper, finding the doubt in her eyes. "It will be all right." He kissed her hand. "You won't get pregnant, I promise you that."

She snatched her hand away and her eyes flew wide open, fixing on him in horror. "Oh, my God," she cried, "No!"

She thrust herself from his body and rolled away. She scrambled to her feet and raced away from the firelight in panic-stricken flight, slamming the bathroom door behind her.

Chapter Seven

Stunned by Lisa's sudden flight, Jake levered himself against the couch, boosting himself to a sitting position. He sat in agony for a few moments, struggling to cool his passion. At last, he floundered to his feet, trying to regain his bearings.

Everything was as it had been, the bright fireplace, the dying candles, the soft lighting. Only the scattered pillows, her blouse and bra remained as evidence of their lovemaking. Why had she run like that? What had he done? What had he said?

He cautiously moved to the bathroom door and knocked gently.

"Lisa? Lisa, what's wrong, love?"

There was no response, but through the heavy door, he could hear her sobbing and his heart caught in his throat. He felt guilty, without having any idea why. He tried the door, but it was locked.

"Lisa," he tried again, more insistently. "Lisa. Please talk to me, love. What's the matter? I have to know what I did."

"Go away," she cried. "Just go home."

"I can't!" he exclaimed desperately. "I can't leave you like this. What happened? I . . . we were so close, love What did I say? Lisa? Are you listening to me?"

"Please . . . please go. It was all a mistake. I never should have let . . . " Jake could hear the hoarseness in her voice, as she struggled to control her violent weeping. "Jake . . . I . . . I know it was all . . . my fault, not yours. I . . .I'm not blaming you for anything. It was wonderful, but I just . . . can't."

He knocked sharply on the door again in frustration. "Lisa, I don't want to talk to you through a closed door. I want you out here, face to face."

There was no reply.

"Honey, I promise I won't touch you. Lisa, please talk to me."

His plea was met with silence.

"Lisa, if you don't come out of there, I'll go and get your brother. Maybe he can talk to you."

She laughed bitterly. "He won't help you. He can't even help himself. Why don't you leave the two of us to our private hell?"

"What in God's name is that supposed to mean?" he demanded.

Again she refused to answer him.

"Lisa, if you don't come out of there, I'll break down the door." Jake derided himself even as he spoke. So now he was going to do himself bodily injury against this heavy door? He'd been watching too many detective shows on television. Besides, in her state, Lisa certainly wouldn't appreciate such macho tactics.

Her voice rose hysterically and broke. "No, you won't. If you try, I'll . . . "

Jake strained to hear her but missed the rest of the sentence, if indeed she had finished it. What would she do? What could she do? Was there some way she could injure herself? Something in the medicine cabinet? He couldn't chance it, he had to diffuse the situation. He stood deep in thought, mulling over various strategies. He slumped against the door frame and sighed.

'Lisa," he spoke softly. Lisa?"

"Yes, what do you want?" She sounded so exhausted. Lord, what had he done to her?

"Are you O.K.?"

"I would be if you would just go away. I feel like such a fool."

"I'll go," Jake assured her, "if you promise me two things."

"What are they?"

"First, that you'll come out as soon as I leave here. I want you to go to bed and cry it out there. I can't leave you to spend the night in there."

"I'm not that much of an idiot, though it may seem like it to you right now," she sniffed and blew her nose. "But I want you to know that you shouldn't plan on tricking me. I'll have to hear the sound of your car going over the old wooden bridge on the river before I come out."

"Can't fool a Norwegian-Italian clarinetist," he teased her.

"Jake! Oh, what's the other thing," she demanded, exasperated with him.

"Promise me that when I call you tomorrow morning, you won't hang up on me."

"Jake, it's better if we end this thing now."

"Damn it, no!" he exploded. He caught himself and began again, quietly and tenderly. "I'm not going to give up on you, Lisa Fratelli, so don't count on it. You might have something you can't tell me about, some secret so horrible that it would turn me away. But I don't think so. I know there's nothing on this earth that you could tell me that could stop me from loving you.

"So you had better promise to answer my phone call tomorrow or I'm going to sit out here all night and all day, if necessary. Maybe even a week, though I don't know how I can handle that, considering you're occupying the only bathroom." He heard her involuntary laugh and grinned in relief. "I will stay as long as I have to, Lisa. And there goes my law practice, and if that goes, there goes the money for the house, there goes your commission, and there goes your business. Lisa, this could ruin the whole Upper Michigan economy!"

Her reluctant chuckle was followed by a sad little sigh. "I guess I'd better agree then. Out of patriotism. But I think you're a fool to bother with me. Jake?"

"Yes, love."

"The Johnsons accepted your offer. Their acceptance is on the mantle."

Jake smiled his satisfaction with himself as he pulled on his shirt and retrieved the document. At least she still wanted him in the same town, if not in the same room. It was a start.

When Lisa heard Jake's car door slam, she began to cry quietly once more. It had been so gloriously beautiful, being with Jake, touching him, loving him, being loved back. Was this truly what making love was all about? She hadn't known it could be like that. She was learning so much about her own sensuality, about her capacity for giving and taking. Everything had been so perfect.

"I won't get you pregnant." Why, oh why, did he have to say that? Did he mean that he would take precautions? She had never thought about it. That was how out of control she had been, she of all people. What had he meant? It didn't matter. "I won't get you pregnant." How many years had it been since she heard those words from another man, how long ago?

"I won't get you pregnant." When Jake spoke, it had seemed as if it were all starting over again, the months of nightmare, the years of agony. She couldn't face the pain, the loss, never again. Better that she stop this thing with Jake before she was hurt again.

But the niggling truth was that she was already suffering the pain and agony of losing Jake. The truth was that she had wanted him as much as he wanted her. Just remembering his mouth on her breast caused her to whimper, aching for the fulfillment she had denied herself. How could she let him go? Oh, she could live with the frustration, with the unfulfilled desire. That was part of living alone. But how could she go on without the laughter, the special moments of sharing?

Why not call him? Why not ask him to come back, to share her bed? It didn't have to be forever. She was no experienced woman who could dazzle him with her sexual expertise. He would soon grow bored and leave her alone. But at least she would have him for a time. At least then she would have something to remember. What did she have now?

She rocked back and forth, holding her knees to her chest in indecision. What if he never called? What if he decided not to buy the Johnson house and she never saw him again? The years behind her and those before her seemed to stretch on forever.

The rattle of the Corvette's wheels on the old bridge brought Lisa out of her tortured reverie. She stood up, stretching her aching muscles. No, she would not call Jake. She had been alone this long. She knew that she would be all right.

She turned on the sink's faucet and bathed her sore eyes with cold water. She could only do what she had always done. Go on.

In the early hours of Sunday morning, Jake woke once more from a restless sleep, frustrated, angry and confused. In his dreams, he relived the scene in front of the fireplace again and again, to wake each time in an agony of thwarted desire.

What had happened? He went over those moments before she so abruptly left him, but found few clues. The memory of their lovemaking, of her incredibly beautiful body lying so close to his, merely added to his frustration. He groaned and rolled over, punching his pillow.

Had he hurt her? No, he had been so careful with her, he knew her fragility. Had he given her pleasure? Yes, he was certain that she had welcomed his touch, no, had encouraged it.

He had said something. What was it? Something about not

getting her pregnant, that was it. He had said it to reassure her, but maybe it had had the opposite effect. Was she that frightened that she might have a baby? Maybe she didn't like the idea of having a family, didn't like kids. No, that wasn't it, he knew that wasn't it. She had been great with the high school students on the rafting trip and the children's area in her office indicated that she liked little ones.

Maybe she was offended, thinking that he wouldn't want her to have his child. God, if only he could give her a baby! He would love to see Lisa pregnant, her belly swollen with his child. She would be so beautiful carrying a baby.

But that was impossible. He should tell her about that, too. He wanted to be honest with her, to let her know what she was getting into before he told her he was in love with her and wanted to marry her. Jake had known her only one short week, yet he knew already that he wanted to spend the rest of his life with her. But most women would want to bear children of their own and that wouldn't be possible for Lisa if she married him.

Lord, he hoped she would be all right. She had been very upset and he shouldn't have left her alone like that. He should have stopped by to see that brother of hers or at least called him. But what could he say to the man? "Hey, buddy, would you check up on your sister. She's upset because I tried to make love with her."

If he's any kind of brother, he would punch my lights out, Jake thought ruefully. Not that I don't deserve it, but it probably wouldn't help matters.

There was something odd about that brother anyway. Why did Lisa feel that she had to take care of him? He certainly should be old enough to take care of himself. And what was that about them being in a private hell?

Jake sat up in his bed, lit the lamp and checked his alarm clock. Three a.m. He switched off the light and lay down again, forcing his eyes to close. He had to get some sleep!

Damn! What had he done? Maybe it was because he had pushed her too far, too fast. Was it because he had asked her to touch him? Was she that innocent? She said she wasn't a virgin. That bothered her, too, but why should it? It certainly didn't matter to him.

But as Jake thought about it, it suddenly did bother him. He was in agony of jealousy. He pictured her face as it had been, strained in passion, flushed with the pleasure she was receiving, but saw another man at her breast. She had been so passionate, so giving, until that last moment. Who had taught her so well? Jake groaned and rolled over yet again.

The faces of some of the men he had met in Norway during the past week flitted before him. Was it one of them? Or was there more than one? He cursed himself, knowing he had no right to wonder about Lisa's past. He had been with more than one woman in his forty years. He could hardly expect a thirty-one-year-old woman, especially one as beautiful as Lisa, to live a celibate life.

But jealousy isn't rational. Jake had a long night.

Lisa's night was as long. After hours of sleeplessness, she simply gave up and left her bed to take a long, hot shower, following it with cold, hoping to clear the cobwebs from her mind. The icy water shot onto her shoulders like tiny needles, invigorating her body, but doing nothing for her emotional state.

Jake must think she was some kind of an idiot. What kind of woman would lock herself in a bathroom like that, as if he were ... some rapist, bent on attacking her. As the early morning light filtered into the cabin, she toweled herself dry and looked at her red eyes in the mirror over the sink. The misted-over reflection of the tiny room mocked her. How melodramatic she had been, she groaned. At the moment, she wanted to lock the door again and never leave the confines of this sanctuary. She could live her life here, slowly starve to death, never to face Jake again. But her sense of humor returned as she thought of herself pining away in a bathroom. Would she be found eventually curling around a toilet bowl or draped gracefully in the tub? She threw on an old terry cloth robe and wandered into the kitchen to brew a fresh pot of very black coffee.

She sipped from her favorite old mug as she dusted, vacuumed and picked up for the night before, blushing as she retrieved her bra and green shirt from the floor in front of the fireplace. How could she have allowed that to happen, she wondered, all the time knowing how it had happened. She had wanted it, wanted it still. Jake, oh Jake, she sighed, as she clutched a patchwork cushion to her breast. What was she going to do? What could she say to him when he called? If he called?

She went to work on her kitchen, cleaning and scrubbing, finding limited relief in hard work. Her home was sparkling by five-thirty. She searched from one end to another for something else to do. Nothing. For a minute, she mulled over the idea of chopping wood or mowing the lawn, but Richard would certainly hear her from his cabin at the foot of the lake and wonder what on earth she could be thinking of. She couldn't bear to answer his questions right now.

She paced through all the rooms one more time before she finally gave up. She threw on a light pink linen dress, grabbed her jacket and purse and left for the office. The thing to do was to immerse herself in work there until it was time for church.

Church! Oh Lord, she would have to face Neil, and worse, Beth. How could she face her friends' well-meaning quizzing? For the first time in years, Lisa considered skipping the Sunday morning services. But if she wasn't in her usual spot in the fourth pew, Beth would be at her cabin early in the afternoon, full of concern and questions. It would be much easier to go to church and bear the mild teasing from the congregation.

As Lisa unlocked the door to her business, the telephone began to ring. She seized the receiver with trembling hands, knowing full well who would be on the end of the line.

"Fratelli Realty," she said, barely audible in her nervousness.

"Damn it, Lisa," Jake exploded. "I thought you were going to wait for my call at home. Do you have any idea what I thought when there was no answer there?"

"No," she whispered.

"That you had . . . Oh, I don't know what I thought," he shouted at her. "You were upset last night, very upset. Do you know what time it is? And do you know what *day* it is? Do you always go to work on Sundays?"

"I thought I'd get some work done," she explained weakly. "I couldn't sleep anyway."

"Join the crowd, babe," he growled sarcastically.

"Was there something you wanted?" she asked coolly, recovering her composure as her anger grew.

"Do you want to re-phrase that? I thought it was obvious last night I wanted you!"

"Well .... Yes. I don't want to talk about it. Was there anything else we have to discuss?"

Jake took a deep breath, calming himself. "I have to see you."

"You can see me when you close on the house."

81

"That's not what I mean. There'll be at least five other people around then."

"I know what exactly what you mean. I don't think being alone with you is such a good idea. One or the other of us would be hurt if I go on dating you. I don't want that, Jake. Please understand."

"What do you want me to say?" he asked in exasperation. "That I promise that you will never be hurt? There are no guarantees in this life, Lisa. We are human. We will say things and do things that cause the other pain without meaning to do them. But I can promise you that I would never knowingly cause you any unhappiness. All I want is the best for you, darling. Isn't that enough? More than enough?"

She swallowed painfully. What could she say to that?

"Lisa? Lisa?"

"Yes, I'm here," she whispered, tears in her eyes.

"When's the closing?"

"W . . . what?"

"When can we have the closing?" he repeated patiently.

"Uh . . . I guess whenever you're ready. I can have the bank's lawyer update the abstract any time you say."

"Friday. I can be ready by Friday, if I have to type the papers myself."

"O.K. Friday, at the bank. Say one p.m. – if I can get everyone there." Lisa was once again the efficient real estate agent. "You'll take care of the insurance and the mortgage?"

"I'm a lawyer, Lisa, and a good one. I'm certain I can handle a simple real estate matter."

"Yes, of course. Well, call me if any problems crop up," she replied lamely.

"Fine," he said briskly. "And Lisa, don't make any plans for Friday night. We're going out to dinner to celebrate my new house and then we're going to start all over. No physical involvement unless you want it. This time, you call the shots." He hung up the phone abruptly before she could refuse.

Lisa stared at the receiver in surprise and it was some moments before she returned it to its cradle.

A hundred times during the next week, Lisa changed her mind about that dinner date. There were times she knew with certainty that she would accept Jake's invitation (if she could call his gruff command an "invitation") and she would whirl around her bedroom, selecting and discarding clothes, singing snatches of love songs.

But most of the time, she thought that there was no way she could allow herself to be drawn into a destructive relationship. After all, she had learned at an early age that loving always led to heartbreak.

Those Lisa loved were inevitably lost to her. Her own parents had left her, first her father, then two years later, her mother. They were two teenagers forced into marriage by an unwanted pregnancy and had little interest in the tiny baby who placed them in that predicament. But their departures, however traumatic for Lisa, left her with her adoring grandmother, Nana.

Then Nana died and no one was able to locate either parent to sign the necessary papers to place Lisa in an adoptive home. She was shunted from foster home to foster home, a tiny, pale child who stared with wide, frightened eyes at the adults around her. She became more and more withdrawn with each move until she ceased to talk at all. At one point, she was diagnosed as disabled and barely escaped being sent to a special school for the handicapped. Lisa tried not to think much about those years.

It was then that the Fratellis had taken her into their little family. After her son's birth, Betty Fratelli could have no more children. She had her heart set on a daughter and she fell in love at first sight with the little girl with white-blond hair and fearful green eyes. She set about giving the child what she needed most – love and security. The wildly exuberant family poured out their love to Lisa and, in time, she came to love them back, especially her big brother, Richard, only two years older than she. The unhappy little girl had grown to be an intelligent, cheerful young woman, secure in the love of those around her. The Fratellis were never able to adopt here, something Betty had her heart set on. It was years later that the social agencies finally established that both of Lisa's parents were dead, one in a traffic accident, the other of a drug overdose. By that time, it was too late.

If only things had stayed the way they were, Lisa thought sadly, as she dressed for the one o'clock closing on Wednesday. But she had lost that family, too, tragically. How could she take another chance on loving and losing? It would be best to discourage Jake now. She pawed through her closet once more, searching for something casual, yet business-like, to show Jake

83

from the start of this meeting that she would not be going out with him. Perhaps a tailored suit, if she could find one plain enough.

She probably had nothing to worry about. Jake must have forgotten all about that date by now. And why not? Why would he, a skilled professional, used to cosmopolitan socialites, want to be saddled with a neurotic small-town woman. For all she knew, he had found someone else in the past few days.

It did seem as if he had lost interest in her. He hadn't contacted her all week and she thought he would. She didn't expect to see him Sunday night, but he might have called. And Monday. He had allowed her Monday nights to wash her hair, but after all! And then there was Tuesday. True, she had band practice on Tuesdays, but she was almost sure she would see Jake waiting at the door of the practice room at the high school as the band finished rehearsing. The rest of the band members had expected him, too, for she was assaulted with various repetitions of the basic question.: "Hey, Lisa, where's Jake?" Knowing that she was supposed to be half of a couple made it doubly difficult to return to her quiet cabin. She tried very hard to be glad Jake had forgotten about her, but she was unsuccessful.

As she was leaving her bedroom, Lisa glanced in her full-length mirror and was shocked to find that she was not dressed casually at all. Neither did she look businesslike. While daydreaming, she had donned a bright ankle-grazing yellow, orange and red print skirt and matched it with a yellow crew neck tank top and poly-chromatic sandals. A brilliant red belt cinched her small waist. This outfit was hardly appropriate for a business meeting. Jake would think she was trying to catch his attention! What had she been thinking of?

But a glance at her watch told Lisa that she simply did not have time to change if she wanted to make her meeting at the bank. Flustered, she dashed out the door, using words Neil and Beth would have deemed inappropriate for a youth group leader.

Jake grinned at Lisa's bright array as she marched into the bank, but quickly erased his smile, becoming a very professional, very serious lawyer. Lisa had never seen him in a truly business capacity before and was impressed. He was strictly an attorney as he carefully and painstakingly read each document presented to him by Lisa, the Johnsons, their lawyer, and the president of the bank, as they all sat around an oak table in a meeting room .

Lisa shyly glanced at Jake, who was awesome in his gray,

double-breasted suit, white shirt and maroon tie. He was a wonderful lawyer, asking intelligent questions of all participants. If only he wouldn't insist on addressing her as Ms. Fratelli!

"Ms. Fratelli, would you happen to have the sales contract with you?"

"Ms. Fratelli, by some chance have you prepared the bill of sale?"

"This seems to be in order, Ms. Fratelli, but I would like to suggest one little addition. Would that be possible, Ms. Fratelli?"

The others looked at the two of them in astonishment. Everyone in town knew they had been dating, so why the formality?

And why was he taking so long with what should be a simple meeting? He was checking and re-checking every figure furnished by Lisa and the others. The business Lisa had thought would take no more than fifteen minutes stretched to an hour and still he read on and on. Everyone concerned looked at their watches as Jake slowly turned page after page. What was he up to now, she wondered.

Jake caught her watching him and winked. She sniffed and turned her gaze out the large window that looked over Main Street. She idly watched the townspeople going up and down the sidewalks and entertained herself by guessing where they might be going. It was easy for someone who knew them all. Mr. Torelli, for instance, was going for an afternoon cup of coffee. He left his car dealership every day at this time, had for the past twenty-five years. And there was Mrs. Jorgenson, hurrying to open the library. Was it two o'clock already? She glared at Jake who was apparently oblivious to the restless movements around him. Lisa looked down the street again.

Neil and Beth came hurrying toward the bank from the direction of the church. Beth was practically running to keep up with Neil's long stride. They seemed to be rushing toward the bank as if they were late and Lisa straightened in concern. What were they doing downtown at this hour? She moved slightly in her chair to watch them through the glass panel at the front of the meeting room, as they entered the bank.

Just then, Jake cleared his throat. "Well, this looks in order," he said briskly.

"Of course it is!" Lisa snapped.

Mr. Fletcher, the bank president, peered at Lisa in wonder, adjusting his wire-rimmed glasses. He knew she was usually the epitome of patience with her customers. Jake caught his eye and shook his head, as if commiserating with him over a temperamental female. Lisa bit her tongue to keep from screaming at the irritating man.

The papers were quickly signed by all the proper parties, the checks were turned over to the Johnson's attorney and the banker, and Jake was now the owner of a Victorian mansion. With newly found haste, he said rapid good-byes to everyone, took Lisa's arm as she was gathering her and portfolio, helped her out of her chair and led her out to the main lobby, all before she realized what he was doing.

"And now for that date you promised me," he began.

"*I* promised you?" she cried, digging her heels into the carpeting and refusing to take another step. "I *never* . . . ."

"Lisa! Jake!" Neil called heartily from the teller's window. "I thought we were going to be late, but here we are, right on time to celebrate with you."

Lisa stared at the minister and his wife blankly. "Celebrate?"

Beth was practically jumping up and down in excitement. "Didn't Jake tell you? We're double dating! We actually found someone to watch the kids and found a night without a church meeting and we're all going to Escanaba to stroll along the lake and have some of the best seafood in the world. It's our anniversary," she confided, hugging Lisa. "You've no idea how hard it is for us to get away for an evening together and when Jake suggested, well I . . ." Her gurgling monologue ended as she noticed Lisa's stunned expression. "Oh dear," Beth said despondently. "Can't you come?"

Neatly cornered by Jake's maneuvering, and not wanting to spoil Beth's happy plans, Lisa tried to recover. "Don't you two want to be alone?"

Beth positively skipped as she led the way out to the street. "Oh, we'll have that time later, when you and Jake go for the moonlight trail ride. I never could get Neil on a horse anyway, so we're going to enjoy a romantic evening by the lake. It will be all the more romantic for being with another couple in love."

"In love? Trail ride? What trail ride? I won't . . . can't! I'm not dressed for a . . . " Lisa shrilly objected as Jake hustled her down the street to Neil's car, a sedate Ford station wagon suitable for a minister's family.

"I've brought clothes for you, love," Jake assured her

86

calmly. "Jeans, shirt, socks, boots. You wouldn't need any special underwear, would you? We could always stop somewhere," he suggested in a low voice.

"Underwear? Jeans? You can't buy clothes for me! I won't have it! And how would you know my size?" she hissed at him.

"Took measurements last week," he whispered, chuckling as she assumed the color of a lobster. He had effectively silenced her.

He settled her in the back seat of the large car and slipped in beside her, sitting much closer to her than was necessary. She tried to move away from him to the far side, but he slid an arm around her waist to keep her next to him.

"What are you trying to do, Jake?" she muttered almost inaudibly as Neil started the old car with a roar.

"I thought that was obvious," said he with a self-satisfied grin. "I'm kidnapping you,"

"I'll have the FBI after you," she threatened with heat.

"It's no use, Lisa. As a competent attorney practicing under the auspices of the Michigan Bar Association, I can assure you that the Mann Act doesn't apply because we are not crossing state lines."

"Aha! You *are* admitting to transport for immoral purposes!"

"Not at all," he cheerfully reassured her, but added, "at least not at the moment. Furthermore, Neil and Beth will swear that you entered this car willingly with no coercion on my part, dressed fit to kill I might add, so you can't cite the Lindbergh Law."

"I was tricked," she cried, hitting him on his solid chest with her tiny fist.

"Ah, but that's not illegal," he answered, catching her flying hand.

"Ooooooh, you!" she fumed, then sputtered into silence when she caught sight of Beth, who was considering them anxiously from the front seat. Lisa forced herself to smile at the redhead and relaxed her body, which allowed Jake to pull her even closer to his side.

She gave Jake her most dazzling smile and said between her teeth, "I'll get you for this, Gannett." Jake grinned at her and gave her a quick but thorough kiss, to Beth's delight.

87

Chapter Eight

The dinner, at an old inn that rested on a pier at the very edge of Lake Michigan, had been hilarious with Lisa's protestations, Jake's placid assumption that she would give in eventually, and the Frankes' well-meant matchmaking. While stuffing herself with lobster, Lisa repeatedly insisted that she would not be going on a trail ride.

"How can you subject poor horses to the torture of carrying such an overload? Would you look at how much we're eating, Jake?"

"You know, you're right," he mused. "We'll have to do something about that."

Jake's solution was a long walk in the moonlight, leaving Neil and Beth behind to their own devices. Before Lisa could open her mouth for the objection she thought was expected of her, Jake explained that it was all "for the good of those poor horses" and what possible exception could she take to that? And to be fair, Jake had behaved himself rather well, snatching only an innocent kiss or two. Jake loosened his tie, took off his jacket, and slipped off his shoes and with only a brief hesitation, she removed her sandals. They strolled down the beach, hand in hand, silent in the beauty of the starlit night.

Stars still reflected in her eyes as, floating along on a cloud of her dreams, Lisa followed where Jake led, even when he steered her to a room of the old inn. There she found an unexpected roommate, Beth, who was changing into a swimsuit. The Frankes were going to swim while the Lisa and Jake took a trail up into the hills.

Beth hugged Lisa excitedly. "Oh, Lisa, I'm so happy for you. It's about time you had your chance for happiness. You'll make him such a wonderful wife."

"Wife?" Lisa exclaimed in alarm. "Beth, you're jumping to conclusions. Jake has never said a word about marriage!"

Beth waved aside that minor technicality. "It's just a matter of time, dear. He's absolutely besotted with you, I can tell. He looks at you the way Neil looks at me sometimes."

Lisa automatically began to change, too intrigued by this conversation to continue her refusal to ride. "What do you mean, the way Neil looks at you? How does he look at you?"

Beth demonstrated a lusty leer that sent Lisa off into gales of laughter.

"Beth, he doesn't! Neil never looks that way."

Beth stuck out her tongue and made a pretense of being offended. "Dear, Neil may be a minister, but believe me, he is a man. My children were not immaculate conceptions, after all."

Flustered, Lisa quickly changed, not wanting to go on with that subject at all! To Beth's amusement and Lisa's embarrassment, Jake had guessed all her sizes correctly. The jeans cupped her derriere lovingly, the pale yellow linen shirt seemed to flow around her breasts. She tied the shirt tails at her waist, but she kept thinking about Neil's leer...and the children.

How could she keep her mind on Neil's sermons after this conversation? She glimpsed Beth's amused face out of the corner of her eye, and began to giggle. She collapsed on the floor, holding her sides with her arms around her, and that was how Jake found her, still laughing helplessly as she tried to don her boots.

The boots fit perfectly and Jake had even furnished some cotton socks, tickling her insteps as he slipped them over her toes.

From his perch on the lanky sorrel, Jake admired Lisa's straight back as she trotted her white mare down the trail in front of him. His eyes caressed the fair head, following the long plait down the curve of her spine. Wisps of hair had escaped their strictures and were glowing silver in the moonlight, forming a halo. She had been an angel all evening, Jake reflected, but if he wanted to keep her from flitting away again like a will-o-wisp, he had better move into the next stage of his battle plan.

He clicked his tongue against the roof of his mouth to signal his horse and dug in his heels. Horse and man moved as one as they followed the white mare.

"Wait up," Jake called to Lisa. She glanced back and reined her horse to a walk. As he drew near, she smiled.

"As much as I hate to admit it, this has been fun, Jake. I haven't been on a horse since last summer. It's not time to go home yet, is it?"

"Wish it didn't have to end, love, but tomorrow is going to be a hard day for me. That's why I wanted this time with you. It's going to be a long, lonely week for me. I'll miss you."

"You're going away?" Was that a pensive note in her voice?

"No, but I'll be too busy to take you out. I'm the owner of a new house, you know."

"I seem to remember something about it," she said dryly.

Jake sighed. "I wish it didn't have to be this way, but Jodi will be coming home on Sunday and I don't want her to return to chaos. Her life has been unsettled enough as it is. I've arranged for our furniture to be moved here from Milwaukee. It should be here by Friday. I'm going to buy a few other things here. We need a new stove and refrigerator and then there's drapes and paint. I've only got three more days to get the place in shape and I have client meetings during the day. That means I have to spend my evenings, shopping, cleaning and painting. Wallpapering, too, I suppose.

"You know how to wallpaper?" she said dubiously.

"I guess I'll have to learn," he replied somberly. "Have you ever done it?" He smiled to himself, keeping his face carefully averted. Only yesterday, Beth had shown him the Sunday school rooms that Lisa had papered.

"Well, yes. There is a trick to it, you know."

"Could you show me how? If you could spare a little time tomorrow night?"

"I suppose so. It shouldn't take long to get you started."

"Great," he exclaimed enthusiastically. "Then I should be able to do three or four rooms by Saturday."

"Three or . . . "

"I might even have time to start building the new bathroom."

"A new bathroom by Sunday?" she gibed. "In your spare time?"

"Well, I might need some help there. A plumber maybe. A carpenter and electrician, too. Do you have any suggestions? You know everyone around here."

"Your best bet would be to get in touch with the Harms family. They contract to do everything, including painting. They're very good. I could call them for you."

"Terrific. Could they get to work right away, do you think? Oh, I don't expect everything to be done in a week. I know better than that. Can I trust them to pick out the paint colors?"

"Heavens, no! All the men in that family are color-blind. They're neat painters, but you have to select your own colors," Lisa decreed.

"Oh." There was no way she would miss his woebegone expression.

"What's the matter?"

"I'm color-blind, too."

"Is that so?" She inspected his sorrowful face with the first glimmerings of suspicion.

"I can get Jodi to pick out the colors," he said quickly. "She always wanted to decorate, I know. She loves anything purple."

Lisa winced. "Maybe I could help you out there."

"Wonderful," he said eagerly. "And what about a housekeeper, or a cleaning woman? I don't know if I could keep up with a house that big.""

"Well, I could make a few phone calls for you tomorrow and round someone up."

"Would you?" he sighed with exaggerated relief. "How about meeting me for supper tomorrow night. We could shop for the stove and refrigerator afterward."

Lisa reined in her horse and eyed his complacency. "Why do I feel like I'm being led down the garden path here?" she demanded.

"What garden path? This is supposed to be a bridle trail, have we gotten off it?" he asked innocently, but thought "a bridal trail" was nearer his intentions.

Lisa put her hand on her hip, glowering at him. He hurried on, "And speaking of gardens. Do you suppose we could find a lawnmower? And do you think it's too late to start a little plot?"

"A little plot? I think you've already started one. No, don't say another word," she admonished him and urged her mount to a walk. "I want to think about this for a moment."

Jake brought his sorrel up beside her mare, watching Lisa anxiously. Was she going to go along with him on this? He sighed. Oh well, if she wouldn't, he'd think of something else. Then he caught sight of the white flash of her teeth.

"I think," she grinned, "we could still plant some beans, lettuce and radishes."

On Saturday night, as Lisa sat in the library of Jake's new home, unpacking the last of his possessions, she observed that it would be much simpler to ask Jake what he wanted of her in the first place and then go along with it, but it was so fascinating to watch him connive, wheedle and try to outsmart her. She had to put up some sort of resistance, they both enjoyed the game so!

92

Together, on Thursday and Friday, they ordered a dining room set, a stove, a refrigerator, and all the towels, sheets and miscellaneous items he thought they might need. She soon stopped worrying about spending his money, and concentrated on convincing him not to buy every silly gadget they encountered. She was soon convinced he was indeed, color blind, and took over all the color coordination. He good-naturedly bowed to her opinions on paint, wallpaper, carpeting and draperies. After they shopped, they spent hours working on the house. She papered, he painted, and they laughed and talked as they worked. The movers brought the furniture and the two of them worked out the room arrangements, arguing amiably. Lisa began to feel more and more as if she had an interest in this old house. It all felt so right.

The only thing Lisa refused to do was select furnishings for Jodi's room. She knew how she would have resented such interference when she was thirteen.

"So what if everything is purple, Jake? You can paint over it when she's older. She needs to express herself." Jake groaned and forecast dire color combinations.

Lisa was becoming very anxious to meet this daughter of Jake's. She knew only that Jodi was blond and slender. Lisa looked across the room at Jake's mop of dark hair, as he bent over his desk, arranging files, reference books, pencils, pens, paper clips and other business paraphernalia. She wondered idly how a man with such a dark complexion could have produced a blond daughter. Jodi must take after her mother. Odd, that. Somehow, Lisa thought that Jake would have imprinted his stamp on any child of his.

All at once, she pictured a tiny baby with blond hair – what there was of it. She could feel the tiny hands moving gently as she held it to her breast . . .

Oh, God, she thought in anguish, don't think about it. She shook her head and forced her mind back to the task at hand, sorting out Jake's books. Fiction. Non-fiction. Law books to one side . . .

Jake was well aware of the agony that marred Lisa's delicate features and wondered anew what secrets she hid from him. He wanted to know everything about this woman yet there were closed places in her mind that she had clearly marked off-limits to him. He shared laughter and camaraderie with her, but it wasn't enough. He wanted her to open herself to the intimacy, both physical emotional, that would allow her to love him as he had come to love her.

He ached for her. He had been so careful with her this past week, but damn, it was frustrating. The glimpse of her softly curving breast through the yellow linen shirt he had bought her was torture. She had tied the shirttails tight under her breasts for coolness on this hot and humid late June evening. He longed to slide his hands around that slender waist and crush her to him. Her hair was piled on the top of her head, but as always, she could never quite control the tendrils that were sticking to the perspiration on her face. From time to time, she ineffectively pushed the curls back. At any time, the mass of hair might collapse and cascade down her back. Jake found himself waiting for it, the suspense part of the excitement that surrounded Lisa.

Jake had never made comparisons between Lisa and Christine before, but now he remembered that Christine had chopped off her long, black hair the day she reached twenty-five, to his great disappointment. She told him that twenty-five was the age at which women cut their hair, it was as simple as that. It was some kind of female rule that men would never understand, Jake mused. He had loved her long hair, but thereafter, Christine went to a beauty salon religiously three times a week, to keep her hair perfectly coiffed. Jake had never dared to touch her hair after that. He considered Lisa as she pored over a novel she had discovered among his books. He doubted that Lisa ever went near a salon unless it was to sell a raffle ticket or put up a poster for a band concert.

To be fair, Christine had been a good wife, a perfect hostess, a perfect housekeeper, a perfect everything that a young lawyer required as he worked to build up his practice. Their apartment was impeccably furnished. She bought Jake the latest fashions to wear in court and checked his appearance before she would allow him to leave the apartment. Jodi always had the correct clothing for every occasion, the best schools, and lessons, in piano, ballet, or whatever was fashionable. Her mother saw to that.

Christine was so organized. She kept lists of everything that pertained to their lives in neat, leather-bound notebooks. Her filing system was better than that in Jake's law office. Whatever they discussed, from possible trips to bathroom fixtures, Christine was sure to have notes on it somewhere. Yes, she insisted on perfection in everything.

There had been times that Jake wished his wife could be a little more spontaneous. He couldn't remember ever seeing Christine in a pair of scruffy jeans, like the pair Lisa wore now. Oh, Christine had jeans all right, designer jeans in the correct shades to match the expensive silk blouses she favored. But her slacks would never be dirtied, she was too immaculate for that. She would never consider sitting on the floor as Lisa was doing, her nose smudged from the dust on the books she was stacking.

"Lisa," he called over. "Let's call it a night and go get something to eat. I'm starved."

"Taco Bell? Hardee's?" she teased. The only restaurants he had taken her to since their evening at the Highway Supper Club had been fast-food joints.

He chuckled. "I guess you do deserve a good meal, but neither of us is dressed for it." He looked ruefully at his own denims, splashed with paint and wallpaper paste. "Want me to drive you home to change?"

"No, thanks, Jake. I understand. Fast food is fine tonight, in fact I think a drive-through would be a better idea. We have so much to do here! But give me a few minutes to finish these books first." She lowered her head to her task again and another lock tumbled down from her topknot. Jake wanted to catch her into his arms and pull out all the hairpins that remained, to feel the hair flow over his arms, to kiss that dirty nose.

How different than Christine she was! Jake remembered how a young legal aide had once jostled against Christine, depositing her into a swimming pool at a Bar Association party. She emerged furious, screaming at Jake to take her home. She never spoke to the culprit again, no matter how often the man tried to make amends. Christine never allowed herself to be less than faultless; that her friends saw her with wet hair and blurred makeup was unforgivable.

Her perfectionism sometimes irritated Jake. Christine had been a good lover, but Jake discovered that they always made love exactly three times a week, neither more nor less. Had she read some magazine article that mandated that schedule? He never found out. But if Jake hadn't reached the weekly quota, Christine would initiate matters. If he tried to exceed it, she would find an excuse to avoid his embraces. It seemed she had a list for that, too.

Jake realized with a start where his mind had taken him. It was terrible to think such disloyal things about a woman who had tried so hard to please him. He had loved Christine in his own way, but she had never accepted that he had loved her for better or for worse. He could have cherished her, whatever her faults or imperfections, but they had never had that kind of marriage. At the heart of the problem were Christine's insecurities, her fear of rejection. Jake never understood, because they never discussed it. He wished now that she could have been open with him. She had never even told him about her heart condition. If he had known, perhaps he could have saved her life.

Lisa was giggling over some silly passage in a novel and Jake glanced at her crinkling nose fondly. She had the one important thing that Christine lacked, a sense of humor. Jake couldn't remember a week when he had laughed more. She was so enthusiastic about everything! She gave as good as she got in the teasing game they played, quickly spotting his little stratagems and erecting her own lighthearted barriers. Each wall he breached was another minor victory that kept him charging toward his final goal – to make her love him.

Lisa was all he wanted in a woman. She was giving and caring, brainy and beautiful. He wanted her so much he was aroused just thinking of her, but he didn't dare touch her for fear of losing her. He didn't know how much longer he could play this waiting game.

In the morning, he would have to pick up Jodi at the Iron Mountain bus depot. What would she think of Lisa? He knew exactly how difficult his daughter could be. She would add another complication. As much as he loved Jodi, he wished she could stay at camp for another week.

To his astonishment, Jodi had settled into camp life. Her brief postcards dealt with necessities, such as money for boat fees, horse rides and souvenirs, and pleas that he send the few toiletries she had forgotten. One card had simply read:

> "Send Misty Peach lipstick.
>   Love, Jodi"

Apparently, Misty Peach was not stocked at the camp store. Jake wasn't absolutely certain that the Lake Hope Girls' Camp allowed lipstick, but he sent a tube anyway. Jodi was touchy enough and he was only happy she hadn't run away from her counselors. He half expected that. Her last card explained her contentment with the camp and the plea for the lipstick – the boys' camp across the lake was holding her interest.

*****

"What on earth is this, Jake?" Lisa exclaimed, peering into a large bag from an Iron Mountain department store. "You've been shopping on your own, haven't you?" she needled him, as she pulled out yards of emerald brocade. "Do I have to watch you all the time?" What wild extravagance had he found this time?

Jake jumped to his feet and reached for her hands, pulling her to her feet. He marched her to the stairs, taking the heavy bag from her and toting it himself.

"I've visualized this since the day you showed me the house," he told Lisa as they ascended the stairs and walked down the hall.

The master bedroom was no longer starkly unfurnished. The green and beige floral drapes they had selected the day before adorned the windows. They had rescued oak furniture from an antique store to compliment the unusual bed. Lisa had polished all the pieces until they glowed. A brass lamp with insets of tinted, etched glass stood on the bedside table, casting a soft light over the ornate carvings on the bed. The animals of the wooden forest seemed to be watching them warily, one squirrel giving every indication of winking. Every hair was in place. The carving was extraordinary.

Jake dropped the sack on the new mattress and drew out the queen-sized emerald bedspread and a mint flannel blanket, as well as floral sheets and pillowcases that matched the curtains. Getting into the spirit immediately, Lisa skipped to the opposite side of the bed. Together, they put on the sheets.

"We work well together, don't we?" he smiled.

"Tuck that corner in tighter," she ordered.

"But Sarge, these are fitted sheets!"

"I meant the top sheet, private! Any more lip and it's back to boot camp for you! Hand me the blanket."

They finished their respective sides of the project at the same moment and rushed back to the door to observe the effect. It was perfect. The room was now complete, a pastoral Eden, the carved animals resting on a carpet of green, eternally watching the invaders of their forest domain.

"Oh, Jake," Lisa squealed happily, "it's beautiful!" She hugged him in her excitement and he quickly enveloped her in his arms, glorying in her closeness. He dropped a hasty kiss on her moist mouth and reluctantly began to widen the distance between them. But his kiss touched the core of her long-felt frustrations.

She swept her arms around his neck to prevent him from moving and enthusiastically kissed him back. His surprised "Oh!" was a warm breath in her mouth.

Jake stood silent. She knew he would touch her only if she demanded it. She timidly touched her tongue to his upper lip, wondering at her own temerity. Jake needed no second invitation. He thrust his tongue into her mouth, only to find her matching his movement. She trembled as his hands glided down the slope of her spine, gently pushing her errant curls aside as he cupped his hands around her curving buttocks, drawing her firmly against his muscled thighs, now pulsating with his need. He shuddered, then brusquely drew away from her. He was breathing heavily as he fought for control.

"Don't play games with me, Lisa," he gasped. "I can't let you do this to me twice. Don't start anything you don't intend to finish."

She dropped her gaze from his only to flush deep red on seeing the evident sign of his arousal. There was no way she could doubt his virility. She raised her eyes in confusion, indecisive, frightened of the consequences of her choice. Her breath caught at the extraordinary depth of feeling in his expressive eyes. It was desire she found there, desire to match her own.

"Lisa?"

She slowly nodded her acceptance to his unspoken question. He tenderly lifted her hand to his lips, kissing her palm. She tentatively brushed a black lock from his forehead and took a step toward him, but he stopped her with a gesture.

"Lisa," he began, his bass voice rumbling with emotion. "I started to tell you something that night and you shut me out. I know it upset you somehow, but it's important that you know this before we go any farther."

Her green eyes glowing with trust, Lisa took his hand, squeezing it to encourage and reassure him.

"Christine and I wanted children very much and we tried for several years . . . "

Lisa withdrew her hand abruptly.

"What's the matter, love?" Jake demanded, lifting her chin with a finger.

"I . . . I don't like to think of you . . . trying . . . with another woman," she confessed.

"I don't like to think of you with another man," he said, "but I can deal with it. Lisa, I loved Christine and I refuse to close

98

her out of my memories. I don't think you can expect that. But that part of my life is over. My heart belongs to you now. It has for some time."

The corners of her mouth turned up at his admission of his love. She reached out to him. He grasped her shoulders firmly to hold her back.

"No, this is important, Lisa. When Christine and I didn't have children, we went through a series of tests and . . . Damn, I still don't like to say it. I was the one. Do you understand me? I couldn't father a child."

Lisa was stunned at the unexpected pronouncement. "You? No, that can't be. I've always thought you were. . . a . . . ."

"Stud?" he teased.

She blushed again, to his amusement. Damn him, all she did lately was blush. And he didn't have to laugh at her! "No! Oh, I don't know."

"I said sterile," he reminded her, "not impotent."

She covered her glowing face with her hands while her mind scrambled to change the subject, but one question sprang before her: "What about Jodi?"

"We adopted Jodi. I've never had the slightest regret about that. But I wanted you to know because it . . . well, it's important that you know."

"Why?"

"Because, first of all, you don't have to worry about becoming pregnant when we make love, and secondly, I wanted you to be aware of it should we decide to have children."

"Should we ever . . . " Open-mouthed, she gaped at him.

"Well, isn't that where this relationship is headed?" he asked mildly. "Marriage, a family, a house with a mortgage."

"Oh, Jake, I love you!" she cried, throwing her arms around his waist and hugging him with all her might.

"Thought I'd never hear you say that," he said and kissed her very gently, not yet allowing a kiss of passion. She knew he was waiting for her response, her commitment.

Lisa's head rested against his throat, her nose inhaling the male scent. She found herself feverishly desperate to rub her fingers through that delicious mat of hair waiting for her just beneath his shirt. With trembling fingers, she began to unbutton the cotton fabric, placing little anxious kisses on his throat as she worked. Jake responded by laving her forehead, licking the little salty drops of perspiration away. She sighed as he slipped his hands to her breasts and cupped them, testing their weight. Then abruptly, he tore his hands away and stepped away from her.

Lisa whimpered, looking at him in astonishment. How could he stop now? Her breasts ached for his touch.

"I'm not seducing you this time, my love," he explained in a husky voice. "I want this to be your decision. Show me you want me." He drew his shirt off and dropped it to the floor. He waited, his bronzed skin gleaming in the lamplight.

Not for an instant did Lisa hesitate. Wasn't this what she wanted? To love and to be loved? She would match him, move for move. She pulled the shirt tails from her linen blouse and dragged it over her head, tossing it aside. She faced him, shy in her lacy bra.

Jake would allow only total commitment. "I'm waiting," he intoned deeply.

Lisa understood him at once and reached beneath her breasts to the front clasp of her bra. She unhooked it and slid the straps from her shoulders. The pink scrap fell unnoticed to the floor. She straightened, her breasts held high, a proud figure of womanhood.

Jake's face was lit up by his smile. He sank to his knees and reached for one of her feet. Caught off balance, she held herself up by grasping his broad shoulders. Entranced by the smooth, warm strength of his sinewy back, she kneaded him as he removed one, then the other sandal. As he finished his task and rose, he could not resist a quick kiss to each of her pert breasts, caressing them with work-roughened fingers as he reluctantly stepped back. He held his breath as he awaited her next move.

Taking her turn, Lisa dropped to her knees before him and removed his tennis shoes, teasing him by tickling his toes.

"Stop that, woman," he commanded gruffly, bringing her to her feet. He tried to remove himself from her seeking hands, but she was firm with him.

"Fair's fair," she declared and bent to taste the male nipples, running her hands through his pelt of wiry hair as she had dreamed of doing so many nights. Jake once again grasped her shoulders to set her away from him. She grinned at the frustration on his face. This game he had set in motion was becoming uncomfortable for him.

He unbuckled his belt, unzipped and dropped his slacks to the floor, kicking them out of the way. He stood before her in navy blue briefs that concealed nothing of his growing desire.

She contemplated his arousal, holding her hands to her glowing cheeks. For one brief moment, she thought that she would go no farther. Their eyes met and in that communion, Jake tried to show all the love he had for her. He reached out to her without moving a muscle, pleaded with her without saying a word. Their souls met and joined and became as one in their need.

Lisa's eyes never left his face as she slipped the jeans over her thighs and daintily stepped out of them. She now wore nothing but her pink bikini panties.

He paused to admire the full length of her, from her shining hair and luminous emerald eyes to her long, slender legs and tiny feet with their pink toenails. Lisa felt exquisite, knowing the pleasure he found in her body.

She inspected him in turn, marveling at the firm muscles of his arms, the strong chest, the hard thighs, the tight calves of his legs. Her fingers ached with the need to touch him.

"What now?" she murmured.

"What do you want, Lisa? Tell me what you want of me."

"Love me," she whispered. "Please love me."

Jake needed no second invitation. He swept her into his arms and carried her off to the bed, laying her tenderly across the green spread. She reached for him but he surprised her by fending off her hands, while he lifted her head to remove her hairpins, working her hair free from its bonds and fanning it against the brocade. He nuzzled her questioning face as he hovered over her.

"I've dreamed of seeing you this way since the day I saw this room," he confessed, sliding his fingers through the wealth of silvery-white waves. "The vision has been with me ever since. I knew from that first day that you would be mine."

"Oh, Jake," she whispered.

"Dearest Lisa, you more than match my dream. You are perfection. Marvelous, wonderful, perfection." He kissed her again, on her lips, her eyes, her cheeks, her throat. Suddenly, he was gone from her side and her eyes flew open to see him standing beside the bed, removing his last barrier of clothing. Her face was warm as she saw his manhood, proudly erect, but she did not turn away. She examined him boldly, learning this last mystery about him, loving his strength. He quickly joined her on the bed, squeezing her hand reassuringly.

"We'll take it slowly, love," he spoke thickly. "I'll do nothing until you're ready for it."

Silently, she reached for him, skimming her hand to his

neck to draw him to her. Their lips met in a soul-shattering kiss that spoke of their mutual adoration in the language of lovers. He ran his fingers up and down her body, lightly finding all the curves and hollows and secret places. She touched the hair on his chest with her fingertips, loving the differences of their bodies, finding the smooth and hard muscles she had envisioned for so long. The quivering between her thighs grew to an ache. She arched toward him, slightly parting her legs to feel his arousal against her quickly dampening panties.

"Slowly, love, remember?" he groaned against her throat. "Be gentle with me, O.K.? I'm a middle-aged man."

"Where? Show me where you're middle-aged?" she chucked so deeply in her throat that she purred. She reached for him but he parried her hand.

"Damn it, Lisa, we've barely started! Do you know what you're doing to me?"

"I was trying to find out," she teased him, "but you won't let me."

"Cheeky wench." Jake pushed her shoulders down on the bed and stopped her joking with his firm lips, setting her to gasping as he found the sensitive hollow at the base of her throat. He quickly found his path, nibbling the delicate bones of her shoulders, then working his way down to the shadowy area between her full breasts. He continued his journey of exploration, licking and nipping the tender underside of one of the plump mounds.

Lisa was going mad, she was sure of it. She wriggled her hands loose from his grasp and firmly took his head in her hands, leading his lips to the summit. He washed the aureole, in broad sweeping strokes of his hot tongue, lifting his head once or twice to watch with fascination as it darkened to a deep, angry hue. Her nipple grew hard, an erect button begging to be taken.

"Please . . . " she begged.

He needed no further urging, but covered her breast with his mouth, sucking and nibbling as she writhed beneath him. He gave her no respite as he turned his attention to its twin. His hand slipped to her waist then found her long legs. His large hand slipped behind a knee to move her leg to one side, giving him access to her inner thighs. He stroked the smooth area still hidden by her silken underwear as he continued to suck at her breasts, bringing them to aching peaks.

"Yes, yes," he murmured in satisfaction as he touched the

hot dampness of her panties. Lisa clasped his hand against her, pleading soundlessly for him to ease that heat. His lips left her breasts, trailing kisses to her stomach. Her hands kneaded his shoulders, urging him on. He found the indentation that was her navel and flicked his tongue over it, nipping her soft stomach as his hands found the waistband of her last garment and eased the flimsy material down over her thighs, as his mouth followed it trail, he quickly discarded the unwanted clothing, Lisa anxiously assisting him in his task.

His hand short out suddenly to seize a pillow from the wreckage of the bed clothing. He smoothly slid an arm under her and raised her hips up, levering the pillow beneath her to give himself better access to her secret desire. She felt herself trembling on the brink of something new, something wonderful. She held onto his shoulders for dear life, as if she would fly from the bed, torn asunder by the sensations rushing through her body. Jake worshiped her mouth slowly and passionately, tasting her tongue, encouraging it to come into his mouth, as he parted her legs and stroked her, bringing her to a point of frenzy.

"Now, oh, please now," she wailed. "I need you. Jake!"

"Soon," he whispered. "Soon."

He drifted down her warm and now slippery body once more, teasing each breast as she arched against him. She felt his hardness against her thigh and twisted sensuously, luring him to her, but he resisted her wiles. He urged her legs farther apart and kissed the tender flesh he found there, listening with pleasure to her gasping little cries. His tongue found the core of her desire and she screamed. She began to pound her fists above his shoulders and thrust herself rhythmically toward him, her eyes closed, her head thrown back.

He raised his head and quickly moved over her, still caressing her. She grasped his haunches, urging him to her, but still he waited, tenderly touching and stroking her.

"Look at me, love," he commanded her softly.

Green eyes, almost black in their passion, gazed at gray eyes. She understood through the haze that controlled her mind that he would never force her. It was still her decision.

She reached for him and seized him firmly. He gasped and struggled for control, but she showed him no mercy as she led him to her. Her hands slipped away to slide up his thighs and then to the hard muscles of his back as he slowly entered her. She held him fast, her nails digging into his hard flesh, spurring him on. He met her silent plea with a sudden thrust, filling her completely.

Jake paused for a moment, allowing her to stretch to accommodate him, searching for the self-restraint he needed.

"My God, Lisa," he groaned, "You're so tight. I don't know if I can . . . " He began to move experimentally, slowly, until he found her moving with him. She urged him on with her hands, making little whimpering cries. He quickened his pace to match her. Her cries became screams and they rocked together, his cries matching hers.

Lisa was no long Lisa. She became a wild creature, arching and bucking wildly, pummeling him, the ache inside her growing, overcoming her. She was reaching, reaching, reaching, climbing with Jake to an unknown place and time. She found what she had been seeking and her world exploded around her and she screamed in ecstasy as he joined her in that glorious release.

Chapter Nine

Jake sprawled beside Lisa, his head propped on an arm, watching her anxiously as her eyes flickered open.

"Are you all right?" he asked huskily. "I thought for a moment there you had fainted." He brushed a wisp of hair from her face.

"I think I might have," she said, her surprise written on her face. Her eyes were enormous as she realized what had taken place. "Is it always like that?"

His hand stilled. He stared at her in astonishment. "Don't you know?"

She turned her head away to avoid his searching gaze.

"Lisa," he growled, forcing her to face him, "you said you weren't a virgin. That was true, wasn't it?"

"Yes," she admitted miserably.

"How much experience have you had?" he demanded. He was angry at himself for forcing this out of her, especially after what they had shared, but he had to know. When she refused to answer, he towered over her, compelling her to look at him. She closed her eyes. He took her shoulders. "Tell me! Just how old were you?"

"Sixteen."

"Oh, my God!" Jake threw himself backward onto the bed, his eyes searching the ceiling, cursing himself for not realizing how innocent she was, how vulnerable. "That's why you were so tense," he said, "why you were so afraid that night in your cabin." He rolled to his side and punched the mattress with a hard fist, swearing until he caught sight of her. She was sitting, her arms wrapped around her body, her eyes. She looked guilty, yet confused.

"You're angry," she whispered. "Because I wasn't a virgin? Or was it because I'm not very experienced? Please Jake, tell me. What did I do?"

Jake struggled to control his thoughts. "Let me get this straight. You haven't been with a man since you were sixteen?"

She nodded and hid her face against her knees.

"My God, Lisa, that's almost fifteen years. I can't believe that in all that time . . ." Then he noticed her quivering body. Lord, what was he saying to her? "Oh, baby, don't cry," he crooned, " I didn't mean that. But can't you see that it's difficult for me to understand how a woman as beautiful as you hasn't had more . . ." A horrible suspicion flew into his mind. He rolled to sit before her and grasped her shoulders. Her head flew up and he examined the tear-drenched eyes.

"Were you raped, Lisa? Is that it?" he demanded fiercely.

He strained to hear her almost inaudible whisper. "I don't think so."

"You . . . what is that supposed to mean?"

She was trying valiantly to control herself. "I . . . never thought about it that way. I mean, we were . . . both so young . . . I didn't know what . . . I didn't want to . . ." She hiccuped.

"How old was he?" He shook her gently when she didn't answer, his self-condemnation driving him on.

"S . . . seventeen. Almost eighteen."

"Just kids." Jake released her and flung himself back against the pillows, rubbing shaking hands over his eyes. In his mind's eye, he saw Lisa as she had been, a few years older than Jodi, a vulnerable little girl playing grownup games and being hurt. It must have been a bad experience if she had never wanted a man since. He cursed himself angrily. He had pushed her relentlessly, never taking this possibility into consideration. No wonder she had been so afraid. Sexually, Lisa was still a child, frozen by a single act to the emotional state of a sixteen-year-old.

"Jake? Jake!" She was openly sobbing now, a miserable ball, her skin ivory against the wrinkled spread. "Jake, I'm sorry. I know I'm naïve. But . . . I could learn. Maybe . . . you could teach me. Don't be angry, please."

"Angry?" he asked in astonishment, finally realizing why she was so distraught. "Oh, Lisa, no! Never! I wasn't angry at you, I'm furious with myself, at my own stupidity!" He jumped to his feet, making her start at his quick departure, and began to pull at the bedclothes beneath her. He bustled about like a naked male nurse, lifting her from one side of the bed to the other as he straightened the spread, blanket and sheet and covered her.

When he was satisfied, he crawled in beside her to gather her into his arms, rocking and comforting her as she sobbed out fifteen years of grief. He whispered little love words to her, rubbed her back, stroked her head, knowing that she must cry it out. All he could do was be there for her.

He lifted her onto his lap and cradled her slender form against him. "It's not your fault, honey, it's mine," he told her gently as her keening began to diminish. "You were wonderful, perfect. You are all woman, my love, and nothing can change that. I shouldn't have yelled at you, especially when you were so vulnerable." He kissed the top of her head tenderly. "Lisa, I was blaming myself for not taking better care of your needs. I wish I'd known all this before we started making love. I would have been more considerate. I would have been gentler with you."

"You mean it would have been better?" She gaped at him in astonishment through her tears.

Laughter rumbled out of his throat. "You're right. It was great, wasn't it?"

She smiled wanly, rubbing the tears away with a fist. "Wonderful. But was it all right for you?" she asked timidly.

"Honey, if it had been any better, it would have killed me."

She caught her breath and was still against his chest. Jake glanced down and saw the fear in her face. "What is it, honey?"

"Could that happen?"

"Lisa! Of course not!"

She buried her head in the mat of hair on his chest. He felt her lips on his skin as she whispered, "I don't want anything to happen to you, Jake. I would never forgive myself if . . ."

"Love, I have the heart of a twenty-year-old. My doctor told me so only three months ago. Here, feel it beating." He held her hand to his chest.

"I love you, Jake," she murmured. "I love you so much. I couldn't bear to lose you." She kissed his cheek.

"Hey," he teased, tiling her chin up. "Listen, you couldn't get rid of me, haven't you noticed that? His hand stilled. "Do you think I'm too old for you, is that it?"

Lisa levered herself up on his chest and glared down at him indignantly. "Do you think I'm too young for you?"

"Of course not."

"Then shut up." She snuggled against him again, murmuring, "Jake, there is one more thing."

"What's that, love?

She ran a finger down his chest, following the path of hair as it narrowed to a trail that led to his stomach. "When . . . when can we do it again?"

In Lisa's dream, she was chasing Jake who was running off with a picnic basket. Lisa was close behind, but never quite catching up. As the dream faded, she realized she was ravenous, somehow having missed her dinner the night before. Jake had several times discussed the possibility of ordering out for pizza, but for some reason, their hunger had been channeled to other things. Her stomach growled. She decided she would have to get up and see about breakfast soon.

She closed her eyes against the strong morning light and stretched, opening her mouth wide to yawn. She heard a chuckle nearby and opened one eye to inspect the frisky squirrel on the headboard. She frowned and thought, wooden squirrels can't laugh, can they? She opened both eyes and met Jake's, sparkling with amusement.

He had donned a light blue sweatshirt and a pair of white jeans that hugged his thighs. Her imagination ran wild as she inspected him. Was he wearing any underwear under those tight pants? Her gaze flicked down his legs to his bare feet and he wiggled his toes. Her eyes flew up to catch his very satisfied smirk. She blushed as she remembered their behavior of the night before.

The mattress sagged as he perched his big frame on the bed. "It's about time you got up," he chided her." I've already showered and dressed and unpacked several more boxes while you were snoring."

"I don't snore!"

"Yes, you do. It's charming. Hurry, woman! I'm starving and there isn't a thing to eat in this house. I need to be fed! And don't forget, we have to pick Jodi up in Iron Mountain at ten-thirty."

Lisa sat up hastily, forgetting her natural state until she noticed that Jake's fascinated eyes were taking in her ample breasts. She raised the sheet demurely and draped it over herself.

"What time is it?" she asked.

"Eight, which gives you time for a quick shower, if you hurry, and if I don't join you. Then we'll run you home to change and go out to eat in Iron Mountain."

"Burger King or McDonalds's?" she asked, with pretended weariness.

"The woman thinks I have no class," Jake groaned. "Come on! I'm a starving man!" He bounced the mattress up and down to emphasize the desperation.

She laughed at him until the realization of her situation dawned on her. "Jake! What will everybody think when we leave here this morning? Oh, no! My car has been in your driveway all night! What if Neil and Beth saw it? Jake, what about the youth group? If one of the kids . . . "

Jake grinned at her. "Lisa, we have been seen at every social event in this town in the last two weeks. You know everyone's been taking bets on when I'd talk you into my bed. If it hadn't happened last night, they would have figured we had already done it somewhere else. If you want to keep a secret . . ."

" . . . you'd better reconsider living in Norway," she finished ruefully.

In one smooth motion, Jake whipped the sheet from her hands, grasped her by the waist and swung her from the bed. Lisa blushed anew when he lowered her to her feet and stepped back to feast his eyes on her rosy body. He winced as he observed the faint purple marks on her breasts.

"Did I do that?" he asked, gently touching them.

"Anybody else in that bed last night?" she answered.

Lisa was surprised at the emotion in Jake's voice. "There better not have been. And there better not be in the future. Got that?" He kissed her soundly, crushing her breasts against his shirt. She clung to him, not wanting to let him go, even for breakfast, hungry as she was.

It was Jake who drew away, sighing. "Jodi will be left at the bus depot if we don't get moving." He caressed her plump breasts and grinned. "You left a few marks yourself, you know."

"I didn't!"

"You did."

"Where?"

Jake rubbed his buttocks in mock pain.

"I don't believe you," she challenged. "Prove it. Show me!"

"Honey," he laughed, turning her around and sending her to the bathroom with a pat on her tender behind, "if I showed you, you wouldn't get any breakfast and neither would I. I'm sure you'll get a chance to examine the wound before the scars heal."

"Count on it."

*****

109

Lisa took a long, warm shower, soaping and soothing parts of her anatomy sore from the unfamiliar exercise of the night before. Beats aerobics, she chuckled, trying to calculate the calories she had burned off.

As the streaming water swept over her, she touched herself delicately, remembering the reverence Jake had shown in his worship of her body. She cupped her breasts, loving them because they had given him such pleasure. She felt the ache between her thighs growing once more. She reveled in her femininity. She would welcome Jake again and again. She would delight in his body and he would delight in hers. It was all as it should be.

I told him I love him, she thought, in awe of this great mystery. It was true.

"I love Jake Gannett and he loves me," she sang making up her own melody, not caring if the sound traveled to the kitchen where he waited for her. " I love Jake and he is planning a future for us." She raised her arms, the water cascaded over her, and she sang her lilting song.

When Lisa finally returned to the bedroom, wrapped in a large fluffy white towel, to look for her clothes, the bed was newly made and empty boxes gave evidence that Jake was still unpacking. As Lisa dressed, she inspected the room, admiring what they had done with it. From his old apartment, Jake had brought a nice selection of pastoral prints that were perfect for the room. In a friend's antique shop, Lisa had unearthed an old armoire that well matched the carved bed and made up for the lack of closet space, always a problem in older homes. She ran a fond hand over the dresser they found in another country store.

Jake had laid out his brushes and toiletries on the bureau that morning, she noticed. She could not resist a little curious snooping. Why, for instance, did Jake have such a wonderful scent. It was unlike any other. What cologne did he use? She sampled several bottles. Why was his hair so thick and springy? Lisa placed her hand on his comb, wondering if she dared to use it on her own snarls. Her hand froze. Behind a wooden jewelry box was a school picture of a young girl with the same white-blond hair as her own, wearing an outrageous purple blouse with far too many plastic necklaces. It was the usual yearly photograph, but the face paralyzed Lisa. Sparkling brown eyes shown in a little round face. The pug nose was liberally sprinkled with freckles. The wide mouth was spread even further by a lopsided grin.

*****

Jake glanced at his watch and realized they were going to be late unless he hurried Lisa along. She would tease him unmercifully if they had to use the drive-through for their breakfast. Where was she? He knew that she was unfailingly prompt. He loped up the steps, sure she would come out of the bedroom to meet him. But she never noticed his noisy entrance, engrossed as she was in Jodi's photo. She held it gingerly, her expression pensive, but unreadable.

She started when Jake spoke behind her. "Cute kid, isn't she," he said with paternal pride.

"Precious," she said absently. "How old did you say Jodi is?"

"Twelve there. She's thirteen now."

"Oh," she said huskily. "That's all right, then." There was a note of relief in her voice, yet there was regret, too, to his bewilderment.

"All right?"

She turned then and saw his puzzlement. She cried out quickly, "Listen, buster, how about that breakfast you promised me?" She tripped down the staircase, teasing him about his fast-food cuisine and soon had him laughing as they dashed out of the house.

But in a corner of his mind, Jake still wondered about her wistful expression as she looked at the photograph of his daughter.

Chapter Ten

Jake had warned her about his daughter's moodiness, so Lisa was relieved to see that Jodi was in high spirits as she bounced off the bus, her face shaded by a big, silly straw hat sporting a bright pink poppy. It clashed wildly with her oversized sweatshirt imprinted with large pieces of tropical fruit. The shirt almost covered her baggy jeans, which were crookedly cut off below the knees. Lisa hid her smile as Jake grimaced at the black high top shoes that completed the ensemble.

"Is that the latest fashion?" he grumbled and shoved away from the white car to greet his daughter.

The girl rushed to exuberantly hug her father. "Daddy," she squealed, "camp was wonderful. I want to go again next year, can I? There were some girls there from Norway. They knew all about the house you bought!" She chattered on about the fun she had, about all she had learned about her new home, about the friends she had made. She was already excited about the summer and the school year ahead of her. Jake could not get in a word. Lisa grinned as she wondered how he would ever introduce her to his daughter. The problem was solved easily, for Jodi stopped in mid-sentence when she spotted Lisa leaning against of the Corvette.

Lisa's hands were ice-cold with tension. She had nervously debated with herself about what to wear for this most important meeting, vacillating between matronly formal and casually youthful. She finally compromised and wore a blue striped cotton shirt, topped by a pale yellow shaker sweater vest, and a cream colored skirt. That settled, she worried about her hair. No matter how much Jake tried to reassure her, she fussed with it until she ran out of time and had to quickly braid it.

Jake meant so much to Lisa. She knew he loved her, but he also loved his daughter. What if Jodi didn't like her? It was so important that they become friends. She clutched the empty McDonalds's bag tighter: because of their rush, they had gotten take-outs at the drive-through after all.

Jodi pulled off her floppy hat and Lisa caught her breath.

113

Now she understood how Jake could have mistaken her for Jodi that first day. Jodi's hair was the same shade and they were almost equal in height. Viewed from behind, they would be nearly identical.

But it was the face that startled Lisa. She knew it so well, that youthful face out of her own past. Even the photo had not prepared her for the reality of this girl. Only the knowledge that Jodi was just thirteen allowed Lisa to straighten up and calmly greet her.

"Jodi, this is Lisa Fratelli. She sold us our house and has been helping me get it ready for you." Jake had agreed with Lisa that Jodi would need a little time to get used to the idea of her father dating again, let alone their true relationship.

Jodi immediately pouted, sticking out her lower lip angrily. Lisa blinked, remembering another sulky visage. It was all so familiar, yet it couldn't be! She had never met this child before, she reminded herself.

"I don't see why you had to go and buy a house without letting me see it first," Jodi complained to her father, shifting her mood dramatically. "If I have to live some place, I should have some say in it."

"Honey," Jake answered patiently, "you know very well that when you left, you told me to buy anything, that you didn't care what I did."

"Well . . . I was mad at you. You shipped me off to camp without giving me any say in that either!" The girl became more and more belligerent as she expounded her grievances.

Jake shrugged helplessly, looking to Lisa for understanding. She, in turn, recognized all the symptoms of an impending tantrum and decided to head it off.

"What camp did you go to?" she quickly interjected.

"Lake Hope," Jodi answered sullenly. She plopped the oversized hat back on her head as if to cut Lisa out of her sight.

"Oh, I always went there when I was a teen," Lisa exclaimed in delights. "Do they still have horses?"

"Yeah?"

"And tennis courts? And canoes?"

Jodi nodded her head slightly while peering at her father from under her hat, as if to say, Who is this person?

"Did you get that hat at the camp store?" Lisa chattered on, acting like a teenager herself. At least Jake was enjoying the show, his lips spreading into a wide grin. "I had a hat like that myself once," she added.

Jodi's eyes shot to the brim of the hat then returned to pin themselves suspiciously on Lisa's face. "Are you making this up?" she demanded.

"Of course not," Lisa retorted indignantly. "Lots of Norway girls end up at the camp. Let me see, I think several from our church were there this month. Kris, Marie, Stacy? Did you met them? They're always together."

"You know them, too?" Jodi considered Lisa skeptically.

"Oh, look, there's Stacy Larson over there." Lisa waved at a skinny brunette dressed even more outrageously than Jodi. Spotting Lisa, the girl left her family and rushed over.

Stacy was like a fountain, constantly bubbling over. "Hi, Lisa! Jodi didn't tell me she knew you! Wow, is this your dad, Jodi! Awesome! Oh, Lisa, how'd the rafting go? Did I miss much?"

"It was terrific!" Lisa quickly interposed, knowing from experience that she had to move swiftly to stop Stacy's flow. "Perfect weather, lots of kids and we all got absolutely soaked. Everyone had a great time. But not to worry, Stace, we're going again next month."

"Next month?" Jake asked in consternation.

Lisa grinned. "Yes. And guess what! We're still short one chaperon. Want the job?"

"No way!" Jodi scoffed. "You could never get Daddy on one of those things, he only swims in pools. But don't ask why, 'cause he refuses to tell."

Jake was signaling desperately to Lisa behind Jodi's back. Lisa did her best. Her mouth quirked up and she covered it with her hand. She broke out in giggles and she clapped her hand over her mouth. But then she saw Jodi's expression, and when Jake began to chuckle, she was lost. They were both laughing when Stacy joined in, with Jodi coming in at the last, though she didn't know what the joke was.

The stove was scheduled to arrive the following day; until then, there would be no cooking at the new house. Jake stopped at his favorite fried chicken restaurant and ordered several helpings of every item on the menu, over Lisa's objections.

"Jake, you don't have a refrigerator either!"

But when the three of them sprawled on a blanket having

their picnic in the back yard of the new house, Lisa saw Jodi in action, she admitted Jake had been wise. His daughter, too, had a "good" mouth.

Jake and Lisa had conducted a whirlwind tour of the house. To Jake's relief, Jodi adored her new home. In fact, "adore" was apparently the latest word in her new set. To an attentive Lisa, Jodi was explaining that she had always lived in an apartment and that she would just adore having so many rooms and a big back yard. She just adored her new bedroom and knew that with the right paint and furniture – something in purple and lavender maybe – it would look totally wild. The girls from Norway would just adore it. She had heard all about the junior high school, too.

"It's a good school," Lisa got in quickly.

"Oh, yeah," Jodi said enthusiastically, "they said they all loved school, especially the math teacher. Are we really going rafting on the river with Daddy? I would adore that."

Jake was shaking his head at the non-stop monologue, wondering how Lisa could keep track of it all, when he caught sight of Gordie Ruggeri peering at them over the back fence, fascinated by the blond girl talking to Lisa. The two did make a fetching picture. Jake motioned to Gordie. With no further urging, the boy grabbed the fence and bounded over. Within a few minutes, he managed to polish off the balance of the chicken dinner and become the new love of Jodi's life. She took him in tow and they ran back into the house for a further series of explorations.

Jake grunted and commented wryly. "There's one little thing you forgot to mention about this house."

"What's that?"

"That Gordie Ruggeri would be living behind us."

"Will he be a problem, do you think?" Lisa asked worriedly. "I thought he was over that puppy love thing. Don't you like him?"

"Oh, I like him all right," Jake sighed. "But I expect that Jodi will 'just adore' him."

Lisa stifled a laugh. "Gordie is one of the nicest boys in Norway. You should count yourself lucky if Jodi is choosing him as a friend."

"Easy for you to say. You're not the parent of a teenage girl."

Lisa gasped, as if she were short of breath. Jake looked at her sharply.

116

She rose to her knees and rapidly gathered up the cardboard boxes, cups and utensils, spilling soda with shaking hands.

"Lisa, look at me."

"You're right, of course." She whisked imaginary crumbs from the blanket, her lashes cast down.

"What is it, Lisa?" Jake demanded. "What did I say?"

She shook her head, but he persisted.

"Lisa, darling, you have to tell me. How can we go on with this relationship if you aren't open with me?"

"Go on?" she asked in horror.

Fool, he said to himself. You thought that if you took her to bed everything would be solved. There are still things you have to learn about this woman, problems we have to iron out. Threatening her is no solution.

He brought her to his side and settled her close to him. "That was a stupid thing to say, honey. Of course our relationship will go on. Forever, I hope. But I wish I could share whatever it is that's troubling you. Can't you tell me?"

Lisa sniffed, crinkling her nose, and searched for the right words. "It's just . . . that . . . I would give anything to have a daughter. I think I've missed that over the years."

Jake carefully wiped a solitary tear away with his thumb as the corners of his mouth curled up. Some solutions were simple. Lord, she was adorable, even with a runny nose.

"We'll have to see what we can do about that, won't we?" he murmured, helping her to blow her nose with his handkerchief. His resolve crystallized. Yes, he certainly would do something about giving Lisa a daughter.

"I don't know why I'm so weepy lately," Lisa apologized with a half-laugh, fingering the neckband of his sweatshirt. "I'm never like this, Jake, believe me."

"You know, I don't mind at all," he smiled. "Cheering you up is so enjoyable." He lowered his lips to hers in a comforting kiss. Lisa raised her trembling fingers to his face, softly caressing his whisker-rough skin. She parted her lips in invitation.

Jake groaned and wrapped his arms around her waist to pull her closer. As her hands slipped to his neck, they heard and outraged cry behind them. The two turned in unison to see Jodi, her long braid flying behind her, run up the back steps, leaving Gordie on the lawn, embarrassed and tongue-tied.

"Oh, damn," Jake rasped. "Now what?"

"Oh, Jake, go after her," Lisa cried in her concern, but Jake was already on his feet, almost charging into the bemused Gordie, who stood on one foot then another, hands in the pockets of his jeans. Jake hesitated, wondering what to say to him.

The boy, his face red, tried his best to be casual. "Uh, I think maybe it's time for me to go home," he muttered, looking across the lawn at Lisa.

Lisa's face was as red a Gordie's as it dawned on her that he had seen her car that morning, and had drawn his own conclusions about that kiss. Jake cursed himself, as she lowered her flaming face to her knees. He realized the position he had placed her in, but his first responsibility was to Jodi right now.

He answered Gordie as calmly as he could. "That probably would be a good idea, Gordie. I'm sure we'll have this all sorted out soon."

At least I hope we do, he thought, as he watched the boy once again vault over the fence.

Jake found his daughter sitting on the steps of the curved staircase, sobbing furiously. He sat beside her on the step and attempted a paternal hug of comfort, but she jerked away, hiding her head against the banister and wailing even louder.

Jake withdrew his arms and lounged back against the wall, watching and waiting for the squall to die down. He knew from experience that it was better to say nothing when Jodi was in this state. He certainly was getting to be an expert on female tears!

He wondered what Lisa was feeling right now. Embarrassment, certainly. Regret? He hoped not. He hated to leave her alone right now, their relationship seemed so fragile, so breakable. He could sense the enormous fear that threatened to overwhelm her. At the height of their lovemaking, she clung to him, almost as if she thought he might disappear. If only he could get to the heart of her anxiety, if only he could find some way to reassure her.

At the moment though, Jodi must be his first concern. He finally judged the time right to try again. The sobs were subsiding.

"About what you saw, Jodi. I'm sorry . . ."

"You should be!" she snuffled. "Mother only died a year ago! You should be ashamed of yourself!" She gave him a scathing look through red-rimmed eyes. "How could you do this to me? And to her!"

118

"You don't understand, Jodi," Jake said decisively. "I'm not at all sorry I kissed, Lisa. I enjoy kissing her and I intend to kiss her again and again and you had better get used to it."

Jodi's tears dried up and her mouth hung open. She was staggered by this revelation.

Jake's voice softened. "Honey, listen to me. I am sorry that you found out about it that way. I knew this would upset you at first. I planned on telling you about Lisa later, when she had gone home. I wanted you to have time to get used to the idea."

"No!" Jodi shouted, jumping up and taking one step down.

"Yes!" he said sternly, rising with her and grasping her forearms to firmly plop her down again on the steps. He towered over her, intimidating her with his height until he was sure she was going to stay put. She stared at him murderously, but she did not move.

Jake lifted a palm in a helpless gesture. Frightening her was no solution. He settled himself on the step again, letting his legs drape themselves carelessly down the stairs to establish a casual air. He began again.

"Jodi, you know that I loved your mother and I love you. But it has been a year, a long and lonely year, since your mother died. Now I've found a woman to fill the void she left. Couldn't you try to be happy for me?" He smiled tentatively, encouraging her to smile back. His attempt was unsuccessful; she continued to scowl. He tried again. "I'm forty years old, baby, and you're growing up so fast. Do you realize that you will be going away to college in only four years? Then where will I be? And after that, some worthless young man will steal you away. I bet you won't give me a second thought when he comes along. I'll need someone of my own, honey."

"I don't care," Jodi sniffed stubbornly. "It isn't right."

Jake studied her obstinate little face. She had been through so much in the last year, the loss of her mother, the realization that she was adopted, her experiences in the drug scene. For a brief moment, he thought about sending Lisa home and waiting a week or two before trying to broach the subject with Jodi again.

Then he thought of Lisa, waiting for him outside, and his resolve returned.

"I intend to marry Lisa," he said firmly. Jodi gasped in outrage, but he charged ahead. "I am going to marry that woman, Jodi, if she will have me, so you better get used to the idea." He patted her hand, pleading with her to understand. "Don't you see, honey, I'm asking your blessing. Isn't that funny? In just a few years from now, you will be asking the same of me, I expect."

Jake gave Jodi a moment to think about what he had said. She wrapped her arms around her legs and rested her chin on her knees, staring into space as her thoughts churned through her head. At that moment, in some indefinable way, she reminded him of Lisa, of her intense concentration when she was wrestling with a problem.

"What if I don't like it?" she asked Jake hesitantly.

"That would make me very unhappy. But whatever you say or feel, I am going to marry Lisa," he said resolutely. "That doesn't mean I love you any less. It only means that I have found a woman I care for, a woman to care for me. Lisa will make an excellent wife and mother for us, Jodi. She'll be as important for you as she is for me. There are so many things I can't help you with as you grow up. You need a woman around the house. So do I."

With cunning, he added the clincher. "Jodi, she can cook."

The girl frowned at him. "I would cook for you if I knew how, Daddy. I could have learned if Mother had shown me, but she would never let me use the kitchen. She said I would make a mess."

"Honey, I know that. She wouldn't let me near it, either." Jake hugged her in relief, knowing the worst was over. He kissed her forehead. "Why don't you ask Lisa to teach you a few things. She loves kids, you know. Gordie will tell you how much fun she is. She likes you already, she told me so. All I ask is that you give her a chance."

In an unconscious imitation of Jake's daughter, Lisa waited on the blanket, rocking back and forth nervously, her arms wrapped around her bare legs, her head resting on her knees. A blue jay chattered saucily at her, urging her to leave so he could examine the picnic leavings, but she never heard him.

She had gathered and stowed all the paper and miscellaneous carry-out paraphernalia and put them in the largest of the boxes. Lisa wondered if she should simply go home. Then she remembered that Jake had brought her there in his Corvette. She silently cursed the lack of a cab service in this small town.

She could ask Gordie's older sister to give her a ride home

– but that would mean explaining why Jake couldn't do it, and Gretchen was a terrible gossip. To ask Beth's help was unthinkable.

She could walk home! Lisa had her own private trail through the hills that she had hiked hundreds of times. She hastily began to rise, but slipped sideways, landing with a resounding thump on her backside. She examined her high-heeled, open-toed sandals, wiggling her toes. No, she would never manage the rocky path.

What was Jake telling Jodi? It was taking him long enough. Her heart wrenched as she pondered the coincidence of the girl's appearance. She looked so much like . . . was it possible? No! Jodi was only thirteen. Besides, there had to be a million kids in the world with blond hair, freckles and crooked grins. It was inevitable that one would come into her life sooner or later, just as it was foreseeable that her heart would go out to such a child.

Lisa sighed and rested her chin on her arms again. She knew it was wishful thinking on her part to expect Jodi to respond to her immediately. They had had a poor beginning. It would be wonderful, though, to be a mother to Jodi, especially if she could have Jake as a husband. She discovered to her surprise that it was possible to envy a dead woman. She was jealous of Christine because she had eighteen years with Jake. Lisa felt she would never be satisfied until she had him for at least an equal length of time.

Lisa looked up at the old house wistfully. It seemed like home to her already, yet until things were decided between the three of them, she could not share the house or the old carved bed with Jake. Jodi would never accept a physical relationship between Lisa and Jake, at least not in her own home. What if Gordie told the girl that the Bronco had been in the driveway the night before? Please, please, Lisa whispered soundlessly, don't let that happen.

Her eyes traveled unerringly to the bedroom windows on the second floor. Jake had said they had a future together, hadn't he? Didn't that mean marriage? Perhaps she would not have long to wait. How marvelous it would be, living in this house with teenagers running in and out, and maybe a baby or two.

But that was impossible. Even if Jake was really serious about wanting her, they would never be able to have children of their own. But couldn't they adopt? It had happened before, in both of their lives. An errant tear slipped down her cheek as she remembered. Darn, she sniffled, why am I so weepy? It was as if the floodgates, long sealed shut, had been opened. Raw emotions had been opened for inspection. She had laughed and cried and loved more these past few days than she ever had in her entire life. Everything centered around one man, the man she wanted.

She closed her eyes against the sun as it came from behind the clouds and set her mind to forget her dreams. She should know better. Early in her life, she had learned the pain of trying to reach for the impossible. Loving led to hurt, as she was well aware. But just the same, visions of a future with the two people in that house kept floating through her head.

Her reverie was interrupted by the slam of the screen door. Jake was striding toward her, smiling confidently. Lisa's questions were written all over her face.

"It's going to be fine," he reassured her.

"Then she doesn't mind about me?"

"I wouldn't go so far as to say that," he admitted. "But she is willing to get to know you better. At least she'll give you a chance. Jodi is always fair, so I think everything will work out."

"Do you really think so?" she said tiredly.

"Of course. It has to. Did you think I would ever let you go? She's going to love you in time, Lisa . . . especially after she tastes your spaghetti sauce."

"Now it all comes out," she cried indignantly. "He doesn't love me for my mind."

"Oh, you do have a few other redeeming qualities besides your ability to cook," he assured her, hugging her to him and nuzzling her neck playfully.

"Jake, stop it! She might see us!"

"She has to get used to it. Besides, she's going to take a nap now. She didn't have a good night's sleep like we did."

"Jake!" She knew without his amused grin she was blushing again.

"She'll probably sleep for an hour or two. The girls in her cabin had an all-night gab session last night. Besides, she has to rest up for tonight."

"Tonight?"

"I'm taking my two girls out to eat at the best restaurant in Iron Mountain."

"Not Kentucky Fried again," she groaned.

Jake punched her lightly on the arm. "I can see I have to prove that I can be sophisticated," he grinned. "Right now, I better run you home. "You'll want to change clothes and I thought I might as well wait for you. Who knows, you might need help with your shower or something."

He kissed her briskly and hoisted her to her feet, adding softly in her ear, "I love my daughter dearly, and it's wonderful to have her home, but I have to admit it's going to put a serious dent in my social life."

Lisa dismissed his problems airily. "I'm sure a man with your background can overcome all obstacles."

"My background?"

She ticked off his attributes on her fingers. "Let me see, you are an intrepid adventurer, a gourmet, a music and art critic, a stage-door johnny and a kidnapper." Jake burst out laughing, but she continued coolly, "Experienced attorney, a super father, but best of all," and she lowered her voice to a husky whisper, "best of all, the greatest lover in the world."

"Then it's best we hurry, love," he said agreeably, as he led her around the house to his car. "After all, it's practice that makes me perfect."

That evening, Lisa found herself once again in Grandma's Old Fashioned Ice Cream Emporium, washing down her cheeseburger and fries with a chocolate shake, as she inspected her reflection in the mirrored wall opposite the booth Jodi had selected.

Lisa thought she might be a little over-dressed for this establishment. She was resplendent in a stylish pale turquoise silk suit with a matching white blouse, graced with a rich ecru collar. Strappy high-heeled sandals showed her tanned legs to their best advantage. She had piled her hair on her head in a rather elaborate French twist and added tiny pearl earrings that matched the buttons on the sleeves of her suit. Her makeup was carefully applied, from the soft pink lipstick to the light turquoise eye shadow that emphasized the emerald eyes that were dancing with mischief.

"You know," she remarked to Jake in a conspiratorial whisper. "I'd never been to Iron Mountain's 'finest restaurant' before you introduced me to it. Do you think my clothes are up to the standards here? I could whip out and buy an evening gown or something. Would long gloves be appropriate?"

"Shhhhhhh," he cautioned, casting a wary eye on the somewhat imposing tartan clad waitress who was charging down the aisle with a huge tray. "I did say I was sorry. I forgot that tonight was Jodi's choice. Look," he suggested apologetically, "I'll make it up to you. How about we go ethnic tomorrow night. I've heard there's a great Mexican restaurant here in Iron Mountain."

"Taco Bell?" she jibed. "Besides, I thought I get to shampoo my hair on Monday nights."

"Ah," he chuckled, "I helped you do that this afternoon."

"Shhhhh!" Lisa reddened as Jodi meandered back from the juke box, where she had been comparing rock tunes in Iron Mountain to her favorites in Milwaukee.

Lisa had enjoyed the afternoon's pleasures, but she hoped Jodi didn't resent the long time Jake had been gone. His "lift home" stretched to two hours! Perhaps he told his daughter that Lisa lived fifty miles out of town. But how had he explained his wet hair?

It had begun innocently enough with a simple kiss. How had they ended up together in a warm shower, lathering each other with her shower soap, rinsing and starting all over, painting pictures on each other's bodies, giggling and shouting with pleasure? Richard would be on the phone tomorrow morning to find out what all that had been about? What on earth should she tell him?

But if she had the chance, she would do it all over again. She was certain Jake would agree. She wondered wistfully if she could throw out her old loofah. It was immensely more pleasurable to have someone to scrub your back . . . and your front.

Jake caught the dreamy expression in Lisa's eyes and the slight parting of her lips. He knew she was thinking of the shower they shared and the following hour in her brass bed. He remembered her purrs of pleasure, her cries of ecstasy. He was not a quiet lover himself. He hoped the sounds of their passion did not carry out over the lake. He certainly hoped her brother never decided to wander over to their hideaway to see what was going on.

Jake sometimes wondered about that brother of hers. Why didn't he have the usual Norway curiosity? Jake was getting pretty curious himself. When would Richard Fratelli make an appearance?

His eyes met Lisa's and suddenly he saw her as she had been that afternoon, damp from the shower, her eyes shining, her mouth swollen from his passionate kisses, her arms held out to him as she waited for him to join her on the bed.

Damn! he swore to himself and moved uncomfortably. He silently blessed the owners of Grandma's Old Fashioned Ice Cream Emporium for having the forethought to place long red-checked tablecloths on each table. He slid forward slightly as Lisa raised an eyebrow at him and grinned.

Jodi slouched over to the booth and slid in next to her father, avoiding conversation with the woman opposite her. Lisa thought of Jodi as a young puppy who had room for only one emotion at a time. Her moods had ranged from anger to enthusiasm during the evening. She loved Grandma's and the food they served. She disliked having Lisa with them. She grudgingly admired Lisa's dress, but she became angry when Jake looked at it with appreciation. She was enthusiastic about the music on the jukebox. She was desolated that Gordie hadn't been able to come with them. Occasionally, there was an air of held-in excitement about her that Lisa did not understand. Jodi expected Jake to do something tonight, that much was clear, but Jake was very nonchalant, draping his big body over the booth. Lisa had come to expect the worst when he acted that way. He was up to something.

Lisa could tell Jodi had been taught some good manners, for even when the girl became sullen, she would never say anything rude. Or perhaps it had been the "little talk" Jake had had with her.

Lisa was drawn to Jodi and she didn't think it was just because of her love for Jake. The girl really was an attractive child, bright and lively. If only they could become friends.

All of a sudden, five waitresses converged at their booth, raucously ringing a fireball and bearing an enormous cake, blazing with candles. They performed a noisy rendition of "Happy Birthday" with various degrees of expertise, with Jake joining in with an adequate baritone. Lisa made a mental note to talk to him about joining the church choir in the fall. She turned to the giggling Jodi.

"Your father forgot to tell me it was your birthday today!"

"It isn't," Jake admitted sheepishly. "With all that's been going on the last few weeks, I forgot all about Jodi's birthday. I had to use my cell phone to make some fast arrangements this afternoon while you were getting ready."

Lisa sat very still, clasping and unclasping hands that had

grown very cold, as she watched Jodi make her wish and blow out the candles. Jake produced, seemingly from nowhere, a package which Jodi opened with squeals and giggles, to reveal another outlandish sweatshirt. She hugged her father and jumped up to model it to her reflection in the mirror.

Like a sleepwalker, Lisa admired the present and extended her good wishes, her words sounding as if they came from another room. Finally, she took a sip from her shake, and in what she hoped was a calm voice, asked the all important question. "When was your birthday, Jodi?"

"I was fourteen on the seventh of June."

The chocolate shake slipped out of Lisa's hand and crashed to the floor.

Chapter Eleven

Jake watched Lisa pacing around the kitchen nervously checking the beef stew for the fourth time since he came home, straightening the new dishes in the cupboards, scrubbing at an imaginary spot on the counter. She had been like this for the past two weeks, edgy as a skittish filly whenever they were alone. Something was bothering her and Jake wished he knew what it was. The easy camaraderie of their first two weeks was gone, their teasing skirmishes a thing of the past. She never seemed to know what to say to him.

He sipped his cup of coffee, relaxing against the old kitchen chair he and Lisa planned to refinish some day. At the moment, she was looking in the refrigerator, straightening a row of jars and bottles in the door, then closing it, apparently forgetting what she was looking for. She wiped her hands nervously on the oversized butcher's apron that covered her navy blue tunic top and white slacks. She had come to his home directly from her office and was dressed in business clothes.

"Would you like more coffee?"

"No, hon. It just cooled off enough to drink. Why don't you sit down and talk?"

"N . . . no. I have to keep an eye on dinner." She whisked off to the stew again.

As soon as the stove and refrigerator were delivered, Lisa began to drop by to cook for Jake and Jodi, worrying about the fast-food fare they had survived on for the past few months. Jake's objections had been few and weak, and she soon felt the kitchen was her own. If she hadn't been secure in the knowledge of his love for her, she would have wondered if he cherished her cooking skills more than any other attributes she might have. She was certain that Jodi's slow acceptance was coming along because she regarded Lisa as a housekeeper-cook and therefore of some use. At this point, Lisa was taking anything she could get.

Inside, Lisa mourned the loss of the intimacy she had had

with Jake. Until that fatal Sunday night, she almost concluded that Jake now knew everything he needed to know about what had happened when she was sixteen. If he had asked her, she would have married him, loved and lived with him for the rest of their lives without ever telling him more. Jake was a mature, intelligent man, too secure in his own masculinity to pry into an affair best forgotten. They would have put the past behind them and lived happily ever after, at least that was what would have happened if this were a fairy tale.

When Jake glanced at her, Lisa suppressed a tiny half-sob, hiding her head in the steam rising from the stew pot. She didn't want to be this way. All she wanted was to rush to his arms and cry it all out. Jake was such a good comforter. For the first time since she was a child, she had someone to cuddle her, to give her solace. But along with the cuddling, Jake would expect her to talk it out. Jake was understanding, but he would not put up with unexplained tears forever.

That was the rub, the reason for her indecision. She couldn't tell him. To do so would mean losing him, because if he found out everything, he could never accept her, not the way she longed to be accepted.

But neither was there an alternative to telling him. Lisa could not live a life with Jake with the secret buried inside her. Besides, when he met Richard, he would soon suspect the truth. Already, Richard was making demands.

So here she was, buying time, trading sexual intimacy for the real communion she wanted. She bit her lip and checked the oven.

Jake's stomach grumbled in anticipation. By now, he knew exactly how good a cook Lisa was. The aroma wafting his way from the stew pot was better than any perfume. Why didn't someone bottle the scent of cooking onions? He would follow that smell anywhere! Lisa had even dropped in that morning to set some dough. When she opened the oven door, the fragrance of freshly baked bread filled the kitchen. Jake had never been so content. He stretched and unbuttoned the top three buttons of his light gray shirt, having flung his jacket and tie on a chair the moment he came home. How wonderful to be greeted by a domestic scene like this! If only he could get Lisa to sit down to share a cup of coffee with him and discuss their respective business days. But she was once more stirring the stew she had stirred not thirty seconds before.

"Where's Jodi?" he asked.

"She went over to look at the junior high with Gordie and Stacy. Stacy's dad is the principal, you know. He's going to show Jodi the school." Lisa buried her head in a cupboard of pots and pans, noisily rearranging them.

Jake shook his head thoughtfully. This restlessness began the day Jodi came home. At first, he figured that Lisa was upset by Jodi's initial reaction to their relationship, but he discounted that idea almost immediately. Lisa like having Jodi around. In fact, the only times Lisa seemed to relax were when Jodi joined them in some activity. When the girl was involved, Lisa poured her whole heart into whatever they were doing. She was constantly thinking of things that Jodi might enjoy, be it a trip to a local beach, a hike in the woods, or an outing with the church group. Whether Jodi appreciated it or not, this woman was her greatest supporter in Norway. The week before, Lisa had rounded up all the teenagers she knew for an impromptu picnic at the park, instantly supplying the girl with new friends.

Jodi no longer grew sullen when Lisa arrived, in part because she found Lisa's cooking so useful, but because she discovered that Lisa had been separated from her own parents and seemed to understand her insecurities. Jake overheard his daughter confiding that she thought her real mother must have died and that was why she had been placed in an adoptive family. Jake knew of her fantasy, but had seen no reason to tell her that her natural mother had simply been another teenager in trouble. It seemed best that Jodi thought as she did, that she make no attempt to open old records and old wounds.

"I think my real mother would have kept me if she had lived, don't you think so?" Jodi asked Lisa.

Lisa had only hugged the girl, saying nothing. Jake saw some indecipherable emotion flit across her face, perhaps a sense of shared sadness, that he would never understand. Lisa did not discuss the conversation with him and he did not press her. She would have to find her own way to Jodi's heart.

It was Lisa who decided that Jodi needed new summer clothes and insisted on a shopping expedition. The two females quickly outdistanced and outpaced Jake and left him at one of his favorite take-out restaurants to nurse a cup of coffee. They returned two hours later laden with boxes and bags, full of treasures for his inspection. He satisfied himself that among the gaudier purchases were a handful of demure dresses. The glow of delight on Jodi's face matched the happiness on Lisa's.

When Jake began to wonder later that evening how Jodi had found so many wonderful bargains on the money he allowed her, he discovered that Lisa had paid for at least half of the clothing. When he asked her about it the next day and tried to repay her, she was visibly upset.

"I wanted to do it, Jake! It gives me pleasure to do things for Jodi, can't you see that? She's a wonderful girl. You've done a sensational job raising her. She couldn't have had a better father. She doesn't realize how lucky she is." Her eyes were misty as she protested. "Please don't try to pay me back. I've enjoyed pretending she was mine this past week. She's everything I could have hoped for in a daughter. Let me do this at least."

In the end, Jake let her have her way, but he knew that Jodi still did not completely accept Lisa. Along with all the other roadblocks, he had to contend with his daughter's stubbornness.

"Does Lisa think she can catch a husband by cozying up to his daughter?" she asked him sarcastically one day.

Jake knew differently. There was no way Lisa could fake the affection she showed, but Jodi would have to discover that for herself.

Jake got up to inspect the stew for himself. Where were those kids? He would starve if they didn't come back soon, waste away to nothing. Lisa gave him a little push as she reached for the salt shaker. He saw his chance and grabbed her, planting a haphazard kiss on her chin when she dodged.

"Hmmmm, that feels good," he murmured, rubbing her breasts against his chest. She could not disguise the hardening of her nipples, the way her hips immediately curved forward to entice his maleness.

No matter what her problem was, their lovemaking was still superb whenever they were able to sneak away. Lisa was a most willing student in that art and even thought of things that almost surprised him. He'd come to love her little cabin in the woods and wondered if they could keep it when . . . "

"Jake, the stew will burn!"

He smiled and let her go, sliding his hand into the pocket of his gray slacks to finger the little box he had secreted there. As he poured himself a fresh cup of coffee, he thought about Lisa envying him because he had a child. Perhaps that was what was bothering her now, the fear that their relationship would end and that she would lose the family she wanted so badly. If so, he could easily remedy the problem.

Lisa broke into a smile as Jodi frisked into the kitchen, followed by the ever-faithful Gordie. The two were inseparable. Jodi even followed the boy on his paper route. Two days after her return from camp, she announced that she absolutely, positively must have a mountain bicycle or her demise was imminent. Gordie agreed that at best she would be a social outcast in his set. If that weren't enough, Lisa joined in with her own arguments for the needed transportation. In the end, over-riding Jake's mild and teasing objections, they all went to purchase the required item. Now Jake seldom knew where Jodi and Gordie were, but Lisa assured him that they would be safe in a community where everyone watched out for each other.

"Lisa, that's just a nice way of saying we're nosy," Gordie interrupted.

"Maybe so, but you two keep it in mind that if you do get into any trouble, somebody is sure to call me and I'll call Jake and your parents, too," Lisa threatened. "You both know the rules, now be sure you follow them."

As long as the two stayed in and around Norway, they would be all right, she felt. Besides, neither of them would ever consider missing a meal, an automatic check on their activities. Whenever Jake was tied up in court or at his office for an entire day, Lisa arranged for the two teenagers to stop in at her office for lunch. Whether or not she was in the middle of a business transaction, the two happily dived into her small kitchen to see what was cooking, sometimes bringing a friend or two along to partake of the largesse.

Lisa knew instinctively what appealed to children of all ages so Jodi and Gordie were the objects of envy in their set. Lisa even took time out to give Jodi a few rudimentary cooking lessons and insisted that Gordie could learn a few things, too. One evening, when Lisa was busy with a band rehearsal, the two surprised Jake by having dinner ready when he came home.

In so many ways, these should have been happy summer days for Lisa, with Jake and Jodi as a sort of temporary family, with her friends and neighbors cheering her on. Even her business was flourishing as never before. But it would all end too soon.

*****

Jodi was poking her nose into every pot on the stove, peeking into the oven to inhale the crusty scent of fresh-baking bread, chattering away, asking Lisa how this or that was made. Jake examined Lisa's animated face as she explained the intricacies of what she was doing. What a wonderful mother she would make! She soon had Jodi and Gordie scurrying around, setting the table, slicing the hot bread, and making small salads. A serious silence fell in the room as the four of them set to work on the stew. With only half his attention on the meal, Jake sorted through his repertoire of excuses he could give for accompanying Lisa home. Jodi figured out early on that Lisa had her own transportation and didn't need his help. From that time on, she kept an eye on her father's comings and goings. A few nights before, he had resorted to sneaking out of the house at midnight, returning a few hours later to creep up the steps past Jodi's bedroom.

"I felt like I was nine-years-old again," he complained to Lisa.

"At least you had some clothes on this time."

Jake chewed on the butter-soaked bread and pondered. It was about time to end this charade. He hadn't shared Lisa's bed in three days and his frustration was building. Who was he trying to kid anyway? There wasn't a soul in Norway who didn't know about them, with the possible exception of Jodi and she had her suspicions.

Furthermore, the whole town was in favor of the match. Everyone was waiting for them to take the next step. He wouldn't be surprised if some folks had bought wedding presents at the sidewalk sale days the week before. Old Mr. Torelli had even gone so far as to accost Jake on the street and ask his intentions. Lisa was right, Norway took care of its own.

The only person who showed no interest in the relationship was Lisa's elusive brother.

"Richard doesn't like much company," she explained. "He's a little shy, too. You'll meet him sooner or later."

"I've always thought he would stop in sometime when I'm visiting. After all, we're not always in bed!"

"Jake! Richard . . . knows about you, sort of. Oh, Jake, I don't want to talk about him. You'll understand when you meet him."

Perhaps that was true, but she certainly didn't seem at all anxious for them to meet. For some reason, she was ashamed of him. Jake reviewed all the possible reasons and none seemed to fit, unless he were an escaped ax murderer or something equally strange.

"I know what we should do!" Gordie shouted enthusiastically, and Jake realized that the other three at the table were making plans for the weekend. "We should tour the old iron mine!" the boy continued. "I haven't done that for a long time, not since I was a kid. I bet Jake and Jodi would like it."

"Who wants to see an old iron mine?" Jake pooh-poohed. "Just going down a bunch of damp tunnels."

"I agree with Gordie," Lisa interjected smoothly. "The mine tour is interesting and I'd like you to see what a big pit is like. The Large Swope is four hundred feet down and . . . "

"What's a swope?" Jodi interrupted.

"It's an enormous mined cavern and it's so deep and wide they don't even try to light it up. I want you to get an idea of how big it is, Jodi, so you'll understand why I keep reminding you not to ramble around in the hills. If you ever fell into something like that, no one would ever find you."

"You walk around in the woods," Jodi objected. "How come you can do it?"

"I only walk on trails I know. My brother spent years teaching me where to go, but even so, I'm mighty careful in the spring when the ground is settling. There is a beautiful trail that I sometimes use when I want to walk to work. Some day, we'll hike to my cabin on that path and we'll have a picnic. But don't you dare try it without me!"

Jodi pouted, her lower lip a flag of warning.

"Listen to her, baby," Jake admonished her. "Lisa knows this area and you don't."

"I am not a baby, Daddy. Don't treat me like one," the girl grumbled.

Jake caressed her shining head and wisely retreated, but he worried about his bull-headed and unpredictable daughter.

Lisa tactfully turned the table talk to the practices for aspiring cheerleaders that were going on down at the high school. Jodi's face brightened immediately but Jake grimaced when Lisa offered to show her some of her old cheers after the meal. He had hoped to have Lisa to himself tonight! It looked like another long evening if he didn't take some action.

"Tell you what, I'll do the dishes," he offered. "You two can do cheers until I'm done and then I'm going for a ride with Lisa. We have to go see about joining the golf club," he invented quickly.

As he stacked the dishes later, he thought about Jodi's surprise at his offer. Christine never allowed either of them in the kitchen. Their meals had been served in the formal dining room. Neither knew anything about the preparations or cleanup. As he rolled up his shirtsleeves, he wondered what Jodi thought about all this. She was seeing her father in a new light. Her old secure world had disappeared with her mother's death and now even her father was different. Did the change disturb her? It might be part of the lingering resentment she felt toward Lisa.

Jake could see that however much Jodi tried to dislike Lisa, she was being won over, though he wished that Lisa didn't have to work so hard at it. Couldn't the girl see, as he had from the first, that Lisa had an oversupply of love to give? Why did Jodi keep fighting Lisa? Perhaps it was all those evil stepmother stories he read to her when she was small.

Jake was deep in thought, his hands in the sudsy dishwater, when a blur of feet flashed in front of the large kitchen window, followed rapidly by a second pair. Hands still covered with foam, he quickly pushed his way out the back screen door to the back porch. To his amazement, Lisa was doing cartwheels, one after another, around and around the back yard, Jodi following her lead, as Gordie loudly counted, "Twenty-four, twenty-five, twenty-six . . . "

Jake burst out laughing as Lisa collapsed on the ground and was passed by a freewheeling Jodi, her arms and legs flying.

He sauntered over to the woman who lay flat on her back on the lawn and peered down at her. Her hair was plastered to her head, her breasts were heaving and she was gasping for breath. He sat down cross-legged beside her.

"And what was that all about?"

"She . . . she . . . she didn't . . . think I could . . . do cartwheels."

"Wouldn't one or two have been enough to prove the point?"

"She . . . she bet me she could . . . . do more in a row than I could."

"She was right." Jake considered her prostate form for a moment, his chin on his hand. "What did you bet?"

Lisa rolled onto her stomach with an effort, unmindful of the effect of the grass on her white slacks, and buried her head in her arms. Jake had to lean over to hear her muffled voice.

"I don't think I want to tell you."

"Tell all." He prodded her in the ribs.

She turned her head slightly toward him, so that he could see one green eye and a conciliatory smile. "Well. . . . Jake, I didn't think she would be able to do cartwheels that well."

"Amazing what five years of gymnastic classes can accomplish, isn't it?"

"Why that little sneak!" Lisa raised herself up to glare across the yard to a smirking Jodi and her gleeful accomplice.

"Pay up! Pay up! PAAAAY UP!" Jodi chanted, jumping high in the air as she cheered.

"YEEEAAAAAH, TEAM!" Gordie yelled in response.

"What did you bet?" Jake asked tolerantly.

Lisa groaned. "You don't want to know."

Now he was alarmed. "Lisa . . ."

"I promised her we'd take them to a drive-in movie tonight. She's never been to one, and the one here is a tradition." She winced at his expression. "Oh, Jake, I'm so sorry, I really am. I know you had other plans for this evening."

"I did."

"Jake, I was the cartwheel champion of Norway. I thought it was a sure thing."

"No such thing, honey."

"I'll make it up to you, I promise."

"I'll hold you to that," he said with resignation. "The drive-in it is. We'll have to sit in the back seat, that's all."

"With Jodi and Gordie in the front seat?" she yelped in horror, sitting up quickly. "Jake!"

Jake chuckled and she glared at him. As he helped her to her feet, he dusted off her clothing, spending too much time on certain parts of her anatomy.

"Stop that," she whispered, looking anxiously at the other two members of the planned foursome, but they were too busy dissecting a bicycle to notice. "Sometimes," she said, "it's hard to tell when you're teasing."

"I was perfectly serious," he said with a straight face, as he led the way back to the kitchen, leaving the back yard to the co-conspirators. "By the way, what's playing?"

"What difference does it make if we're going to be in the back seat," she parried.

Jake whipped an arm around her waist as she tried to slip past him and pinned her against the cupboard, a hand on the counter on each side of her. "You know," he said, studying her, "you're about as good at evading my questions as Jodi is. You two are alike in a lot of ways."

Lisa choked, coughing until she turned red. Jake slapped her back until she managed to catch her breath.

"Body snatchers!" she blurted.

"Huh?" he grunted, not following the quick change of subject.

"B . .. body snatchers. I think the movie has something to do with body snatchers." She twisted in his arms to face the sink. She thrust her hands into the cooling dishwater.

"Oh, great! Is this by any chance something that any serious critic would even remotely approve of?" He reached for a towel.

"I think they even did a special show about it," she smiled encouragingly.

"Really?"

"I think it was named Dog of the Year."

Jake laughed and flicked her with the towel.

Jake was such a good sport, Lisa thought, as they watched what surely must have been the worst movie ever made. The evening at the drive-in was not the romantic interlude he had planned, but he happily did the best he could with the situation she had handed him. Even Lisa was amazed at the popcorn, soda and pizza Jodi and Gordie could consume. Jake craftily furnished them with carefully doled out money that ensured the two would spend a great deal of their time at the refreshment stand. The beauty of the strategy was that because of their numerous trips, the teenagers were constantly entering and re-entering the two-door Bronco and it was only logical that Jake and Lisa move into the back seat.

The master strategist reached for his prey as the two teenagers left on their third scavenging expedition. The victim grasped with laughter. "Don't you think they're getting suspicious?"

"If they haven't figured out by now why this is called a passion pit, they're a lot denser than I think they are." His lips found hers in the darkness as he glided his hands up under her tunic to capture her breasts.

"Jake," she reproved. "I haven't hooked my bra from their last snack break."

"Wonderful." His teeth gleamed white in the darkness surrounding them. "Saves time."

Her glazed eyes fixed on the zombies marching across the enormous screen as his thumbs stroked her erect nipples and his teeth nibbled on the sensitive cord of her throat. She swallowed convulsively and tried to hold on to her sanity. "Do you have any idea what this movie is about?" she demanded in a high, shrill squeal.

"Do you think we'll be called on to critique it?" His voice was muffled. Oh God, she thought, my shirt will be stretched all out of shape. He ran his fingers along her leg, seeking the softness of her inner thighs.

"Oooooo . . ." she moaned. "This is torture."

She jumped at the playful nip. "Good. It's what you deserve, woman, gambling away our evening." His mouth closed over her plump breast.

"Revenge? This is revenge?" she squeaked.

With a wicked laugh, he pushed her down against the seat, and kissed her firmly. "It's about time you realized who the master is here, wench."

"Master!" she exclaimed.

"Of course. The male is dominant in this species," he teased, "or at least in drive-ins. Besides, isn't it every woman's fantasy to be dominated by the man she loves?" He lowered his head to her breast once more.

"Yes, yes . . oh, yes," she cooed sweetly. "I just love a big, strong, domineering male." She slipped her hand up his thigh, sliding upward until he gasped.

"Damn it, Lisa!" He moved uncomfortably.

She inched her fingers up to his zipper.

"Lisa, they might be back any minute."

She unzipped his slacks and slipped her hand inside.

He groaned.

"I just love," she repeated, "a big, strong male."

Just before dawn the birds began to chatter noisily, announcing the new day. Jake began to kiss Lisa awake. Out of sheer frustration, he had driven back to her cabin in the middle of the night after he was sure his daughter was asleep. Lisa had been waiting for him in her bedroom, turning down the corner of the blanket to welcome him to her bed and to her body, wanting him as much as he wanted her.

As he watched her sleep, he felt the familiar stirrings, but willed them away. He hoped to be home before Jodi discovered his absence, but first he had some important business to transact.

"Lisa," he whispered into her delicate ear. "Wake up, honey, it's almost morning."

Her eyelids flickered for a moment, then she snuggled back under the blankets, curling into a tight little ball. Jake smiled, thinking that she slept the same way Jodi did. He shook her again, biting gently on her fragile shoulders.

Lisa's lips curved upward slightly. Her dimple made a brief appearance, though she kept her eyes stubbornly shut. Her hand slowly inched across the sheet to find his thigh. Her fingers touched denim and she frowned, opening her eyes to see Jake fully clothed. She was obviously disappointed. Jake could read the question in her eyes: would he consider taking his clothes off again?

He grinned and poured her a cup of freshly brewed coffee as she organized all the pillows into a cushion she could rest against. She draped the sheet around her waist to cover her legs, but her delightfully rumpled hair was the only covering she needed for her breasts. He gloried in the view, as she intended he should, but he carefully forced all lustful thoughts from his mind.

He sipped from his own mug and perched on the end of the bed, which creaked out its objections.

"Honey, I know you realize as well as I do that we can't go on like this," he began.

Lisa's eyes flew up in horror.

He was quick to reassure her. "You know I shouldn't be leaving Jodi at home alone like I did last night. You don't approve of it and neither do I, but Lord, Lisa, I want to be with you." He tenderly touched her lips, still a rosy pink from the passionate kisses of the night before.

"You're right," she said quickly. "We'll have to find some other way. What if you and I arranged to meet here some time during the day?"

"Nooners?" he asked derisively. "No way. I'm not going to sneak around any more, Lisa. I want the world to know that I'm your man. Heck, Jodi's the only person in Norway that doesn't know that already. No," he continued, taking her cup and giving her the tiny box, "the only solution is this."

With trembling fingers, Lisa opened the box and found an exquisite engagement ring, a perfect emerald surrounded by small but beautifully cut diamonds. Instead of snatching the ring from its container, as he had expected, she touched it with a shaking finger, her lips expressionless. Then suddenly, to Jake's surprise, she snapped the box shut and sagged back on her pillows, staring at him, her eyes strangely damp.

If Jake had anticipated any response, it certainly had not been this! His eyes narrowed. What is it, love?"

She breathed a sigh, "Oh, Jake. How I wish you hadn't . . . done this."

"You don't like the ring? I thought it would be right. It reminded me of your eyes." It was unreasonable to be hurt, he knew, but just the same, he was. "We can pick out another."

"It's not that! The ring is exquisite."

"What, then?"

"I . . . I don't know what to tell you," she stammered, hiding her eyes from him.

"Yes," he told her sternly. "That's all you need to say, 'yes'. Lisa, I love you! I want you to be my wife. I want to have you in my life during the day, in my bed at night. I need you. Jodi needs you. Why can't you say 'yes'?"

Lisa made a helpless little gesture, a sob catching in her throat.

"Are you telling me you don't love me?" he asked wearily.

"Oh, Jake, of course I love you!" she cried vehemently. "How could you doubt it?"

"Then why the hesitation? Was it conceited of me to think that you would want this as much as I do?"

"We've only known each other four weeks!"

"So what?"

"You don't know that much about me."

"I know more about you in four weeks than I knew about Christine in eighteen years!"

"No, you don't!"

"I know that you are all I want. You're a loving, caring woman. Besides that," he teased, ticking off her virtues on his fingers, "you're a crafty business woman, a talented musician, an intrepid adventurer, a gourmet chef, and . . . " he lowered his voice to a husky murmur, "an imaginative and merciless lover."

139

She refused to smile, her face bleak. He bowed his head in despair, to fix his eyes on the braided rug. "Are you refusing me, Lisa? Is that it?"

"No!" she cried, "Oh, no!"

"Then you are saying yes?"

"No! At least . . . Jake, I need a little more time to think about this."

"How much time?"

"A month?" she tried tentatively.

"A month!"

"Is that so much to ask?"

"Yes!" he said emphatically. "Lisa, don't you see? I want to settle matters between us. I want to give Jodi the security of a regular home life. I would be willing to wait, for as long as you want, if you could tell me why you're hesitating. Can you tell me that at least?"

"I don't know . . . Oh, Jake, if only . . . I . . . " Lisa stumbled to a halt, breathing deeply, an emotion he could not understand tearing at her. She covered her face with her hands. A long minute passed. He ached for her, yet he could not console her, not now. The time had come for answers.

At last, Lisa raised her head and met his confused eyes. "I'd like to be alone tonight, Jake."

"Just a min. . . "

"Just tonight. Please, I need time to think about . . . well, things." She silently pleaded with him for understanding.

"Tonight is all you're asking for?" He considered her seriously.

"Just tonight," she repeated. "Then I'll come to your house tomorrow night, and we'll talk about it."

"And you'll give me a definite yes or no?"

"It may not be simple."

"What do you mean?"

"It could be," she said slowly, staring into space, "you won't want me." She picked up the little box and held it out to him.

Jake grasped her hands in both of his, closing her fingers around the container so firmly she winced.

"I'll want you, you can bet on it."

Chapter Twelve

When Jake was gone, Lisa lay huddled beneath the blankets in the gray half-light of early morning, clutching the ring box and staring sightlessly at the walls of her room, facing the future with dread. What an unlikely and unlucky hand fate had dealt her!

On one hand, she was fortunate to have fallen in love with Jake, a mature and understanding man who could accept that what had happened so many years ago was not important to their future. Under other circumstances, she would have shared everything with him, secure in his love. They would have put the past behind them and looked forward to a happy home and family.

But fate had taken a quirky twist, making it impossible for her to ignore the past. Try as she might, she could come up with no other solution than to place the whole problem in Jake's lap.

No, that wasn't true. She could tell him she didn't love him and never wanted to see him again. But that would never work. He would never believe she didn't love him, they had gone too far for him to believe otherwise. Besides, to never see Jodi and Jake again, or worse, to see them occasionally around Norway . . . well, she would die a little more each day. It would be worse than anything that had gone before.

Jodi. What should she do about Jodi? How she would love to have her as a daughter, not a fantasy child, but a real daughter. What if she often treated Lisa like some housekeeper that Jake needed only temporarily? She could see beyond the sulleness and hostility to the intelligent, sweet girl Jodi could be, given time and someone to help her.

Time. If only Jake had given her a month, even one more week, time to treasure the two of them, the family she would never have now. Tomorrow she would tell Jake everything, if she could. He had the right to know. There was just one more problem to deal with and then she would be ready. She lifted the telephone from the bedside stand and placed it beside her on the bed, dialing the well-known number. The phone rang on the other end. And rang. And rang. Lisa waited patiently, knowing that her brother would need time to answer. On the tenth ring, she heard the familiar click, followed by the hollow sound that meant he had switched on the speaker phone.

"Richard Fratelli here," he said cheerfully.

"Richard," she half-sobbed. "I have to talk to you."

Jake jumped to his feet to pace his living room one more time. He paused to look out the bay window into the setting sun, searching the street for a sign of Lisa's car. Nothing. He stalked into the kitchen for a cold beer, opened it as he returned to the window, then forgot to taste it. The television made soft noises behind him. He had no idea what he had been watching. He walked over, switched the set off and resumed his position at the window.

Where was she? She said she would be here tonight but not specified what time. He tried to call her all day to find out. Oh, be honest with yourself, he almost said aloud, it was just to talk to her and hear her voice. You can't go a day without her. You're a Lisa addict and you wanted a fix.

There had been no answer at her home and only her answering machine at the office. She had turned off her cellphone. He left message after message, teasing her at first, becoming impatient, and finally shouting his frustration at a recording device. She did not return his calls, if she ever received them.

And then there was the problem of Jodi. The night before, she had awakened to discover her father was missing. When he arrived home at dawn, he found her crying frantically, worrying about him. She was angry, too, because she had called the Norway police, who had only laughed, telling her Jake would be home eventually, as if it were normal behavior for her father!

When Jake explained, too precipitously, where he had been, she was outraged. In one way, he agreed with her, because he knew she was right to object to his leaving without telling her where he was going. But he was, after all, an adult, and he refused to feel guilty about his relationship with Lisa. He tried to reason with Jodi, promising not to leave her alone again without warning.

Jodi was not to be placated. She tore apart Lisa's character, using language that surprised Jake. Where had she learned that vocabulary? He demanded she stop using profanity. She retaliated with worse expletives. He grew angry. She grew angrier. He shouted at her. She screamed at him. He sent her to bed and she stormed off to her room, slamming the door and locking it behind her. Today, there was an armed truce in the house and Jake felt he hadn't a friend in the world.

And where the hell was Lisa? His fingertips tapped out a beat on a windowpane.

He had decided she meant she would be there for dinner and brought home a choice selection of items from a take-out Chinese restaurant. He was sure that she would tease him about it, but he looked forward to the verbal sparring they always enjoyed. She didn't come. Gordie and Jodi weren't able to finish all the food, so he stored the balance of the cartons in the refrigerator. He wasn't hungry himself.

What was wrong with Lisa anyhow? He had been so certain she would marry him. Jake did not consider himself a conceited man, but it had never entered his mind that she would react that way to his proposal. Though he never thought of himself as particularly handsome, not in the classical sense, he wasn't bad looking. At least he didn't frighten small children and dogs.

He was a relatively successful attorney, or would be when he built up his practice again. He knew that she didn't need or care about his money, but at least she could be sure he wouldn't become a financial burden to her.

He didn't consider himself a male chauvinist. He'd always assumed that Lisa would want to continue her real estate business after they were married. She was a terrific realtor. She'd sold him this house, hadn't she? She could even steer some business his way. Should he have told her that?

Was it because she did all the cooking? He tried to help out around the kitchen, but she knew how incompetent he was when he got anywhere near the stove. But he would take cooking lessons if it meant she would marry him!

Her hesitation wasn't because of Jodi, he was sure of that. Lisa practically drooled over the girl. She was always patient and cheerful, no matter how sullen and moody Jodi became, thinking of ways to bring her out of her "blue funks". Lisa had slowly been winning over his daughter, though now that Jodi knew he had been sleeping at her cabin, he didn't care to think of their next confrontation.

He tried to think of anything that he could have done to upset Lisa. Did she regret that they had become intimate so quickly? No, she had been ready for that, what's more, she loved the times they shared a bed. She had turned into a temptress who initiated matters as often as he did.

Lisa told him once that she had to make up for all the years she had missed, but after a few lengthy orgies, she might be satiated. He doubted that. He chuckled, picturing the two of them as an old married couple. At seventy, she would still be trying to lure her crotchety husband into bed. He only hoped he would be able to keep up with her. He sighed. All he asked was a chance to try. He only wanted to grow old with her, was that so much to ask?

Deep in thought, Jake barely heard her soft and hesitant knock at the front door. It was repeated before he reacted. As he hurried into the hallway, he realized he had not heard her car. He thrust the door wide open, eager to hold her in his arms again.

He stopped short, for a moment speechless, as he examined her. Beneath the golden tan, there was an unhealthy pallor, and her eyes seemed smudged because of the dark half-circles beneath them. He understood immediately that she had not slept the night before. Strings of hair were flying loose from her braid. Bits of leaves and grass covered her entire body. Her old jeans were battered, her blue windbreaker was grass-stained, her cotton shirt was rumpled. She was tired, she was miserable, and she was beautiful.

"Where the hell have you been?" he barked as he pulled her into the living room. "I've been calling all day. Don't you ever check your machine? What have you been doing?"

"Walking." Her face was a landscape of sadness with faint tints of fear.

"All day, damn it?"

She nodded and sighed.

"Where?" he interrogated her sharply, and regretted it immediately as she cringed. She didn't need his anger. But hell, he had been worried!

"I don't know," she murmured. "By the lake. In the hills. I walked here from my place. I know it's late, later than I'd planned, but I needed time to think."

"But that's dangerous, Lisa! It's not safe up there in the hills."

"I know them, Jake," she told him bleakly. "You don't have to worry about me."

He softened his attack, sensing the sorrow in her voice. She was so fragile. He hugged her abruptly, trying to join her wherever her thoughts were taking her. But she would have none of it. She bore his embrace patiently but coolly, not allowing herself to respond. He kissed her soft lips, but she turned her head away before he could find that core of passion that was always waiting for him.

"We have to talk," she told him quietly.

He released her reluctantly and clasped her hand to lead her to the old Chippendale love seat in front of the bay window.

She sank down wearily, resting her head against the ancient cushions, closing her eyes for a moment. Jake joined her, warming her cold hands with his, waiting patiently. She took a long breath and fumbled in her jacket pocket to bring out the little box that held his ring. She contemplated it as if she could see its contents. He wanted to snatch it from her, to tear out the ring and force her to wear it. She raised her eyes.

"Where's Jodi?" she asked tiredly.

"At Gordie's, where else?"

"Oh." Her attention was once more on the box.

"What's wrong, love?" He carefully brushed the strands of hair from her forehead, anchoring them behind her ears, hoping his touch, his caring, would reassure her that he would always be there for her.

She swallowed and tried to start, but only a hoarse sigh filled the silence of the waiting room.

"What could you possibly have to tell me that's frightening you so?" Jake demanded at last. "By now, you surely must know how much I love you. If you're worried that Jodi won't accept you . . ."

She shook her head emphatically.

"Then is it me?" Is there something wrong with me? Tell me. I can change."

"You're perfect, Jake," she laughed a little hysterically. "I don't deserve someone as wonderful as you."

"That's great for my oversized ego, but it doesn't solve the problem. I'll turn into a louse if you want."

She smiled sadly at his attempts to cheer her. "The problem isn't you, Jake. It's me . . . what I am and was."

145

"What do you mean? You have to tell me, you know that, so why not get it over so we can get on with our lives."

"Yes, yes . . . of course you're right. I should start at the beginning."

"That would be best," he teased.

"You know that I had . . . been with someone else when . . ."

"When you were sixteen," he interrupted impatiently. "Go on." Jake felt as if he were being torn apart from the inside out simply thinking of her with someone else. Couldn't she see that it was best they put that behind them? He was mature enough to do it.

Her lips trembled. "I . . . I . . ."

"For God's sake, tell me and get it over with," he demanded hoarsely, his patience disappearing entirely.

"I got pregnant," she blurted and bit her lower lip as two tears welled into her eyes, soon followed by others.

Jake's hand tightened on hers convulsively. "Oh, love," he groaned, his compassion exploding to surround her. He dragged her onto his lap, wrapping his long arms around her, tucking her legs on the love seat against his thighs. He crooned to her as he tried to comfort her. As he held her sobbing body to him, he thought about her as she must have been, a girl growing up before her time, only two years older than Jodi. He peered into her past, trying to picture her as a young mother. The image of the baby, held in her arms, burned into his mind. He tried to accept the painful reality. Some teenage boy had taken Lisa brutally and given her a baby. And Jake would never be able to have a child with her. The injustice of it tore him apart.

"What happened to your baby?"

She was shaking violently, as she lived her old, bitter grief. "They made me put her up for adoption." Her tears melted against the warmth of his shoulder. "They wouldn't let me keep her."

"They . . . ?"

"The social workers." At his sudden stillness, she peeped up at him and saw the questions in his eyes. "My parents were dead," she explained shakily. "They were . . ."

"Yes?"

"They were killed in a car accident before . . . before the baby was born."

"So you were . . . what? In foster care?"

She nodded bleakly.

He crushed her to him again. "And you gave up your baby at the same time you lost your family. Oh Lisa, no wonder you're so crazy about kids." He held her without passion, wanting only to comfort this beautiful, sensitive woman, who so needed all the love he could give.

It was some time before Lisa was able to calm herself, and he steeled himself for the questions he must yet ask her.

"Lisa," he finally asked, "is that why you're hesitant about marrying me? Is it because I can't give you give you a baby to replace the one you lost?"

"Jake!" she exclaimed, straightening. "Of course not! I never even thought of that."

"Then what is it? Did you think that something that happened so long ago would make the slightest difference at all to me? It doesn't, you know. I love you and nothing will change that."

Lisa's eyes were fixed on him and he suddenly understood that there was more, some other secret. For a moment, Jake wanted to stop her. She didn't have to tell him anything else. But it was no longer any good. Now that he knew about it, now that she had started this emotional ride, nothing else but the truth would do. What kind of marriage would it be with this between them? He would always be aware that she was hiding something from him. It was better to find out now. He winced as she dug her nails into his shoulder.

"Lisa . . . Lisa?" He lifted her chin and searched her stricken eyes. "There's more, isn't there?"

"Yes," she whispered, the muscles in her throat working convulsively as she tried to swallow.

"What is it?"

Lisa extricated her hand from his and slid from his lap, moving to the far side of the settee to avoid touching him. She stared into the empty fireplace so intensely, Jake almost imagined that there was really a blaze there. She swallowed again.

"Jake? Where was Jodi born?"

She had changed the subject. Now he was totally confused. "What's that got to do with anything."

"Where Jake?" she grated. "It's important, believe me. It was in Menominee, wasn't it? Menominee County, Michigan? June 7 at 7:22 p.m.?" She continued to rap out her questions harshly, paying no attention to his gasp of disbelief. "The attending physician was named Freed. James Freed, if you check

147

the certificate?"

"How do you know all that?" His voice was hoarse. It couldn't be. Not Jodi! Not his Jodi!

"My daughter was born in Menominee, Michigan on June 7 at 7:22 p.m. fourteen years ago." Lisa spoke softly and wistfully, ignoring Jake now as she returned to another time, another place. "They gave her to me to hold afterward. The people who she was going to did not want that to happen, they didn't want to know anything about me. I was never supposed to see her at all, they were supposed to take her away immediately. I had agreed to that. But someone made a mistake and gave her to me. She was the most beautiful baby. Her hair was blond . . . even then I could tell . . . what little there was of it . . . her fingers and toes were perfect, so tiny . . . and . . . "

All at once, Jake was released from the mist that had captured his mind. He grasped her shoulders so tightly she cried out and shook her roughly. "What are you trying to tell me, for God's sake?"

"That Jodi was that baby. She's my daughter!"

"No! She can't be!"

Lisa raised her chin defiantly. "She is, Jake," she insisted. "I knew it from the moment I saw her picture."

"But . . . "

A shrill cry interrupted anything Jake might have said. He and Lisa turned together to see an unnaturally pale Jodi at the kitchen door, a fistful of cookies rapidly turning into crumbs. Her whimper became a moan and then she found her voice.

"It's a lie."

"Jodi," Lisa whispered in agony.

"It isn't true! You aren't . . . my mother. My real mother is dead! My real mother wouldn't just . . . give me away!"

"It wasn't like that," Lisa objected.

"No!" the teenager screamed.

Jake rose to go to his daughter, but she waved him away and screamed at Lisa again.

"You're just saying all that. You're just saying that so he'll marry you. That's why you were being so nice to me, wasn't it? That's why you cooked all this stuff." She threw the remains of the cookies on the floor. Her voice became shriller as her hysteria mounted. Jake tried to grapple her flaying arms as she ranted on. "You tried sleeping with my father and that didn't work either. I know what's been going on. You're nothing but a slut, you're a whore, you're . . . "

Jake's hand connected with her cheek ending her tirade. Lisa cried out in shock as Jodi's eyes filled with tears. Horrified at what he had done, Jake tried to touch the reddening mark on Jodi's face, as if he could erase what he had done, but she spun away, ducking under his arm and hurtling herself up the curving staircase. A moment alter, he heard the door of her room slam shut.

The old house was silent except for the soft ticking of the grandfather clock in the hallway and the sound of far-off sobs. Jake clenched his fists, ashamed himself for what he had done to his daughter and overwhelmed by the bombshell Lisa had dropped on them. His plans, his dreams were shattered. He reacted in illogical fury at the injustice of it all.

He started toward the stairs to go to his daughter's room. Lisa stood up. "Jake."

"Sit down," he commanded angrily.

"No Jake, let me go and talk to her."

He grunted and kept going. "I'm her father."

"And I'm her mother!"

Jake gritted his teeth and paused on the third step without looking back. "No, you're not," he rasped. "You haven't been her mother since the day she was born."

Ignoring Lisa's anguished cry, he ascended the staircase with heavy footsteps.

Lisa was still on the loveseat when Jake came down the stairs again an hour later. She had collapsed into a miserable ball, her arms wrapped around her legs, her head on a quilted pillow she had given him as a house warming present. Her red-rimmed eyes fixed on him as he strode into the room.

Jake flung himself into an easy chair across the coffee table from her, scrutinizing her with narrowed eyes. He looks so unforgiving, she thought. But after the hour he had just spent with Jodi, she could hardly blame him. Every cry, every scream that echoed down the stairs was etched in her mind. She tiredly unwrapped her legs and slid them to the floor and sat up, still clutching the tiny box in her fist.

"What happens now?" she asked in a small voice, not looking at him directly.

149

"I don't know," he muttered, running his hand through his unruly hair.

"Is she going to be all right?"

"She cried herself to sleep. I don't know what she'll be like when she wakes up. She's pretty upset and I can understand that. I'm upset, too." He stood again and paced to the big window, looking out at the street lights. "I've never hit her before, ever. I hope she can forgive me for that."

"Oh, Jake," Lisa cried. "Of course she will."

"It was unforgivable."

"She was hysterical!"

"I didn't slap her because she was hysterical, it was for what she was saying about you."   Jake whirled to glare at her. "And it wasn't entirely untrue!"

"Don't say that! I didn't do any of those things to trap you!"

"Didn't you? Then why didn't you tell me all this before tonight?" he demanded furiously.

"I didn't know! At least until the day she came home. I had no way of knowing until I saw her picture and even then . . ."

"Other than the hair, she doesn't look like you," Jake said in a dangerously quiet tone. "Does that mean she looks like her fa . . . like him?"

"Yes," she whispered miserably.

"So you claim that you didn't know?" He assessed her with courtroom calm. Lisa felt the unleashed tension and braced herself for his attack. It was as if he could shatter her into a million pieces with a few words.

"Jake, I didn't know," she began with pretended calm. "Even after I looked at the photograph on your dresser, I thought . . . You said she was thirteen and I thought I had to be wrong. Then at the ice cream parlor, she told me how old . . . " Lisa floundered to a stop under his icy stare. How could she explain how she felt when she couldn't pinpoint her rapidly fluctuating emotions for herself. She sighed and rubbed her tired eyes with the back of her hand. "What difference did it make then? By then, I'd already fallen in love with you."

His laugh held no humor and she flinched at the harsh sound.

"In love with me? Really? It all seem too neat somehow. Why didn't you tell me all this two weeks ago when you found out?

150

You could have!"

"I know."

"Then why didn't you?"

"I didn't know how you would react! I thought you might be upset!"

"I am!" he shouted.

They retreated, catching their breaths, like two prizefighters who had been through a brutal skirmish. Lisa calmed herself with an effort. She didn't want to fight with Jake, she wanted him to understand. She tried again.

"Jake, try to see things my way. I hadn't seen my baby since the day she was born. I know it was wrong not to tell you, but I wanted to have her, to know her, for just a few days. Can't you understand how much that meant to me?"

"She's mine! She's *my* daughter," he barked possessively. "Mine and Christine's."

"I never said she wasn't," she said tonelessly, staring at the floor.

Jake strode to her and jerked her to her feet, coldly assessing her tear-stained face. "There's one little thing you haven't told me, lady. Who is her father . . . no, let me re-phrase that. Who got you pregnant?" When she would have turned away, his large hands grasped her head, making her look at him.

"Don't ask me that," she pleaded.

"Why not? You started this. Besides, don't you think I have a right to know?"

"No, you don't. You didn't want to know when Jodi was born and you don't now. And I promised I wouldn't tell!"

"Tell me!" he roared. "Tell who the man is!"

"I can't tell you!"

"What's the matter? Are you still sleeping with him?"

Her hand flew to her mouth in horror. She broke away from him and stumbled to the hallway. He was right behind her and his hand shot out to hold the front door when she would have opened it.

"Where do you think you're going?" he demanded.

Lisa refused to turn away from the door, not wanting him to see the fresh tears that were welling into her eyes.

In a softer tone, he asked, "Lisa, where would you go?"

"I don't know. Home, I guess." Her head was bowed in sorrow for what they had once shared.

"I'll drive you home," he offered. "You don't have your car here."

"No . . . no. You should be here with Jodi. She might wake up and you have to be here. I can walk." She twisted around in his arms, bracing herself against the door. "Let me go, Jake."

He straightened reluctantly, dropping his hands to his side. "It's dark. You shouldn't be out there alone."

"There's a full moon. And I'm using to being alone. No matter what you think," she told him defiantly.

"Look, I was out of line. I'm sorry. It was a stupid thing to say." He was embarrassed at his emotional outburst, so out of character for him. Lisa saw the confusion and agony on his face. How can I hurt him this way, she thought? How could I hurt Jodi? The two people I care most about in the world.

"Lisa, I don't want to . . . "

He swallowed with difficulty and threw his head to one side. He's trying to find the words, she surmised. He wants to end this and doesn't know how. I can do this for him. I can give him this one last gift.

"It's all right, Jake. I'm leaving now." She faced him proudly, head thrown back. "I think I always knew it would end this way. I'll be fine. For fourteen years, I've wondered, you know. I wondered in the winter, when it snowed, if someone would take her sledding, or in the summer, if someone would teach her how to swim. I thought about her thousands . . .no, millions of times. I celebrated every one of her birthdays. Can you understand that, Jake? I'd walk off into the woods somewhere and sing . . ." She sobbed and quickly held her hand to her mouth, fighting to control herself.

"But I always knew I would go through my life without her. I'd accepted that. So nothing's changed for me. I'll go on, so you don't have to worry about me." She smiled brightly through her tears. "At least now I'll know she's all right with you. At least I'll have that."

She became aware of the box she still held in her hand. She thrust it toward Jake. He shook his head, his eyes luminous. Those are tears, she thought in wonder. "Lisa, no . . ." His voice caught. "Lisa, I don't think this is the end between us. But maybe it would be best if we let things rest for a week or so, until Jodi and I come to terms with this. We need time to think. "

She smiled at his gesture. Did he feel that he should let her down easily? A swift, clean break was better for them all. She took his hand, gently placed the box in it and closed his fingers over it. She caressed them as she slowly stepped away and dropped her hands. Any words he might said were caught in his throat and he could only beseech her mutely.

She shrugged her shoulders and turned to slip out the door. Jake stood alone in the silent hallway, a solitary tear slowly sliding down his face.

Chapter Thirteen

Although it was cool for an early August evening, the weather was perfect for a Norway City Band performance, the stars like jewels, the moon silvery bright, and a light wind that held off the mosquitoes. The grassy square in front of the band shell was filled with some people in lawn chairs and others who wandered around to find and chat with neighbors and friends. It was a typical Tuesday evening in Norway.

For the first time, the bright lights of the shell hurt Lisa's eyes as she struggled to follow the music. If she couldn't do better than this, she would lose the first clarinet spot and be relegated to a back seat. Not that she cared much any more. Not even "Stars and Stripes Forever" could rouse her from her aching lethargy. It was all she could do to keep up with the beat, much less to hit every note she was supposed to. What was wrong with her? She was alternately sweaty and frozen. Her fingers were stiff on her instrument. Neil was looking at her from the trombone section, quizzing her with his eyebrows. She knew she must look ghastly. She tried to concentrate, but her eyes barely focused.

Nothing had gone right for her since Jake found out about Jodi. The agony of that night came rushing back to her, not for the first time. She cried the night away, and morning found her too ill to get up, too miserable to care about her business, her church or any of her other responsibilities. She had a bad bout of the flu and ended up staying in bed for almost a week, getting up only to run to the bathroom where she was violently sick.

When she missed a band rehearsal for the first time in anyone's memory, Neil called her. Despite her weak arguments and subterfuges, Beth arrived that same night, to take Lisa in hand and make sure she was fed, bathed and clothed. Beth also asked approximately five thousand questions, but Lisa pretended she was too ill to answer. She would have locked the door to the minister and his wife, if they had not also become her prime source of information about Jake and Jodi. It was amazing how much snooping Beth could accomplish under the guise of pastoral visits! Lisa didn't care, as long as she had some connection, however tenuous, with the two Gannetts.

Lisa went into a panic when she learned that Jake and Jodi had reverted to their take-out diet.

"They'll get sick!" she moaned to Beth.

"I know," Beth said thoughtfully. "I think you should go back to cooking for them."

"Beth!"

"Well, why not? What happened between you and Jake?" she asked again.

Lisa sighed and pulled the covers over her head.

"It's not that you aren't in love with him," Beth mused. "And he's crazy about you. He doesn't ask about you, but he sure doesn't change the subject when I talk about you either. So that leaves Jodi. Are the two of you going to let that girl wreck your lives? Lisa?" She poked at the blanket. "Lisa, I know you can hear me, and sooner or later, I'm going to figure out what happened between you."

Lisa lowered the blanket three inches and gave her a baleful glance. "Does it ever occur to you to mind your own business, Beth?"

"Nope. Not when two of the nicest people I know are managing to throw away something good. Besides, we haven't had a wedding since June. I'm trying to drum up business for Neil."

"There's always funerals and baptisms. He can make a living that way."

"But weddings are so much nicer than funerals and bap . . . "Beth was quiet and after a long minute, Lisa slid the covers down. Beth was examining her fingernails with an absent air.

"What are you up to now?"

"Me?" the redhead said innocently. "Nothing . . nothing. Say," she asked briskly, rising to straighten the bedclothes. "How are you feeling now?"

"Better. I haven't thrown up since this morning," Lisa said. "That's improvement, anyway."

"Yes, I'd say we were making some progress," Beth said thoughtfully. "Well, dear, I'm going to make you some toast and tea, and then I'm going home to my family. You'll be fine in a day or two, but I'd stick to light breakfasts for a while."

Lisa did not try to hide her relief. "I can make the toast myself, Beth. I'm feeling much better. Go on home. Besides, aren't you supposed to tell me it's in God's hands,? she teased.

"Oh, I definitely would say that," the redhead grinned. "He does have a knack of taking care of his own. Well, I have things to work on at home. I'm planning a party for the end of this month."

"At the church?"

"Of course."

"Anything I can help with?"

"Oh, you'll have plenty to do, believe me," Beth laughed, as she walked to the bedroom door.

"Beth? Do you suppose you could . . . ?"

"What is it?"

"About Jake and Jodi. Do you think . . . you could?" Lisa's face had color for the first time in days.

"Oh." Beth understood at once. "You want me to cook something for them?"

"Do you think you could?"

"One seven-layer casserole coming up. And I'll expect to see you on the bandstand Tuesday night. Neil said rehearsal didn't go well, too many members missing. They'll have to cancel the concert if you don't come, Lisa. It's too important a tradition for this town to let it slide."

So here she was, despite her flu. Beth had insisted she be here, actually harped on it until, driven by guilt, Lisa had gotten out of bed. She wiped her sweaty head when she came to a rest in the music. The queasy feeling in her stomach returned. Would she never feel better?

Was Jake out there somewhere in the darkness, listening? She knew he could hear the music from his home. Would it draw him to the square?

He had not called her since that night, but then, did she expect him to? It was better to make a clean break. How she ached for him though! She peered out into the shadowed audience. Was Jodi there? She clutched her clarinet convulsively. God, she felt lousy!

Across the street, standing in the shadow of a brick storefront. Jake listened to the rousing Sousa march, but his eyes were fastened on one musician. He was greedy for the least glimpse of her, hungry for the sound of her voice. Last week he had even called her office late at night, just to listen to her recording device.

She's thinner, and so pale! he thought in alarm. He knew she'd been ill, he'd gotten that much from Beth, along with a tongue lashing, which he'd deserved, and more questions every time she came over, which was almost every day. The woman would make a great courtroom lawyer, though he'd fended off the worst of her inquisitiveness. How could he discuss what had happened with anyone but Lisa?

He couldn't resent Beth's interference, however, because she truly cared about them and had the best intentions. After all, she was taking care of Lisa while she had the flu and for that he would be eternally grateful. He should have been there doing it himself.

Jake had wanted to call Lisa a hundred times, but he was still embarrassed about his behavior. What could he say that would make things right between them? He had shouted at her, saying terrible things to her and he knew none of them were true. She wasn't promiscuous. She hadn't plotted to take Jodi from him. Everything Lisa did she did out of love. In the simplest terms possible, she loved him and he loved her and they both loved Jodi. Why couldn't everything be that simple?

He was still trying to analyze why he had attacked her that night. He hated to admit it to himself, but part of it was plain sexual jealousy, no matter how puerile that sounded.

That another man had given Lisa a child was bad enough. That that child was his Jodi was intolerable. Who was Jodi's natural father anyway? He glanced around the square at the shadowy figures in the audience. It could be any of the men around him. Of late, he had taken to watching the males of the town who were in the right age group, studying them for any resemblance to his daughter. He even considered Neil Franke until he discovered the minister was a relative newcomer to the area.

Jake had struggled with himself over the past weeks, trying to put all thought of the other man behind him, but it was no use. He and Lisa must come to terms with what had happened, and part of that process was his knowing about Jodi's parentage.

The other part was the problem of Jodi herself. Right now, she was somewhere off in the darkness, with Gordie Ruggeri no doubt. The girl had been in a foul frame of mind for two weeks after that dramatic night, refusing to talk to Jake at all and making Gordie's life miserable with her wild mood shifts. She either moped around or went into rages, especially if the boy tried to defend Lisa.

A week ago, Gordie had had enough. He refused to come over when Jodi called and told her he had other plans. She spent the day in tears, wandering through the house aimlessly and reproaching Jake with tragic eyes whenever he dared to cross her path.

"What's wrong?" he was foolish enough to ask .

The floodgates opened. No one loved her any more. No one cared if she lived or died. He loved Lisa and he didn't love her. Gordie had abandoned her. She was going to go to her room and starve herself to death, then they would all see! So there!

After that emotional performance, Jake checked the refrigerator, found the usual depletion of food, and escaped into the back yard. Gordie was already there, mournfully leaning over the fence. The two abused males commiserated with each other.

Gordie was perplexed. "I sure don't get what her problem is, Mr. Gannett. Why wouldn't she want you to marry Lisa? None of the kids around here can figure Jodi out. What's the big deal?"

"You all think I should marry Lisa?"

Gordie reddened. "Oh. It's none of our business, right? We thought you already asked her . . . or something." He paused, then blurted, "Aren't you going to?"

"I don't know. The way Jodi is right now . . . "

"Jodi's nuts!" the boy exclaimed. "Don't pay any attention to her. Any normal kid would jump at the chance to get Lisa for a mother. She's O.K. She always listens to us and she never loses her temper no matter how dumb we act, she always thinks of great stuff to do, and besides," he added, unconsciously echoing Jake, "she can cook."

Jake solemnly promised that he would consider Gordie's recommendations, though he had no idea how he would implement them.

After one afternoon without Gordie's company, Jodi miraculously came out of her blue funk and stopped her vituperative attacks on Lisa. She even began to talk to Jake. If she still bore her natural mother any ill will, she had the sense to keep her thoughts on that matter to herself.

Deep in thought, Jake straightened and strolled across the street, wondering how to proceed. He wanted to start mending his relationship with Lisa tonight. He glanced at her again and found her eyes fastened on him. She quickly bent her fair head to her music, but it was too late, he had caught the pained desperation in her eyes. He took an impulsive step toward her but checked himself. Not now. Not in front of the entire town. He would have to wait for the concert to finish.

Perhaps he should find Gordie's father and buy another bouquet of carnations. Or maybe roses would be better. Yes, that was it! He eagerly searched the perimeter of the square for the florist. He started to grin, now that he had a plan of action. He would play stage-door-johnny again. He would tease her the way he used to and they would laugh and start all . . .

A cry from the band shell interrupted his train of thought. He twisted back to see Lisa sliding from her chair to a crumpled heap on the wooden floor, her folding chair collapsing with a clatter behind her. Her clarinet flew from her hand and rolled to the edge of the stage. Jake froze in place as the townspeople flew past him to the platform, hurrying to see what they could do to help.

"God, no!" The cry swelled inside him and erupted. He hurled himself forward, shoving people rudely in his urgency to reach her. He threw himself onto the stage and rushed to her side, kneeling beside Neil and others in the band, who had parted to make room for him. He took her hand. It was frozen!

"Lisa!" he cried hoarsely. She was so pale, so still!

As the lights of an oncoming car flashed over the interior of the Corvette, Jake glanced over at the woman in the passenger seat. Lisa seemed to be totally recovered from her fainting spell. There was a healthy glow about her, a faint blush in her cheeks. Her wide eyes were snapping with suppressed excitement and happiness. Yet not an hour ago before she had looked like death warmed over. Perplexed, he returned his attention to the road.

In the middle of the confusion, a staff doctor from the Dickinson County Hospital, only two blocks away, who had stopped by on to listen to the music, arrived at the bandstand as Lisa's eyes fluttered open. Dozens of musicians and members of the audience were milling around, yet she found Jake unerringly. Her lips curved in a wistful smile.

"I love you," she murmured and lifted a hand to caress away the lines of concern from his forehead.

160

The entire population of Norway, Michigan, sighed a collective sigh as Jake gently kissed the woman he loved.

The unromantic doctor, however, seized her wrist to take her pulse and after a cursory check, asked for volunteers to carry Lisa to a more private place for an examination, deciding there was no need to call out an ambulance. Jake waved everyone else away and immediately lifted her into his arms, overriding her objections with action, and carried her the short half-block to Neil and Beth's parsonage. They led a parade of followers that included the doctor, the Frankes and their children, Jodi and Gordie. Jodi tugged at her father's windbreaker once and tried out an objection, but a stern command from Jake and Gordie's hand on her arm silenced her.

Jake placed his precious burden on the bed in the room Beth directed them to and with a firm kiss, left her with the young doctor. He had only five minutes to pace around the living room before the intern returned, grinning reassurance, his eyes twinkling with mischief. Despite Jake's protests, he headed for the front door, telling Jake to make sure Lisa saw her own doctor soon.

"She's fine," he assured Jake over and over. "There's no problem at all. I've prescribed something for the nausea. She'll tell you all about it herself, I'm sure."

"Tell me what?" Jake demanded. "What nausea?"

The young man only laughed, slapped Jake on the back and pushed past him to escape through the door. Growling about incompetent physicians and contemplating his first Michigan malpractice suit, Jake rushed back into the bedroom, only to find Lisa staring intently in front of Beth's dressing table mirror as she re-braided her hair.

"Don't you think you should be lying down?"

"Actually," she told him serenely, "I think it would be better if you took me home."

So here he was, carefully negotiating the curves of the dark forest road, Lisa beside him, as they so often had been before. It was as if they had never quarreled. He marveled at how easily their private time together had been arranged. Beth insisted that Jodi spend the night at the parsonage. Jake mildly objected at first, but Beth smiled mysteriously and blithely decided that Jodi could help plan the big party they would be giving on Saturday.

Jake was given no time to discuss any of this with his furious daughter. Lisa and he were hustled out to the Corvette,

161

which Neil had fetched for them, and were cheered on by a crowd of band members and other well-wishers who shouted cries of congratulations.

"I feel like I should give a speech," Jake said to Neil. "This is a lot like leaving for a honeymoon."

For some reason, their audience thought this was hilarious. Jake felt he was the only person in Norway, with the possible exception of Jodi, who was ignorant of a wonderful secret. Lisa certainly had left with a knowing smile.

"Are you sure you're all right?" he asked her for the third time.

He heard her chuckle throatily into the darkness. "I'm perfectly fine, Jake." She reached over to brush her fingers over his hand.

"What's so funny?"

"You are. I'm thinking about fainting every time we have an argument. It makes you so agreeable." The gurgle of laughter ended on a pensive sigh. "We have to talk over a few things, Jake," she said seriously. "There is something I think you don't know."

He pulled the car into her driveway, groaning inwardly. He didn't like the sound of that. "Lisa," he said, "all I know is that when you keeled over on that stage, I realized that I could lose everything that gave my life meaning." He turned off the motor and slipped his arm over the back of the seat to find her. "I love you, darling," he whispered as he lowered his head, "I love you for all time."

Lisa met him eagerly, darting her tongue out immediately to trace his lower lip. A wave of emotion swept over him and he drew her to him, only to find their passion thwarted by the shift mechanism.

Suddenly, the most important thing in the world was for them to get into that cabin. Jake thrust Lisa away and threw his car door open, leaping out and rushing around the front of the Corvette to get her, only to find her hurrying to meet him. He grabbed her hand and they ran to the cabin door together, comically tangling themselves in the doorway, untangling themselves, laughing and giggling like children as they swept directly to the bedroom, making no pretenses about their needs.

They stopped short in front of the bed, for a moment uncertain of each other's moods. Lisa's glowing green eyes shyly questioned his. His hand lingered on hers, squeezing tightly in reassurance. All at once, they were in a frenzy again, tearing their

162

clothes off in their eagerness. A button flew from his shirt as he ripped it from his body impatiently. He cursed when his slacks were hung up on shoes he had forgotten to take off. Lisa was laughing again. For a moment, he was the picture of an offended male until he noticed that she had slipped out of everything but her white tennis shoes. Then his laughter matched hers as their last clothes were joyfully flung aside. He threw her on the bed and straddled her, pinning her arms to her sides, glaring at her with mock anger.

"And what are you laughing at, lady?" he growled ferociously, nipping at her delectable ear.

"At you!" she giggled, laughing even harder when he gave her a little shake. "At both us! At everything! At the whole world!" Her arms managed to escape his clutches and she threw them around his neck, capturing him in turn and bringing his mouth down to hers in a tender and affirming kiss.

"Oh, Jake," she whispered, her voice shaking with emotion, "I've missed you so much."

Exuberant, he kissed her again. He eagerly ran his hands over her beloved body, revisiting his favorite haunts. He gleefully found her full breasts and felt them immediately leap to life, the nipples hardening to tight points. Lisa moaned and encouraged his voyage down her body, grasping his head to direct him as his lips found a soft mound and closed around it. She cried out as he sucked the erect nipple, then moved to the other. She thrust her hips at him provocatively, urging him on. His hand parted her thighs and found her warm center unerringly as he continued to tease and suckle her sensitive breasts. She thrashed wildly. He felt the sudden warmth between her thighs as she screamed his name and collapsed.

Startled at her unexpected and violent response, Jake raised himself on his arms and scanned her face and body. Her slender frame was relaxed, one leg curving inward against the other, an arm draped over her abdomen. Her breasts rose and fell as her breathing slowed. She was smiling the satisfied cat smile had had come to know so well. She opened slumberous eyes to gaze at him lovingly. She blushed scarlet when she noticed his surprise.

"I'm sorry," she apologized hesitantly. Jake waited. She hurried to explain. "My body seems to be very . . . sensitive now. When you touch me, I . . . can't help myself. You see. . ."

"It's been too long for me, too," he finished for her, anxious now to experiment with this new Lisa. "You've turned into a wild woman, but I think I can just about deal with that!" He nibbled at her breast tentatively and felt her waken beneath him again. His body quickened in response.

"What a night this is going to be!" He grinned.

Jake gradually became aware of the smell of freshly brewed coffee. H stretched, yawned and turned over, trying vainly to pull the sheet over his head. It seemed to be stuck on the other side of the bed. He gave up on the project. It was too much trouble. He would have gone back to sleep save for the irritating little pokes he was receiving in his ribs. He opened one eye and examined the Aubrey Beardsley print over the oak dresser, a poster for some event that had taken place over a century ago. Missed it, he thought lazily, deciding he didn't care for the art-deco style, and he closed the eye again. He stretched lazily and moved away from the irritation at his side, but it followed him until he had reached the very edge of the mattress. He sighed and rolled onto his back, opening the eye once more to meet Lisa's solemn perusal. The second gray eye snapped open to fully appreciate what he considered a true work of art.

She was sitting cross-legged on the bed, wearing an oversized green and yellow football jersey he recognized as one he had left behind here early one July morning. It formed soft folds over her slender frame, emphasizing her delicate fragility, and fell over her thighs without concealing the long, graceful legs. Her hair was a shimmering waterfall over her shoulders. This was true beauty, he thought, beauty beyond compare.

Lisa was sipping on her coffee cup as if it contained much-needed courage. When she saw he was awake, she reached for a second mug for Jake. He groaned and tiredly pulled himself up, propping some pillows behind his back and leaning into them, uncaring that the sheets no longer covered his nudity. He took the proffered cup, waiting while Lisa filled it from the thermos pitcher from the nightstand.

"Woman," he signed, relishing the first black coffee of the morning, "I think you may have finally driven me to celibacy. Too many more nights like the last one and you'll be able to add impotency to sterility."

Lisa's lips compressed to a thin line and Jake realized his attempt at lightening her mood had failed. She was troubled about

164

something, and he knew what it was. He wished they could put this behind them. Did they have to discuss it now? If only they could have today, just a few hours to pretend nothing had come between them.

Jake leaned forward for a morning kiss, but Lisa fended him off, brushing his arm aside and dodging his lips. Their eyes locked and he knew that she would allow no distractions this time. He collapsed back against the headboard and took a long fortifying drink from the mug. She had forgotten to add sugar to his coffee, a sure sign she was preoccupied, but he said nothing.

"Jake, we have to talk."

"I agree."

"Jake . . . "

"Lisa . . . "

They laughed self-consciously.

Lisa tried again. "Jake, why did you stay away so long?"

"Why didn't you come to me?"

"You told me we shouldn't see each other, that we should have time to think."

"I said a lot of things that night. I thought that you would come back, sort of . . . stop by, after a week. Or I would drop into your office. But you were never there. You could have called me, too, Lisa. It works both ways."

"I didn't think you wanted me any more." She stared into her cup, biting her lower lip.

"How could you think that?" he exploded. "No, don't say anything!" he quickly interjected when she would have replied. "I know I said some cruel things to you. But I was so upset Lisa, I wasn't thinking. It wasn't just Jodi, either, though that's part of it." He tried to smooth back his hair and rumpled it more.

"I don't understand."

"I don't understand myself these days. Look," he said quietly, seizing her cup and putting it, with his own, on the bedside table. He took her hands. "When I met you I wanted you, almost from the first. You showed me the house, my house. It was far too big for Jodi and me, but all I could picture, all I can still picture, is you and me together, living there with our family. And Jodi wouldn't be our only child! I imagined you with a baby in your arms, standing in the nursery next to our bedroom. Yes," he replied to her questioning smile, "I think of it as a nursery, not a small storage room."

"And it would be our bedroom?"

"Of course." Jake ignored her happy sigh. "But most of all, I find myself imagining you in that long white cotton smock you wear. You turn to me and you're pregnant and I reach out to feel my child moving in your belly." He slipped his hand under the football jersey to caress her stomach. Lisa quickly joined her hand to his, trying to hold him to her, but he drew his breath in sharply and pulled away.

"The only thing wrong with that picture is that I know that I will never be able to give you a baby. No wait," he demanded, when she would speak. "Let me finish. I want you to know how I was feeling, how I could say such rotten things to you."

Jake was silent for a moment as he struggled to form his thoughts into some coherent order. Lisa watched him anxiously. He wanted to erase the lines of worry from her brow, but what must be said had to be said. "My first feeling," he finally said," when you told me you had had a baby was extreme rage that I wasn't the man to give you a child. I could have strangled the man with my bare hands for doing that to you. Then, when I found out this guy had fathered my daughter, my Jodi, the child I've always thought of as my own, that was a blow to my pride. Chauvinistic, perhaps, but it's what I felt. I still feel that way, I can't help it."

"I understand, Jake, but . . . ."

"Do you? Do you know how jealous I was that night? I was so hurt, and I had to lash out at someone. It should have been the guy who . . . impregnated you, but he wasn't there, so I attacked you."

"Oh, Jake, I'm so sorry," Lisa agonized. "But you aren't . ...."

He interrupted her once again. "I have to know, Lisa. I wonder about it all the time. Maybe I have no right to ask, but it's driving me crazy. Who was he? Tell me.""

"I can't tell you, Jake. He isn't ready yet and he made me promise not to . . . "

"What?" he exclaimed. "You've talked to him about it?"

She mutely nodded.

"He knows about Jodi?"

"Well, yes," she said, in a tiny voice.

"Great!" he snorted in exasperation. "Some guy in this town," he looked at her to verify his supposition, "knows all about my daughter and about me and you. It could be anybody I see day in or day out and you won't tell me!"

166

"I can't! Not yet!"

"Have you any suggestions on how I should deal with that?"

Lisa was quiet for a moment, struggling with thoughts he could guess at. She sighed. "Jake, he isn't a bad man, I can promise you that. You might even like him. He needs time to come to terms with this, just like I did. He'll want to meet Jodi, soon, I think, but it's . . . "

"Damn it all!" Jake exploded wrathfully. "What are you trying to say? Jodi has to meet another parent? Didn't you see how it tore her apart just finding out about you?" Lisa winced, but his anger drove him on. "What is my role going to be in all this? I'm her father, I should have some say about what happens to her. Or do you two expect me to step back and let you steal her from me? Damn it, Lisa, she's the only child I have!"

"But Jake, that isn't . . . ."

"And no one, no one, is going to take her away from me, got that?" Jake towered over Lisa, the covers thrown back, bellowing out his hurt and anger.

"I never said . . . "

"This guy has no right to Jodi. She's been been mine for fourteen years and she'll be mine forever! It's not as if I can go out and have a child like you two did."

"That isn't true!" she cried.

"What isn't true?"

"That you can't have a child."

"What in hell is that supposed to mean?" he snarled.

"I'm pregnant!"

Chapter Fourteen

Lisa's blurted words effectively silenced Jake's tirade. She silently berated herself as he gaped open-mouthed at her. This certainly was not the way she had intended to tell him, shouting the news at him, like that! She reached her arms out to him to hug him, to let him share this miracle. But when her hands touched his waist, he grasped her wrists, crushing them as he forced her away.

"Oh!" she cried out in surprise and pain.

He slid from the bed and stalked about in fury, gathering his clothes from the far reaches of the room where they had been flung the night before.

"Say something!" Lisa implored, kneeling on the bed.

"What do you want me to say?" he asked sarcastically, pulling on his briefs and reaching for his jeans. "Congratulations!"

"For starters!" she exclaimed. "I thought you would be pleased."

"Guess again."

Lisa jumped off the bed and seized the shirt he was trying to pull right side out, jerking it from him, trying to get his full attention. "You're supposed to be happy!" she insisted, holding the material to her breast almost as if it were the baby they argued about. "What's wrong with you? Isn't this what you wanted, what you dreamed about?"

"Except for one thing."

"What?"

"It's not my baby." He whipped the shirt from her hands with one sudden movement and turned his back on her as he donned it.

"It is!" she exclaimed, stamping her bare foot on the wooden floor in frustration and hurt.

"I'm sterile, remember?"

"I'm proof you're not!"

Jake smiled sardonically as he examined his shirt and looked for the missing buttons. He brushed past Lisa as if she weren't there, talking more to himself than to her. "I was married for eighteen years and I never managed to get Christine pregnant. Eighteen years! And it wasn't for lack of trying either!"

Lisa winced and turned away as Jake sat at the edge of the bed to put on his shoes. She held back her tears with effort. "Jake, I don't like to hear about that."

"Hear what? That I slept with another woman? She was my wife."

His words lashed Lisa like a whip. Her fingers twisted convulsively as she clasped her hands together. There was no way to reach him. He believed terrible things about her, and there was nothing she could do about it. It was her worst nightmare relived in broad daylight. She tried it once more.

"I understand you were married, and I try to deal with it, truly I do, Jake."

"At least I could be sure that Christine was faithful. That's more than I can say for you. "

"Don't say that!" she screamed at him. Then, quieter, she made another attempt. "I thought we were going to be married. That's what you've always said. I thought . . . "

"Well, you can stop thinking about it!"

Lisa flushed and clenched her fists, her terrible hurt turning into anger. She controlled her rising temper with an effort, saying in a soft, strained voice, "Jake, you are wrong. You are the father of my child. You are not now and never have been sterile."

"You're forgetting the tests."

"Tests can be wrong!"

"No, that won't work." He finished dressing and reached down to retrieve a button he spotted on the floor. "Christine arranged for a second test, using the same samples so I wouldn't be humiliated again. I'll never forget how difficult it was for Christine when she had to tell me the results. She never cried, she never did that, but she was so upset that day, it took me hours to calm her down."

It took Lisa a moment to grasp what he had said, "She told you?" she asked incredulously. "Didn't you see the results for yourself?"

"Christine was so hysterical, she destroyed them, but it

didn't matter. I didn't want to see them! I didn't even want to think about it!"

"But what if she lied!" Lisa cried.

Jake turned on her in fury. "Damn it, Christine was my wife! In eighteen years, I never found a reason to doubt her." Jake strode into the living room, Lisa trailing behind. Tears of helplessness were streaming down her face.

"Where are you going?" she demanded.

"Home. To my daughter."

"What about me?"

"What about you?"

"Can't you at least have the tests done one more time? Give me the benefit of the doubt?" she pleaded, her question ending in a sob.

"Just how much do you think a man can take? It's bad enough that apparently all the people in town are thinking that Miss Innocent has been impregnated by Yours Truly. Straightening that misconception out is not going to be amusing at all."

"Damn you, Jake!" she cried in horror, seeing her reputation tarnished in her own community.

He halted abruptly on the porch. Lisa almost collided with him. She took a step backward to stand in the doorway and looked up at him mutely. His face twisted in a sneer.

"One question, Lisa." He thrust his hand into his pockets, looking deceptively casual. "Who else have you been sleeping with? The same guy?"

"You bastard." She pushed him so violently he stumbled, almost falling down the steep steps, catching himself at the last moment on the railing. She slammed the screen door and cried, "Go away then! I never want to see you as long as I live!"

Jake made no reaction. He looked at her through the mesh door as though she had ceased to exist, then swung around to descend the long flight of steps.

Lisa was stunned by his actions as well as her own. They were both acting like first class fools, throwing away something precious. She couldn't let him get away without one more attempt. She threw her pride to the wind, flung open the door and chased him down the staircase, catching him at the bottom and clutching at his shirt.

"Jake!" she begged him. "Please!"

He paid her no attention as he searched his pockets for the keys to the Corvette.

"Jake," she pleaded again. "I'm sorry I pushed you. Please stay and talk to me. I'm begging you! You can't walk away. You owe me something, you must realize that. You owe me a hearing."

Jake noticed the keys in the ignition, and, as if remembering his haste of the night before, smile wryly. He pushed Lisa aside and slid into the car, closing the door with a resounding thump, nearly catching her in it.

She pounded on the glass that separated them, slumping against the side of the shiny exterior. "You fool," she wept bitterly. "You stupid, blind fool."

She withered for a moment under his icy gray stare, then her pride reasserted itself. She straightened and lifted her chin. "All right then, it will be my baby," she said levelly. "Do you hear me, Jake?" she said louder through the glass. "This baby will be mine alone. I'll raise him myself. At least I'll get to keep this one! Isn't that a laugh? You took my baby and now I'll keep yours!"

She whirled around and ran back up the staircase into her cabin, slamming the door behind herself.

Jake's emotions were frozen as he watched Lisa rushing away from him. He was too numb to know what he felt about her. It was best to go home and think about it later. He shook his head slightly as he turned over the motor and put the Corvette in gear. He already was backing it out of her short driveway when he caught sight of the light blue van turning into the roadway that connected the two lakeside properties. As he braked the car and waited for the van to pass, Jake glanced into his rear view mirror, catching sight of the driver, a dark-haired woman, and a laughing passenger who for some reason sat not in the right hand seat but behind his chauffeur.

The van smoothly passed Lisa's driveway to rest next to the second cabin. Jake threw the Corvette into reverse, spinning backwards to the road. He sped off faster than he had ever traversed the old road before and was over a mile away, approaching the ancient wooden bridge, when he thought about that male face in the van. He wondered why it seemed so familiar to him. He idly cataloged the features: a laughing face, with crinkling brown eyes, a crooked grin. The hair was white, prematurely, Jake thought, because the face was youthful. No, it was the freckles that made the face young. And the lopsided ......

The sports car screeched to a halt, throwing dirt across the little bridge and into the woods. Clouds of dust flew up, almost obliterating the white car.

The dust had long settled when Jake turned the Corvette around and drove back to the two cabins. This time, he passed the first building without so much as a glance and parked his car next to the van. He paused to give it a cursory examination before striding down the paved path. He noted that there were no steps leading up to the entrance, only a gentle incline. He knocked at the door sharply, hearing voices inside.

A petite dark-haired woman appeared at the door. "We've been expecting you," she said and smiled.

Lisa sobbed her fury and hurt into her pillow. She cursed Jake Gannett for throwing away the happiness that might have been theirs. What was wrong with that man anyhow? Why did he have to leave without listening? Did he really have such a low opinion of her that he could believe that she would take another lover? And how could he think that she would lie about whose baby she was carrying? He told her so many times he loved her. Didn't love include respect and trust?

Damn him! She viciously punched the pillow his head had rested on. Several feathers flew up to float gracefully in a sunbeam before settling to the floor. I'm better off without him, she thought, then sobbed afresh, because she knew it wasn't true.

Some minutes later, she sniffed a few times and finally judged herself to be all cried out, at least for the moment. She sat up on the bed to think about what she should do next. Go on, she told herself miserably, hugging her legs, go on. Get dressed, go to the office. You still have to make a living. You have responsibilities, even more so now.

She thought about the new beginning she held inside her and rested her hands over her stomach. She tried to picture this child. Jake was dark. Would the baby look like him? She conjured up an image of a sturdy little boy with gray eyes and unruly black hair, demanding a hamburger, fries and a shake, and she almost started wailing again.

No! She had to consider practical matters. She wiped away her tears defiantly and started to consider her problem. First, how could she cope with this pregnancy? She remembered her first pregnancy, which had been difficult, with long bouts of nausea and occasional fainting. Perhaps that had been because she had been upset. But she was just as upset now and the early indications weren't good. The "flu" of the preceding weeks was now explained.

If she constantly felt ill, would she be able to continue her business? Perhaps it was time she took a partner. Richard had been urging her to do it for some time now, though his idea had been that she should have time to travel and enjoy herself. He certainly hadn't meant that she should go out and get pregnant.

What would it be like raising a child by herself? Would this cabin be large enough for two? She studied the bedroom, pondering the problem of moving the furniture to accommodate a crib and perhaps a changing table. She wondered if she had kept enough matching material to make a little quilt to match hers.

She found herself cradling a pillow and smiled mistily. For so long, her thoughts had been centered on her daughter, watching her grow in her imagination, even before seeing her photograph on Jake's dresser. Now she remembered the baby she had held in her arms for such a short time so many years ago. She smoothed the end of the pillow as if it were that child's downy head. A new baby would be wonderful, but it would never replace the little girl she had lost.

She still wanted Jake and Jodi desperately, but she would have to learn to deal with that. Would Jake want to remain in Norway? How would both families manage to live in the same town, she carrying an illegitimate baby that everyone would know was his, and Jake trying to raise a daughter he now knew belonged to her? Lisa decided that Jake would have to agree to seeing her at least once more to discuss what they should do.

Jodi was settling down so well in Norway, making friends and enjoying small town life. It would be cruel to uproot her again. Lisa still wanted the best possible life for her daughter. If there was no other solution, she, her new child, and possibly Richard, could make a new life for themselves elsewhere. She was an old hand at starting over.

Lisa became aware of that familiar and painful rumbling emanating from her stomach. She rose wearily and padded to the kitchen. The best thing for this slight morning queasiness would be some toast and if that stayed down, perhaps some coffee.

She was sitting at the kitchen table tentatively nibbling the toast and waiting for the fresh pot to finish perking when she heard a frantic knocking at her door. She dived into the bedroom to slip a pair of disreputable jeans under Jake's shirt before answering the pounding. It was Gordie, his sandy hair flying every which way, worry, written all over his usually placid face.

"Lisa, have you seen Jodi? Her bike's not here," he said hoarsely.

"Jodi?" Lisa stared at him stupidly, wondering why on earth he thought Jodi would be at her cabin. She was the last person Jodi would consider visiting.

"Where's Jake? I gotta talk to him. " Gordie was perspiring profusely, his face red with exertion. She could see his mountain bicycle behind him at the bottom of the steps, thrown carelessly thrown on the ground.

"Jake's not here."

"I know he's here. I gotta talk to him," Gordie insisted.

"But he left almost a half hour ago!" Lisa exclaimed, embarrassed that even Gordie knew where Jake had spent the night.

"Look, Lisa, I know he's here!" Gordie blushed and muttered almost inaudibly, "If he's got to get dressed or something, I can wait out here, but it's important that I talk to him. I think Jodi's missing."

Lisa seized the boy's arms, searching his blue eyes. "What do you mean, she's missing? She's with Neil and Beth, isn't she?"

"She was, but when Jake didn't come to get her when he said he would this morning, she went home and got her bike. Then she came over to my house and told me she was going to come here. I think she wanted to talk Jake into going home. She was really upset that he . . . uh, spent the night here. I told her she was crazy, Lisa, but she wouldn't listen to me, she never does. She took off on her bike and I followed her. I thought I was right behind her but she isn't here. I don't see how I could have lost her, there's just the one set of roads." There were tears in the boy's eyes. "I think she took your shortcut over the hills."

"Oh, no, she could be lost! And there are old mine shafts up there!"

"That's why I gotta talk to Jake," Gordie repeated.

"But I've told you, he's not here!" Lisa cried.

"Then why is his car here?"

Lisa pushed Gordie out of the doorway and rushed to the porch railing to discover the white Corvette shining in the sun, parked next to Richard's van. She clutched at the wooden trellis, struggling to control the churning in her stomach.

"Oh, no, what now?" she groaned, unmindful of the boy.

She took a step toward the steps, then shook her head. Jodi, she thought, think about Jodi first, then worry about all that must be happening at Richard's cabin.

She quickly took charge of the situation. "Gordie," she rapped out sharply, "I want you to go to my brother's cabin and get Jake. Tell him I'm on the way to find my daughter. I'm going to take along one of those cans of orange spray paint we used to make signs with for the car wash in May. I'll mark the trail so you can follow me."

She continue to shout out instructions to him as she raced through the cabin, grabbing a pair of tennis shoes, the aerosol can of paint, a length of strong but lightweight rope, and her cell phone.

"Tell Jake to be sure to follow the marks. It would be too dangerous for him to go to either side of the path. Oh yes, tell him to bring along Richard's first aid kit and call the sheriff's department for help. We may have to organize a search if she isn't along the trail. Oh, and don't let him forget his cell phone."

Lisa sat on the steps to pull on her shoes as Gordie hovered at the bottom of the stairway.

"Gordie," she exclaimed impatiently, "did you get all I told you?"

"Yes, ma'am."

"Then get going!" The boy still hesitated, looking at her with troubled eyes. Lisa gave him a shove as she rose, but he took only a few steps before he turned back to her.

"Lisa?"

"What is it?" she groaned.

"Did you say . . . your daughter?"

Lisa hesitated for only a split second before raising her chin in pride. "Yes," she said firmly. "Jodi is my daughter, my true daughter, but please keep that to yourself for the time being. I don't have time to explain it all to you. Right now, I intend to find her whether she wants me as a mother or not. Hurry! And tell Jake not to miss my marks. He doesn't know the way any better than you do."

She waved the boy on his way and sped off down the shadowy trail.

Chapter Fifteen

Though his long frame had collapsed into the depths of a soft easy chair, Jake was anything but relaxed. His disbelieving eyes were riveted on the man in the wheelchair. Now that he was close to Richard Fratelli, Jake could see the lines of sadness and pain etched on his face. Straps held him in his metal prison, a modern contraption with devices that enabled him to control his movements around the room, but a prison nonetheless. His hands lay helplessly on the tray before him, making occasional spasmodic movements that he could not control. His immobile legs, useless, rested on metal supports. Richard Fratelli was a quadriplegic.

"More coffee?" the deceptively petite brunette asked. Marlene Anderson, Richard's nurse-secretary-friend, had already demonstrated her remarkable strength while going about her usual duties.

Jake shook his head and surveyed the cabin, realizing now why it had been built so much closer to the road level than Lisa's cabin. All the rooms were constructed with its wheelchair occupant in mind. Doors were wider, counters and table tops lower. From his position in his easy chair, Jake noticed how many things, books, binoculars, cameras, were placed precisely in a way to give Lisa's brother easy access. In her whirlwind tour of the place, Marlene had demonstrated all the clever innovations that Richard and Lisa had devised to make life easier for a quadriplegic. Using only his head and facial muscles, Richard could do a great deal for himself.

A sliding glass door opened to a deck with a closely fitted board floor that would pose no problems for the wheelchair. The railings on the deck were mounted with countless bird feeders. At the moment, several gaudy hummingbirds were vying for the nectar in a bright red and yellow container.

"Richard writes books about wildlife," Marlene explained as she pushed a tray of sweet rolls at Jake. "It's amazing how much we can see from the deck. It's a regular observation post.

So many animals and birds live around the lake, all we have to do is watch."

"We both write," Richard interrupted. "We co-author the books. Marlene does most of the photography though I manage a good digital photo now and then."

"Richard dictates the articles," Marlene amended. "He has more imagination than I do. But I can spell better!"

Jake took another sip from his cup. It was a perfect home for a man like Richard Fratelli, but as fascinating as it was, his eyes were drawn back again to the two framed pictures that rested on the bookshelf beside Richard Fratelli's desk. The first was a school picture of Jodi. Lisa must have spirited it from his home during their unpacking stage. Next to it was an old photograph of two children, a sandy-haired boy of perhaps twelve and a younger blond girl, apparently Lisa, if he could judge by the emerald eyes. It was the boy that held Jake's attention. Other than his sex, he was Jodi's twin, with identical eyes, nose and mouth. Those features, in a more mature form, were repeated on the face of the man in the wheelchair.

Richard Fratelli was frowning. "I wasn't ready for this," he muttered.

"When would you have been ready?" Marlene demanded snappishly. "You put Lisa in a lousy spot, making her promise not to tell Jake about you. She deserved better than that and you know it."

The handicapped man flinched at her attack. His hands moved convulsively on the tray attached to the wheelchair. "Can you understand why?" he whispered. He followed Jake's eyes as they examined the photographs again. "I was so happy to find out about that little girl, to know that something good came out of the mess I'd caused. She's beautiful, isn't she? Lisa says she's bright, too, and . . ."

"Lisa brags about her, and that's a fact," Marlene interrupted. "If you can believe her, Jodi is the most wonderful teenager on the face of the earth."

"I know how she feels," Richard said. "I wish I could see her for myself. But I don't know how to face her. How would she react to . . . what I am?"

"I still don't understand this," Jake said, dazed. "You're Lisa's brother, yet . ."

"Foster brother. My parents took Lisa in when they found out that I was the only natural child they could have. I was eight and Lisa was six when she came to us." The wheelchair-bound man sighed. "We were all crazy about her, right from the start. You would understand if you had seen her. She was such a little thing with such big eyes. She was scared to death of all of us and everything around her. We were pretty boisterous. It took her a while to get used to that. She must have had some lousy experiences in those other foster homes she'd been staying in because she wouldn't talk at all at first.

"But my mother was one of those hugging Italians with lots of love for everyone. Mom just kept loving Lisa and working with her until she started coming around. Do you know, the social workers told us Lisa was marginally retarded? Lisa!" Richard snorted.

"It's hard to believe anybody could be so stupid," Marlene agreed.

"Then she started tagging along after me," Richard continued. "I would take her along when I went on explorations in the woods. She got to know these hills better than I did after a while. She still spends all of her free time out there. I think she finds peace." Richard stared pensively out the large window at the deep blue lake. "I envy her that.

"The two of us grew up together and did everything you can think of. We were inseparable. There wasn't a thing I asked of Lisa that she wouldn't try to do. She trusted me completely, you see. And I betrayed that trust."

"But . . . are you Jodi's father?" Jake cut in impatiently.

"Yes, of course, I just told you that. You can see it for yourself in the pictures."

"You better tell me about it," Jake said grimly. Here was the man who had haunted his dreams, a man he had hated, a man he had wanted to slug for what he had done to Lisa. And here he was, a man who sat in a wheelchair, unable to defend himself from the least attack. Jake clenched his fists in frustration.

Fratelli avoided Jake's eyes. "You have to understand what we were like then to even begin to comprehend what happened. I was a crazy kid, only seventeen, trying every fool thing that came up. Do you remember what you were like at that age?"

"Go on," Jake growled, admitting to nothing.

"I discovered girls about that time. To be blunt, I discovered sex. I chased everything in skirts in this county, I guess. But the girl that drove me crazy was my own sister. She was the most beautiful girl in Norway. She still is," he said, glancing

179

slyly at Jake. "Remember when you condemn me, that she has a similar effect on you. And she lived in my house, even shared a bathroom with me. Seemed like she was always in that bathroom, half-naked, whenever I walked in. It was all I could do to control myself. I dreamed about her at night, I thought about her all day. My grades were getting worse, I started to lose interest in everything, even basketball!"

He met Jake's scornful glare with defiance. "Look, I can only say this in my defense: other guys my age were having the same problems with their hormones. I bet there were at least fifty other guys in the Norway high school who were in love with Lisa. But I had to live with her day in and day out, and knowing that she was no blood relation made it even worse!"

Richard lowered his head as Jake rose and paced around the room, running his hands through his hair. He walked out to the veranda for a long moment, pounding a fist against the railing. He didn't want to hear this, yet it must be faced. He had to know. He spun on his heel and returned to the living room and an ashen-faced Richard. Marlene was hovering nearby, not knowing how to comfort the man.

"It's O.K.," Jake told her brusquely. "I'm ready to listen now. Let's get it over with." He threw himself back into the chair, gripping the armrests as if he could thus hold on to his sanity.

Richard winced. "I know it's no excuse, but I'd been drinking. I'd been to a beer party, you know the kind. A bunch of kids with a couple of kegs at a stone quarry way out in the woods. The whole object was to see who could get the most bombed out." He grimaced. "I guess I won. Somehow I got home, I don't know how. Maybe somebody dumped me off, I don't remember. Mom and Dad were gone that weekend, and Lisa was waiting for me, wearing this pretty little nightgown, all white and ruffly. She took one look at me and started to put me to bed. Lisa always tried to take care of me, worrying about my grades, nagging me about my friends, my drinking, and so on. She mothered me and that made it worse. She never though of me as anything but a brother, you see."

"But you took her anyway," Jake snarled, holding on to his temper only marginally.

"She fought me, but I guess in the long run, it was just that she never could refuse me anything I wanted. And I wanted her." The paralyzed man shifted his eyes to the floor, avoiding Jake's reproachful stare. "I think I hurt her pretty badly. I heard her crying the next morning . . . Look, it was a bad time for both of us. I hate myself even more than you do whenever I think of it and I think of it all the time."

Jake swallowed painfully, but the taste of bile remained. He wanted to cry, for himself, for Lisa, and strangely, for this man, who had suffered as much as anyone. But he couldn't let it rest, he had to know the whole story.

"What did you do when you found out she was pregnant?" he demanded.

"My mother figured it out first, noticed a few things. I think Lisa was too naive to know what was going on. My mother certainly never told her much. Anyway, Lisa was just a kid and she hadn't even dated yet. She was only sixteen and my parents were protective."

"She must have gone through hell!"

"Don't you think I know that?" Richard cried.

"What happened then?"

"Mom told Dad. We were all up here then. My parents owned this land and we used to camp out over night. They always planned to build a cabin here some day, it was a dream they'd always shared." His eyes glistened with tears and Jake realized, with a start, that the man could not wipe away the drop that slipped down his cheek. "We were out there, just about on the curve of the road when it came out.

"My parents were emotional Italians. They started getting upset. They were shouting and yelling at Lisa, asking her to name the father. She refused to tell them. She knew that they would be furious at me, and she didn't want that at all. Even then, she was protecting me, taking care of me. But by the way she was looking at me, they figured I knew something about it and they started in on me."

"And?"

"I didn't tell them. I just kept my mouth shut."

"You said nothing? You let her take it?"

"I really was a jerk." Richard muttered.

"Then what?"

"My father ordered us all in the car and started to drive us home. Lisa was huddled up in a little ball in the back seat. I was back there, too. My parents were crying, yelling, cursing, I don't know what all. They both were turned in the seat, looking back at us. Lisa just sat there, sobbing, and then . . . " Richard's face was a study in agony, as he relived those terrible moments.

"Yes?" Jake prompted grimly.

"A deer ran out of the woods, right in front of the car. Dad swerved to avoid it. Maybe he could have avoided the accident if he'd been watching the road, I don't know, but as it was, we hit a tree, head on."

"My God! Were you all . . . "

"None of us were wearing seat belts. You can guess the rest."

"You were . . . "

"I was thrown out of the car. The spinal cord is completely severed and I've been like this ever since."

"Lisa?" Jake asked hoarsely. My God, he thought, what this must have done to her! His memory played back that first night at the Highway Supper Club and how upset she had been at her careless driving. She had never recovered from this accident, he realized.

"Lisa had a slight concussion, nothing more," Richard sighed. "She didn't even lose the baby. I'm glad about that now, though at the time it didn't seem much of a blessing. No, Lisa came through the accident with only a few bumps, and she was out of the hospital the next day. But in some ways, she was damaged as much as I was. She had to walk out of these woods to find help for me, all the time knowing . . . "

"Your parents?"

"Killed on impact. So I have that on my conscience as well." He openly sobbed as Marlene rose to gently wipe away his tears.

Jake slumped back into his chair, stunned at the enormity of what Lisa had endured. And there was still more, it hadn't ended with the accident. Like a prosecuting attorney, he drove on relentlessly. "What happened after that? Lisa was having your baby. Did you ever think about marriage? At least you could have offered her that!"

"How?" Richard laughed bitterly, looking down at his body. "Even if I hadn't been injured, we were both minors, wards of the state. I had no other relatives, neither did Lisa! She was put into another foster home almost immediately, her worst nightmare come true. And after the hospital and funeral bills were paid, there was almost no money left in my parents' estate, so I was placed in a state hospital. For rehabilitation, they said, though I only wanted to die.

"The next time Lisa and I saw each other again, she was

eighteen. The baby had been put up for adoption and she was finally let loose from the social services system. I was a basket case when she found me. If I could have arranged it, I would have committed suicide. If there had been a plug to pull, I would have pulled it. When Lisa showed up at the hospital, I refused to see her. "

"But you're together now," Jake said, "and you seem to be coping with your disability."

Richard gave a short laugh. "Lisa's a determined woman, or hadn't you noticed? She just charged into that hospital and told me that I was all she had in the world and that we were going to stick together. She refused to listen to anything I or any of the hospital staff had to say. She took charge of me and I haven't managed to escape her yet. In a way," he added thoughtfully, "I think I may have saved her sanity. I became a replacement for her baby. I was someone she could take care of."

" But how did you manage? I don't suppose either of you had a high school diploma."

"She's an amazing woman, Jake Gannett, and don't you ever forget it. She got a job as a waitress while she worked at getting her high school equivalency diploma, then studied for her broker's license. She's been working on a college degree as well, did she tell you that? Top grades, too. And all the time doing her best for the both of us. It took her a while, but she got me out of the state hospital and into private rehabilitation. She managed to get this land back and had the two homes built. The second, the one she's living in now, was my idea. I though if Marlene could take over here, Lisa would find a life for herself." He added, "You'll notice there's no ramp there, I insisted on that. I wanted her to feel free to have dates visit her."

"It worked, didn't it?" Marlene laughed.

"So Lisa doesn't take care of you any more?" Jake asked.

"Oh, I wouldn't say that," Richard objected. "She's still around here every day, and whenever Marlene needs a break, Lisa is right here to spell her." He considered Jake slyly. "Though with one thing and another, Marlene hasn't had many breaks the last couple of months."

"I haven't minded a bit," his companion said. "It's about time Lisa had some fun. You're exactly what she's needed. I was happy to see your car parked over there. But what we both want to know now is what you plan on doing next."

"What do you mean?" Jake asked blankly.

"Are you going to marry my sister?" Richard asked mildly. "I believe this is known as asking your intentions."

"You better or I'll take a shotgun to you," Marlene threatened.

"Then you know . . . ?"

"That Lisa is pregnant?" the woman grinned. "Oh, yes. Not that she's said anything, mind you, but I can figure out morning sickness as well as the next person." Marlene struck a threatening pose, her hands on her hips. "So what do you intend to do about it?"

"Nothing."

"What do you mean, nothing?" Richard asked in astonishment.

"Just that," Jake said with deceptive calm. "It's not my baby, after all."

Richard's hands made spasmodic tattoos on his tray. "Marlene," he cried in frustration. "Punch him in the nose for me."

The brunette looked as though she were willing to do just that. "What in hell do you mean, it's not your baby?"

"I am physically incapable of being the father," Jake grated, hating this conversation. Must he be humiliated over and over again? He was being made to feel less than a man. "The baby isn't mine," he repeated. "I was tested fifteen years ago. That's why we adopted Jodi."

"I think it's time to have the tests done again," Richard suggested mildly. "If Lisa says you're the father, believe me, you are the father. Lisa doesn't lie."

"You don't think that there's someone around here that . . ."

"Damn it, Lisa's not like that!" Richard bellowed. "I was astonished enough that she had anything to do with you! And other than watching the woods around here, what do you think I have to do? There's only been one other car in our driveway in the last three months and that's your Corvette. I can give you dates and times. And if you don't believe me, you can ask anyone in Norway. You can be sure they've been keeping tabs on both of you."

"What exactly did those tests show anyhow?" Marlene demanded.

"I never saw them, so I'm not sure . . . " Jake began slowly.

"You never saw them! So you don't know anything, do you!" Marlene cried. "Let me tell you something, Jake Gannett, a

184

lot of interesting research has been done in the last two decades. Doctors have found out that there are very few cases of out-and-out sterility. Low sperm counts maybe, but all it takes is one, buster. So unless you and Lisa have been spending those nights in her cabin discussing Great Works, I suggest you have those tests done again," Marlene insisted.

Jake reddened. "You want me to go through that humiliation again?"

"Humiliation! No, you don't have to . You can just take Lisa's word for it, that would be the simplest thing. Instead, you're turning away from your own child when you could verify whether the baby is yours or not with one simple visit to a doctor." Marlene rose and stalked away in disgust.

Richard was speechless in the face of such stupidity.

Jake looked from one to the other, his mind flying back to the day when he had come home to a distraught Christine, who had, only moments before, returned from the clinic where they had both been tested. She had gone back, without him, to find out the results of their tests, and at the time, he did not question her reasons.

He remembered her tear-stained face, her untidy hair, her rumpled clothing. His perfectly coiffed, beautifully dressed Christine, the perfect housekeeper, hostess, and wife, who never allowed herself to be anything less than the best.

How would she have reacted to being told that she could never be a mother? That she had a physical imperfection? Would she have admitted it to him or to herself? Had she told him the truth?

Or had she lied to him, told him that he was the one at fault? Just as she had kept her heart problem a secret from him? As she had kept Jodi's adoption a secret from her?

Could he have been wrong? Was Lisa really carrying his child? Would she ever forgive him for his accusations?

He cleared his throat to admit his doubts to Richard, when they were interrupted by a window-rattling knock on the door. Marlene did not even have time to turn before a disheveled Gordie burst into the room.

"Jake, Jodi's missing! Lisa's gone to find her!"

Chapter Sixteen

Lisa trekked up the steep incline through the forest, following the faint trail that marked her private shortcut, pacing herself with smooth, strong strides while pushing herself to go as quickly as possible. From time to time, she sprayed a bush or tree with a slash of Day-Glo orange from the aerosol can of paint once used for a youth group project. She winced as she made each mark: she hated defacing her cherished path, yet it was the fastest way to point the way to those that followed her. She prayed that the paint would last.

The path curved and twisted for an easier, more gradual passage, but continued to climb higher and higher into the hills. Lisa paused to catch her breath. On another day, she would have enjoyed the sunlight gleaming against the broad assortment of greens and would have tarried for the occasional glimpses of brooks and ponds. But now she hurried on, worrying about her little girl. Jodi needed her, she was sure of it. All of her instincts told her so.

Far below, she heard Jake's rumbling shout, calling her name, and the tenor echo that must be Gordie. Good! They were following her and she could plan on their help if she needed it, but she could not wait. If Gordie was right, and she suspected he was, Jodi had taken this trail, dragging her bicycle along. If she had strayed, Lisa should be able to find the spot and begin her search there. It was possible she was only lost. The sheriff's department could help them if that were the case.

But there were so many other things the girl could have stumbled into! Lisa had always appreciated the dangers of this wilderness. For starters, there were the animals: besides the deer, moose, beaver and other harmless creatures, there were potentially dangerous predators. What if Jodi met a female bear and her cub? They were very common in these northern woods. Lisa had spotted twin cubs in this area recently. Would Jodi have the sense to back away? Would she know enough to leave apparently unattended cubs alone? Mother bears were fiercely protective: Lisa knew exactly how they felt!

And what about bobcats and mountain lions? They should have plentiful food supplies and would be wary of a human, Lisa assured herself. Jodi would be all right as long as she left them alone.

But what if one of the old mines had collapsed? There had been several severe thunderstorms in the past few weeks, real downpours. Sometimes that would be enough to loosen the soil and allow the earth to follow its natural gravitational course inward. Lisa always carefully tested the ground with her walking stick along the paths after rainstorms. Some of the old mine tunnels were dangerously close to the surface, waiting for the inevitable collapses that would fill them in, returning the land to its natural state. If Jodi had fallen into one of those . . . but Lisa refused to think about it any more. She would deal with whatever had happened when she found Jodi.

She hurried on, no longer listening to the sounds of Jake and Gordie thrashing through the woods as they tried to catch up with her. She strained to hear her daughter's cry, trying to block out the sounds of nature, the sigh of the wind through the pines, the songs of the birds.

Now she began to call herself. "Jodi! Jodi, where are you?" she shouted. "I'm coming for you, baby!"

She paused once more, but heard her own voice echoing down through the valleys. Even Jake and Gordie were silent. She sprayed another Day-Glo mark and rushed on, calling from time to time. She saw nothing of the beauty of the hills. She thought only of her daughter, the child she had cherished in her heart all those years. Dear God, she prayed silently, don't take her away from me now.

Jake raced upward, gasping for breath as he adjusted to the higher altitude, Gordie and Marlene at his heels. Fear clutched at Jake's heart as he searched for the bright splashes that meant Lisa was ahead of them. Jodi was up there somewhere in the hills and something had happened to her, if Gordie was right. Lisa was up there, too, he could hear her shouting. She was in no condition to be running through the woods. She had fainted only last night and Marlene said it wasn't the first time it had happened.

How dare Lisa risk her life and the life of his child! When he got his hands on her, he thought .... then half-laughed, half-sobbed. When he got his hands on her, he would hug and kiss her senseless, then drop on his knees in abject apology. For now he knew beyond all doubt that it was his baby she carried. Richard was right, Lisa would never lie to him, could never go willingly to another man's bed. Any doubts had been because of his own insecurities, and if he had concentrated on Lisa's character, he would have realized the truth at once.

He was going to be a father! Tears blurred Jake's vision as he struggled to catch his breath. Before the end of this day, he stood to lose everything that meant anything to him. Where were Lisa and Jodi? Jake quickened his pace and in his haste missed an orange mark. Gordie's quick call brought him back to the pathway.

"Jake, we've got to pay more attention!" the boy gasped. "We could end up at the bottom of some mine shaft."

Jake paled, as he pictured his daughter, her body crushed and broken in the darkness of some pit. He slowed his pace and shouted at the hills, "Lisa, Jodi, where are you?"

No answer came back. Lisa was no longer crying out above them. The hills were silent, revealing none of their secrets. Jake shuddered and reached out to touch another bright slash of paint on a small pine tree. It was still wet. Lisa wasn't far ahead of them.

Lisa heard the frightened whimpering before she noticed the fresh cut in the earth near the trail. She stopped immediately and listened intently to the soft cries that easily could have been those of a wounded animal. She dropped to her knees, inching closer and closer to the jagged rip in the clearing in front of her. She noticed that several trees were tilting toward the opening and that the ground felt spongy beneath her. There was a tremor beneath her and she froze as she heard a shrill scream. She could venture no further without some kind of support.

"Jodi!" she called softly. "Jodi? Are you there?"

"Who is it? Lisa? Where's Daddy?" The girl was terrified, her voice breaking in fear.

"Where are you, honey? Can you tell me exactly?"

"I want my daddy. Where is he?" she sobbed.

Lisa struggled to maintain a calm note, keeping her voice low and soothing. "He'll be here in a few minutes, Jodi. Don't worry, he and Gordie are following right behind me, I can hear them coming. Where are you, baby? Are you all right?"

Jodi was nearly hysterical, her voice screeching wildly. "I'm in this hole! Of course I'm not all right, can't you see that? I fell in here with my bike but the bike went in all the way." She sobbed for a moment and Lisa almost missed her choked out, "Lisa?"

"Yes, dear?"

"It fell for a long time before it hit anything." Jodi half-whispered.

Oh, my God, Lisa agonized, she's at the top of a swope. But at least she hadn't followed the path of her bicycle. "Where are you, Jodi?" she repeated hoarsely. "Are you on some sort of ledge?"

"No, I'm hanging on to some kind of tree root, I think, and there's nothing below me but this hole. Please tell Daddy to hurry. I can't hold on much longer and I don't think this root is very strong. It moved a little while ago. What if it's pulling loose? Oh!" the girl shrieked. "It's happening again!"

One of the tilting birch trees swayed slightly, its leaves shimmering in the sunlight as they moved. Lisa caught her breath as she realized that the day was windless. Carefully keeping any note of panic out of her voice, she called out, "I'll be down to help you in a minute so hang on!"

"I want my daddy," Jodi sobbed, "please send my daddy."

"We'll be along, baby, but I think we can get started while we wait. Hang on!" Lisa chattered on, cheerfully explaining what she was doing as she searched the edge of the small clearing for something solid to use as a base. "Think what a great adventure this will be to tell your friends about!" she exclaimed.

"Don't you dare tell anyone!" Jodi yelled. "I'd die if they found out about it! I'd feel so dumb!"

At least her mind is on something else, Lisa mused as she worked around the hole. There was an old maple tree some feet away that still stood straight and felt firm no matter how much Lisa pushed at it. Lisa quickly tied one end of her rope around a sturdy branch, using a boy scout knot whose name she had forgotten. Gordie had taught her how to tie knots in his puppy love days and she hoped and prayed that he had known what he was doing and that she was following his instructions properly. She tested the line, yanking at it with all her might, and to her relief, it held. She fastened the other end around her waist. As she worked, she shouted encouragement to the child below her, describing her movements and suggesting silly explanations Jodi could give her friends as to why she had been in that old hole.

"Maybe you were planning on running away to the circus and this is part of your acrobat act," she trilled. "No? How about you wanted Gordie to dash to your rescue, like a Tom Cruise or Brad Pitt?"

"No way!" but Jodi's half-giggle floated up. "Justin Bieber."

"I stand corrected!" Lisa laughed as she at last grasped the rope, and hand over hand, began to back slowly toward the hill. She made one last gigantic slash with her can of paint, with a point at the end to form an arrow on the ground. She could not wait for Jake and Gordie, time was too important. Besides, she was the logical choice to go down. She would never risk Gordie's life this way and Jake was too big a man. She wasn't sure the line would hold his weight. There was no sense in waiting for them and spending useless time arguing about it. She finished her bright orange warning to them and tossed the paint can aside.

"Jodi, listen carefully," she called into the yawning aperture. "I want you to watch for me. I don't want to land on top of you, so you'll have to give me some direction. Let me know if I'm coming down O.K."

"I want my daddy to come," the girl said stubbornly and Lisa could almost see the pout on her face.

"He's on his way, honey, but I think we'd better start without him. That'll teach him to be on time for rescues! Anyway, we'll need his muscle to get us out of here. Now, I have to go slowly and some of this dirt might drop on you. You can close your eyes, but whatever you do, don't let go!"

Lisa worked her way backwards on her hands and knees over the spongy area, praying constantly that the ground above Jodi would not collapse. Oh Lord, what if she killed her own child? But what choice did she have? Jodi wouldn't be able to hang on much longer, she must have been dangling down there for at least half an hour already. Lisa could hear Jake's frantic shouts from the trail. He could be as much as five minutes away. She must go for Jodi now.

She slid backwards over the lip of the opening, working hand over hand, one leg wrapped firmly around the line. The darkness opened its ugly mouth to engulf her and for a second she hesitated, fearing the moment when she would be swallowed up in it. Jodi whimpered and Lisa moved at once from the sunlit outside world into the dark bowels of the earth. Now her feet were dangling over the vast nothingness, small pieces of dirt flying down beside her. She knew she must be very careful.

She judged that she was now in Jodi's line of vision. "Can you see me?" she called.

"Yes! Yes, I can!" the girl cried eagerly.

"Am I anywhere near you?"

"You're just to the right and above me. About six feet, I

think. I'm so glad to see another person!"

Even if that person is me, Lisa thought. "Has any of this dirt been falling on you?"

"No. It's over to the side."

At least collapsing soil would not endanger Jodi. Lisa resumed her slow descent, making numerous pauses to ascertain Jodi's position in relationship to her. Fine particles of dirt continued to filter down from the edge of the pit, clinging to the rope and making her grip even more tenuous. She soon realized that she would never be able to pull the two of them up, the rope would be too slippery. The best she could do was to rescue Jodi from her perch and hold on to her. She heard the girl moan and knew how her arms must be aching. If only this line was long enough to reach her! She hoped that Jake would arrive soon.

"Hang on, honey," she called again. "I'll be there in a little bit."

"Hurry! Please hurry!"

Lisa resisted the urge to comply with the girl's pleas, reminding herself to move gingerly.

But as she worked her way down the side of the sliding sandy soil, Lisa had yet another fear. She was beginning to feel dizzy again, just as she had at the band concert the night before. Swaying back and forth over the enormous void wasn't helping at all. She paused for a moment and struggled to control her nausea. Oh baby, she whispered to the small life growing inside her, don't do this to us. Your big sister needs me. She shook her head to clear it, pausing for a few seconds to regain her strength.

"Lisa?" Jodi said plaintively.

"Yes . . . yes, honey, I'm coming," Lisa replied and began to move again. She had to hang on, had to get her daughter out of there.

"Oh, Jake," she murmured under her breath, "please hurry. We need you. I need you."

"Lisa!" Jodi cried out suddenly, startling Lisa so much she almost lost her grip. "Your foot is right next to my head. I could almost touch . . . "

"No! Don't let go yet! I want to be next to you. Hang on just a little longer." Lisa calmed herself with an effort. She would not hurry herself into catastrophe, though the vertigo threatened her more and more as the wall of collapsing loam disappeared beneath her feet. Now only her upper torso had any contact with the earth. She inched down the muddy rope and with barely two feet of line left, she was finally face to face with her daughter, only a yard away.

"Hello, honey," Lisa smiled encouragingly. Her eyes were becoming accustomed to the half-light in the pit and she could see the frightened eyes gleaming in the dirt-covered, tear-stained little face. Jodi's shorts outfit was so filthy it was almost impossible to make out its yellow color. Lisa caught her breath at the scratch that ran along one of the girl's legs. It must hurt like the blazes. She had lost one of her tennis shoes, too. Blood from the scratch dripped down to color her toes a vivid red. Lisa's eyes filled with tears.

"Hello," Jodi whispered back. For the first time since their violent confrontation, mother and daughter were face to face. Jodi's hands clenched the root so tightly that even in the gloomy light, Lisa could see the ivory-white knuckles through the grime on her hands. How she loved this child!

"Jodi, listen to me carefully," she said, no longer trying to hide her emotion, "I want you to hang on tight for now, don't try to move. I've got to swing over and grab you. Some of this dirt will fall on us, so close your eyes until you feel me next to you."

"What do I do then?"

"As soon as you know I'm holding you, I want you to wrap your legs around my waist then put your arms around my neck. Your father and Gordie are going to be here any moment and they can pull us both up." Lisa tried to sound more confident than she felt. There was a buzzing in her ears and she was cold all over. Her grip on the rope was tenuous, yet she could not stop now.

She bumped and pushed along, swinging closer and closer to the child. A clump of sod whizzed past her head, painfully glancing off her should to fall below. Lisa listened and to her horror observed that she could not hear it hit below them. This shaft must be over a cavern similar to the Large Swope in the iron mine tour. God knew where the bottom was. Oh Jodi, Jodi, she silently chided her daughter, didn't I warn you about this very thing?

Lisa grunted softly as she collided with her daughter. She hadn't realized she was so near! Tears of relief came into her eyes as she quickly gathered Jodi into her left arm, protectively winding the line around her.

"Now, Jodi," she said calmly. "I'm going to help you let go of that root."

The girl, staring wildly at Lisa, didn't move.

193

"Jodi, I have you! You're going to have to let go now."

"I can't!" The girl's voice was shrill with fear. Her hands were frozen on the gnarled wood, which now seemed more secure to her than the swinging rope.

"You must!" Lisa insisted. "This line is solid, that root isn't." Lisa held her daughter even more tightly to her. "Jodi, try sliding your legs around my waist first. Please trust me, baby."

"I'm not your baby!"

"Oh, Jodi!"

"I'm not," the girl cried, "and even this won't make it so!"

Lisa furiously blinked away her tears of hurt and said evenly, "Have it your own way, Jodi, but whoever I am, I'm the one who is going to get you out of here. Your father would never forgive me if I let you fall now. So do us all a favor and help me. Hold on to me until they can get us out of here. Please?"

"Listen!" Jodi cried, paying no attention to her. From above came the sound of a rumbling male voice. Jake and Gordie had finally come!

"Jake!" Lisa screamed with all the force she could muster. "Don't come any closer. The ground isn't stable!"

"Lisa? Jodi! Are you both all right?"

"I'm O.K., Daddy," the girl called. "Please get me out of here. I want to go home."

"Tell us what to do, Lisa," Gordie called. "Marlene's with us, too, and the sheriff is on his way. Mr. Fratelli is watching from his window to direct him."

"Great," Lisa said weakly. "Marlene can help you pull us up, but wait a minute. Jodi's hanging on to a tree root and I'm right next to her. She's going to have to let go of the root and grab me before . . ." Lisa's voice trailed off. Her mind was getting so fuzzy! She tried again. "Let me know when you're ready to . . . start hauling us up. I'll . . . try . . . to . . . " She knew that they had barely heard her. Jodi was looking at her with such a strange expression. Her stomach churned and she lowered her head tiredly to her daughter's shoulder. Now needing her support as much as Jodi needed hers, she hung on for dear life.

"Daddy! Something's wrong with Lisa!"

"Damn it!" Jake groaned. "What's happening down there? I'm coming down."

"No!" Feeling Jake's hands on the clothesline, Lisa shook her head violently to revive herself once more. "This rope won't hold three of us, Jake! Don't think of trying it, you'd kill us all."

"My God, Lisa!" he cried.

"Jodi," Lisa begged, "you must do what I say. Now!"

"We're ready here," Jake yelled into the pit. "Jodi, follow Lisa's instructions. We're going to get you out of there now."

"Now, Jodi!" Lisa commanded. "Wrap your legs around my waist."

Lisa steadied herself and the girl, winding the rope even more tightly around the two of them. Jodi carefully positioned her legs as she had been instructed but her fingers were still wrapped around her precious handhold.

"Just one arm, honey," Lisa prompted her. "Do it for me."

"N . . . no," the girl sobbed. "I can't."

"Come on," Gordie ordered. "Jodi, don't be such an idiot!"

"Oooooh, you . . " the girl sputtered, but she unclenched one fist and slipped it hesitantly around Lisa's neck. More gravel and rocks began to slide down into the dark abyss, painfully pelting them. Jodi screamed and finally relinquished her hold, wildly swinging her other hand around her mother's neck in a desperate lunge.

"Now, Jake!" Lisa cried as the two of them spun in a circle over the void, debris dropping around them like hail, as the three people above strained to bring them upward to the light. All of them raised prayers, spoken and unspoken, that the line would not break from the strain.

Jake, who was the closest to the edge of the gaping chasm, was the first to sense the change in the line. Then Gordie and Marlene felt it, too: their burden had in some way become heavier. The three dug their heels into the ground and paused in their struggles, fearfully looking at each other. Something terrible had happened down there.

"Lisa!" Jake shouted.

"Daddy!" Jodi cried hysterically. "There's something wrong with Lisa. I . . . I think she fainted."

"Oh, no!" Marlene whispered. Jake glanced over his shoulder at her white face.

He took charge "Hang on to her, Jodi! We're going to have you both out of there as fast as we can." Jake grimly resumed his hand-over-hand efforts, determination written in his knotted muscles. He knew that he needed no tests, no other reassurances. He was bringing back his daughter, his own unborn child, and the woman he loved.

Chapter Seventeen

There was an acrid taste in Lisa's mouth as the sizzling sound that presaged consciousness stilled, and she became aware of the gentle sobbing beside her. Her eyelids flickered and opened, but slammed shut to close out the painful glare of the bright light from an open window. She groaned at the shooting spears of pain that shot out from somewhere in the middle of her head. It would be much easier to return to the dark world she had just left!

But the sobbing had stopped abruptly and when her curiosity got the better of her, Lisa forced her eyes open again. As her eyes focused to the brightness of the room, Lisa was amazed to find herself gazing into the tear-bright brown eyes of her daughter.

"Oh, Lisa!" Jodi cried. "You're awake! Are you all right?" Without waiting for a reply, the girl threw her head onto the crisp white sheets of the bed Lisa was lying on and wailed brokenly, "I'm so sorry. I'm so sorry. It was all my fault."

Lisa placed a hand that was strangely weak and shaking on her daughter's blond head, stroking it gently as she gazed around the room in bewilderment. Where was she? In some sort of room, she could see that, but where? Pale yellow walls cheerfully reflected the light from two large windows, whose institutional beige drapes were pulled back. She examined the functional furniture around her and slowly came to the realization that her head and back were slightly inclined on a hospital bed. This was a hospital room!

What was she doing here? The mine shaft, she remembered now. She and Jodi were dangling over that black void. Jake must have gotten them out then, but what happened after that? There was something she needed to know and she tried to force her confused brain into action. It was no use, Jodi's soft cries were too distracting. Why was she crying? And why was she here anyway?

Lisa frowned as she smoothed Jodi's rumpled hair once

197

more. It was so dirty! And though the girl had washed her hands and face, she still wore the yellow shorts set, though its color would be doubtful to those who had never seen it before. Who was taking care of Jodi, for heaven's sake? She must see about getting the girl into a shower.

She wondered what she looked like. Surely as filthy as Jodi! But no, her hands were clean . . . and she was in a hospital gown. When had that happened? She reached a week hand to her hair, gathered in a loose pony tail. It was combed out, though it was still a little dirty. How long had she been there? If only she could . . . remember. What was it that she had forgotten? Something to do with Jake.

A movement at the open doorway caught her attention and she shifted her head with painful effort. Jake, a happy smile on his unshaven face, strode to her bedside to present her with a deeply thorough kiss, to her embarrassment. She pushed at his muscular body, motioning at Jodi's wide-mouth stare, but Jake ignored her.

"Awake at last," he scolded her. "Have you any idea how worried we all were?" He found her mouth again and pressed her back into the pillow, neatly preventing her escape, his big hands resting firmly at her waist.

"What happened?" she asked hoarsely, when he gave a chance to breath. To her surprise, she found talking difficult. "I know I fainted, but then what . . ?"

"The dashing hero came to your rescue. We had to drag you out of that hole and bring you here." Jake took her left hand and perched on the bed, leaving the other side for Jodi. There really isn't much room left on here for me, Lisa thought irritably. It would serve him right if I got up and left. And what is the man grinning about? What's going on here? Though she had every intention of frowning, his grin was infectious and Lisa had to smile back. Everything was going to be fine now, she knew it by looking at the man. Even Jodi was smiling at the two of them through her tears, her adorable little nose crinkling. My little girl, Lisa thought with love, my own . . .

"Jake," she gasped, as her concern came to her as a quicksilver flash. "My baby! Is it . . . ?" Her free hand flew to her stomach.

"*Our* baby," Jake corrected her quickly, "is fine. He'll make his appearance as scheduled, come spring."

"He?" she quirked an eyebrow at him. Did he know something she didn't?

"Or she. It doesn't make any difference," he chuckled, waving his hand airily. "What's important is that you are both going to be all right now. I think you should give me some credit for having the forethought to bring along a trained nurse. If Marlene hadn't been there, I don't know what would have happened to you."

"What did happen?"

"There was a little bleeding."

"Oh, no," Lisa cried in horror.

Jake hastened to reassure her. "We had you out of those hills so fast we'll probably get some kind of mention in the Book of World Records. The sheriff's department sent for a helicopter. It was all very exciting, worth at least two columns in the local paper."

"But the baby will live," she repeated with satisfaction and relaxed against her pillow.

"Absolutely. You are going to have to rest for a day or two, and I expect you to take it easy for the next seven months, but the doctors are sure you'll carry our baby to term."

"Our baby?" Lisa's attention was caught by those words. "Our baby? You . . . believe me now? Have you . . . ? Were more . . . tests done?" Lisa wondered how she could discuss the matter with Jodi sitting there, absorbing every word.

"Why bother? I know it's mine. I may be a little bit slower than the residents of our town, but I figure things out eventually. With a little verbal kick from your brother, of course."

"Oh!" Lisa exclaimed. "Richard!" What else had happened while she was unconscious, she wondered, glancing fearfully at Jodi.

"By the way," Jake continued blithely, "I did have one little test run. Actually, two."

"Oh?"

"I had the doctors take some samples for our blood tests, just to expedite matters. We have to be married on Saturday."

"Have to . . . on *Saturday*?" Lisa squealed.

"Well, of course," he said patiently, as if explaining a simple matter to a child. "Beth has the wedding all planned. Neil will officiate, naturally, and the reception is at the parsonage. You'll have to shop for a dress, but I think Beth has everything else worked out. She's invited almost everyone in Norway."

"But Jake," she objected, struggling to sit up. "Don't I have anything to say about this? What if I refuse?"

"*You* have to face Beth." He grinned at her as he pushed the control button that raised her head.

"I told you we were doomed," she grumbled. "But why the rush?" She felt a little dizzy and it wasn't only because of her pregnancy and the sudden movement of the bed.

"I don't believe in long engagements and you've been wearing my ring for over an hour now."

Lisa's startled eyes finally beheld the sparkle of emeralds and diamonds on the hand Jake held so tenderly. He raised it to his lips in a tender tribute. "I've asked Richard to be my best man," he murmured.

"Oh!" Would the man ever stop pulling surprises out of his bag of tricks? Lisa questioned Jodi with a troubled glance.

"I know all about it," the girl quickly said and blushed. "I talked to . . . Richard . . . a little before I came to the hospital. There wasn't room for us all on the helicopter so Marlene took me to his house and he told me. He's very nice, isn't he?"

"Yes. Yes, he is. Then you know. . . ?"

"Yes, Lisa," Jodi nodded her head vigorously. "I know he's my real father."

"Oh no, Jodi!" Lisa cried. "Jake is your real father, don't ever think otherwise." She felt his hand tighten on hers and knew the pain he still felt. "Richard would tell you that himself," she insisted.

"He did," Jodi said pensively. "He said he'd just as soon be my uncle and that's the way I should look at him now."

"Oh, Jodi," Lisa said, her voice catching on a tiny sob, "he loves you as much as I do, always remember that. Do you forgive us?"

"I guess so," Jodi answered honestly. "I still feel a little confused about it. It's not easy."

"I can understand that," Lisa said sadly. "I know how confused I was when it all happened. I was only sixteen, but losing you was the worst hurt in my life. All I wanted was to keep you and love you. You were such a beautiful baby. But I gave you to good parents, didn't I?"

With a soft cry, Jodi threw herself into Lisa's arms. How right, how right, Lisa thought through her own tears, that I should be holding my baby again here in a hospital. My life has gone full circle.

She caught sight of Jake's shimmering eyes over the blond head at her shoulder. She smiled at him, her joy overflowing. She had everything she had dreamed of.

But there was one more thing to straighten out. She gave Jodi a quick hug and gently raised her up. She put the question to her squarely. "Jodi, do we have your blessing? I want you to be happy, too, when we take our vows on Saturday."

"Oh, sure, Lisa, it's fine with me," the girl said stoutly, but lowered her eyes, reddening as something flew into her mind.

"What is it, darling?" Lisa asked quickly.

"I should call you Mother now, shouldn't I?" Lisa almost missed the mumbled words, words that spoke of resignation but not total acceptance. Jodi was remembering the mother she had loved, still loved. She was not ready to betray the memory of that woman.

Lisa caressed Jodi's cheek tenderly. She had been given so much in the past few minutes; she could wait a little longer for this. "Jodi," she began slowly, "your mother was the woman who took care of you for me all these years and you are right to cherish her. I can never replace her. Don't call me 'Mother', save that title for her. But someday, when you feel that I've earned the right, maybe you could call me Mom. Until then, 'Lisa' is fine."

Jodi agreed without speaking, gripping Lisa's hand tightly to secure their bond. At that moment, Lisa looked into the future and saw the strong woman the girl would become and her heart swelled in love and pride. She glanced at Jake and saw the tears in his eyes.

"We have it all, don't we love," he said, his voice catching. Recovering, he added, "Now can I call Beth and tell her there will be a bride?"

"Oh, yes! But there's one more thing."

"What now?" he groaned.

"Jodi? I will need a maid of honor on Saturday. Do you want the job?"

"Oh, Lisa?" the girl bounced in excitement, as all signs of womanhood disappeared. "Does that mean I get a new dress?"

"That means you get the most beautiful dress to be found. You have to go shopping with me as soon as I'm out of here."

Jake grinned at the two of them. "Leaving me at home, I hope. Well, that's all finally settled. It took a while, but I think we may all live happily ever after. Who would have thought it would all work out this well?"

Lisa chuckled at that. "Probably everyone in Norway."

Jodi smiled happily. "Gordie told me over a week ago that

it would end this way," she informed her father. "He had it all worked out. He said Lisa would be the perfect wife for you."

"I agree with him," Jake said curiously, "but how did Gordie figure it out?"

"He said Lisa could run her business out of the house. And since she'd be there all day, we could set up a recreation room in the basement and all the kids could spend time there, too. He said Lisa would like having them."

"What am I getting myself into?" Jake groaned. "Along with a wife, do I get the entire teenage population of Norway?"

"The way I see it," Jodi continued as Lisa smothered a laugh, "he forgot the most important thing of all!!"

"Yes?" Jake quirked an eyebrow.

"Lisa can cook!"

Joshua Richard Gannett cocked an inquisitive gray eye at the bushy-tailed fox that pranced on the headboard of his parents' bed. He inspected the carved sly face for only a moment then ignored it as he attended to the serious business of breakfast.

Lisa started as he ferociously attacked her nipple. She smiled fondly at the dark head at her breast. After two months, she should be used to her son's appetite. He had inherited a "good mouth" from his parents, that was certain. She settled against the pillows once more, enjoying the gentle caress of her baby's hands against her skin as he greedily sucked.

Lisa heard the muted sound of the kitchen door closing as Jake left for his early morning run. He had taken up jogging when they brought Joshua home, trying to lose some of the "sympathetic" weight he gained during her pregnancy and figuring it would occupy him while the baby fed. He always rose immediately at his son's first angry wail, quickly changed the wet diaper and handed the baby to his sleepy wife.

Jake always glanced at Lisa's naked breasts and sighed wistfully as he took to the stairs. Too bad, Lisa chuckled to herself, idly arranging her child's meager hair. Jake's turn comes later.

Lisa hummed a lazy lullaby as she waited for her son to finish. The early sunlight of this spring morning filtered through the drapes. She looked forward to another wonderful day, planning out her busy schedule.

All of her days had been wonderful since Jake brought her here on her wedding day. Together, they had renovated this old house and turned it into a true mansion, the showcase of the city.

Each room had been carefully planned and researched. They scoured libraries and museums for ideas, haunted antique stores and learned the names of all the craftsmen in the northern woods. The constant upheavals had been wearing, but worth it.

Following Gordie's plan, Lisa moved her office into the old pantry next to the kitchen and found, to her surprise, that her business improved. Many of the curious citizens came to do business with her just to get a glimpse at what she and Jake were accomplishing in the old house. She despaired of keeping up with all her added responsibilities, until Beth surprised her by asking for a job.

"I can type, file and handle the telephone calls, and I can take courses to get my broker's license. What do you think?"

"Beth, I'd love it, but can you handle it, with the church and everything?"

"Minister's wives do have careers these days, you know!" Beth said firmly, and proved it. She had been wonderful during the early difficult days of Lisa's pregnancy, taking over the office, answering the phone, handling most of the correspondence, and arranging Lisa's schedule of showings to coincide with her nausea-free moments. Now Beth was working on her own license and the two women would soon have a full partnership.

Jodi "just adored" everything about her new school and would have joined every new club and activity if Jake would have permitted it. She finally settled on being a cheerleader, and to Lisa's delight, was working hard at trumpet lessons. Before another year passed, she would be a member of the Norway City Band. Lisa was hard put not to brag of her talents at practices.

She snuggled into the blankets as Joshua showed signs of finishing his meal. Jodi still slept on in her own bedroom down the hall. Lisa was so proud of her. She was a terrific sister, daughter and friend. She truly loved her tiny brother and did her best to spoil him by catering to his every whim. On Christmas Eve, she had given Lisa the best present ever, the coveted title of "Mom". Jodi brought joy and laughter to this old house, which was filled most afternoons after school with teenagers eating, arguing and working in the basement recreation room. Jake had decreed that if they wanted space in his house, they would have to do some of the work. It was the noisiest decorating crew ever put together and it was a marvel that baby Joshua managed to sleep through it all.

Richard had become Jodi's favorite visitor. Jake had

insisted on adding a ramp to the back porch as the first important step in renovation. Now Richard and Marlene's van frequently was parked in the long drive. Occasionally, Jodi and Gordie would take a long bicycle ride to Richard's cabin to spend a quiet afternoon with him, watching the lake and woods for interesting forest residents. Jodi never again tried to take a shortcut.

Lisa grinned when Joshua made a very unbabylike belch. She wondered how much longer she should breastfeed him. Jake did not press her about it, but she knew how much he longed to take an overdue honeymoon. From time to time this winter, he had mentioned that he would like to get her away from business, children, the youth group, and above all, the curious citizens of Norway, and "have his way with her".

Joshua was fast asleep in his crib when Jake returned to their bedroom.

"The daffodils you planted last fall are blooming," he informed Lisa, "and the tulips are budding." His voice was muffled as he pulled his shirt over his head.

"Oh, Jake," she said excitedly and threw back the blankets to rise, "I want to look at them."

"No way!" he exclaimed sternly, catching her up and tossing her back on the bed. "You've waited all winter, you can wait an hour."

"But, Jake . . . "

"No 'buts'. Jodi will be up in half an hour for school, Joshua just went to sleep and I have no intention of sharing this time with a bunch of flowers."

With his usual gift of persuasion, Jake Gannett convinced his wife of the benefits, both mental and physical, of an extra half-hour in bed.

Colleen Sutherland is a storyteller, musician, writer and journalist from the Midwest. Her short stories can be read at http://blackcoffee.fiction.blogspot.com. She and Wade Peterson collected the best of these stories in **Black Coffee Fiction**, available at Amazon.com.

Her daily blog is at http://storytellingtrailandtales.blogpot.com.

She is currently working on another novel and short story collection.

26144515R00114

Made in the USA
Lexington, KY
19 September 2013